LIST OF ALL POSSIBLE DESIRES

BOOKS BY DYLAN LANDIS

Normal People Don't Live Like This
Rainey Royal
List of All Possible Desires

LIST OF ALL POSSIBLE DESIRES

. . .

DYLAN LANDIS

Published by
Soho Press, Inc.
227 W 17th Street
New York, NY 10011
www.sohopress.com

Copyright © 2026 by Dylan Landis
All rights reserved.

This is a work of fiction. The characters, dialogue, and incidents depicted are a product of the author's imagination. Any resemblance to actual events or persons, living or dead, is entirely coincidental.

The author wishes to thank the editors of the magazines and periodicals in which many of the stories in this book first appeared, sometimes in earlier versions: *BOMB*: "Embouchure," "Mr. Apology," and "Tattoo"; and *Santa Monica Review*: "List of All Possible Desires" and "String Tension."

Library of Congress Cataloging-in-Publication Data

Names: Landis, Dylan, 1956- author
Title: List of all possible desires / Dylan Landis.
Description: New York : Soho Press, Inc, 2026.

ISBN: 978-1-64129-732-5
eISBN: 978-1-64129-733-2

Subjects: LCGFT: Bildungsromans | Novels | Fiction
Classification: LCC PS3612.A5482 L57 2026
LC record available at https://lccn.loc.gov/2025052470

Printed in the United States of America

10 9 8 7 6 5 4 3 2 1

To Jim Krusoe

Teacher, mentor, friend

LIST OF ALL POSSIBLE DESIRES

CONTENTS

La Nounou	1
List of All Possible Desires	23
Embouchure	43
The Wise and the Honest	61
Fear Knot	87
String Tension	109
Mr. Apology	139
Life is Like That	159
The Water or the Fish	177
Bernard Landry, Save Me	195
How to Steal a Family	221
Tattoo	239
Heart Jammed Open	259

LA NOUNOU

1947

Howard Royal, eleven and two months, sat on his parents' bed and watched his *nounou* at his mother's dressing table draw a ruby lipstick over her opulent lower lip. His own mouth hung open, a chalice of joy and shock. A Saturday in July: His mother was out browsing the Champs-Élysées.

It was not just the appropriation of his mother's prized makeup that had Howard in thrall but the willowy spine of his babysitter, the low opening of the silk butterfly-print robe she had so easily assumed from his mother's bedpost, the tumble of her gingery ringlets. His mother was ecstatic to have found a *nounou* in Paris whom her son seemed to like, who did not steal, or arrive late, who was satisfied with her modest wages and also with, his mother said affectionately, her difficult charge.

Howard didn't see what made him difficult. He was just a boy bored to death on summer break, except in the late afternoons when he got to play the downstairs neighbor's upright piano, which wasn't the same as the grand piano at home in New York but was better than no piano at all. His *nounou* took his boredom as a challenge. *Odile Odile Odile.* Her name ran through his brain as he watched her lining those unblinking doll-like eyes with a pencil in the vanity mirror.

Odile swiveled on the velvet stool. Lavishly wrapped in the robe, she planted her knees apart. It gave her an alarming authority. She had just finished her *lycée*, so Howard guessed she might be eighteen, grown enough to tell him what to do. Her skin was bright, her eyes had the clarity of penlights, and she had the strangest notions about how to spend their days. She took bubble baths in his parents' tub after his father had gone to the cafés and his mother left on her daylong excursions. Often she kept the door open, invited him in to talk.

"'Ow*ard*," she said, "we are going to have a delicious afternoon." She held in her palm a crystal bottle of his mother's perfume, *Réplique.*

He sat frozen on the bed. Sometimes she made him lie down on it. He didn't always want to. This was not what people did. Would this afternoon involve the removal of the robe? He prayed that it would; he prayed it would not. The robe looked very different on his mother, who pulled the lapels close to her neck. He was supposed to speak French to Odile, though she always answered in her perfect lycée English. His parents and he had moved to France for a year so his father could make a name here in jazz, which was having a renaissance in the cabarets and nightclubs. A houseboy was taking care of the townhouse on West Tenth Street. Howard struggled a moment with the future tense, then said, "*Que ferons-nous?*" as he had learned in the American school. *What will we do?*

Odile pulled the lapels of the robe even further apart, tipped the perfume bottle and righted it, plucked the wet stopper, and touched it to the furrow between her bosoms. Her black brassiere served as a shelf for two astonishing globes. "*Une balconette*," she said mysteriously, seeing him try not to stare, as if answering a question he had not asked. She dabbed again. A little balcony? What was that? He had often seen her raid his mother's chest of drawers; to whom did this brassiere belong? Hopefully not to his mother, whose own *balcony* mysteriously protruded and was always well covered. Whereas Odile's bosom seemed the more magnificent for being only partially concealed.

Howard was too young to stay home alone, especially in a strange country: That was what his mother said, though his father believed he could handle himself just fine, radio being good amusement whatever language it spoke. Howard might learn some French from it, he said. But Lala had won out over Buddy, a jazz trombonist who left around noon each day to drink in cafés with his fellow musicians till it was time to rehearse and then play in the clubs after dark, which was how Howard had ended up with *la nounou*. He had a vague idea that next fall he'd confide in a boy from school he thought he trusted, or perhaps the idea was to brag—there might not be much difference.

Odile rose from the dressing table. She sank a front tooth thoughtfully into her scarlet lower lip. "'O*ward*, do you love me?"

A dab of scarlet had imprinted on the tooth. Did he love her? He feared and adored her. But this was not a thing he could begin to explain. He looked at the floor. "Kind of," he said. What was that in French? *Comme ci, comme ça?*

"*Bon.*" Soberly, she kissed her index fingertip and pressed it to his mouth, a gesture that seemed designed to seal his silence. Then she stepped out of his mother's robe and hung it back on the bedpost. He could not look directly at her, lest it blind him, yet he saw that her garters dangled, bereft of nylons, and her skin was the glass of milk he drank that morning, the curves of her hips the mountain-pass switchbacks his father had driven with them in the Alps, the Fiat Topolino adhering tight to the camber of the road.

"*Allons-y*," she said. "I am taking you someplace from *un cauchemar*. A bad dream. Go! Get ready."

Fantastic, Howard thought in his bedroom, yanking up his knee-high socks, lacing his shoes. A place from a nightmare—surely not another cemetery? They'd twice been to Père-Lachaise, but that was hardly the gates of hell. His favorite grave had a little piano on it, and the creepiest one had a bronze man holding up the head of his dead wife. Well, it was a mask, actually, Odile had said, but it looked like her actual head. Howard was not a believer, though the American school had chapel twice a

· LA NOUNOU ·

week. His parents were *dissolute*, as his father, Buddy, had said, laughing.

He presented himself in the foyer for inspection and Odile checked behind his ears, making a scoff of displeasure but saying nothing. She had zipped herself into a full-skirted, black-and-white-checked sundress, not unlike the dresses his mother brought home but copied in a watered-down way, the skirt less extravagant, cotton with a petticoat instead of taffeta. A run in her nylons had been stopped with soap. Her shoes were pink and white with a curvy heel, and on second look Howard recognized them from his mother's closet. She took his hand and did a twirl, and he wondered if in some way he did not entirely understand *la nounou* might be his sweetheart.

With the money that Lala Royal left for them each week, they took the Métro to the Pont de l'Alma. He knew that all through France people scrimped by on ration cards, but Lala had money from the States—Howard's grandfather produced a top children's-shoe brand called Kiddo Kicks. Howard wore Kiddo Kicks. He liked them fine. A lot of his grandfather's money flowed down through Lala and put cake on the table, as she liked to say, and let Buddy live his life in the arts, as he liked to say. Howard's mother bought delicacies on the black market, much to Cook's delight, but unless his parents were arguing about it Howard never paid much attention to money. The only thing he had asked for in France was piano lessons, and his mother had immediately found him a respected *professeur de piano*.

They got out of the Métro on the Right Bank, and as they

crossed the Seine on foot, Odile pointed out four massive military statues on the stone piers under the bridge. "That one," she said, lifting her chin, "is the Zouave. When the river comes to his ankles, everyone knows it is not safe to walk on the path. If it comes to his"—she patted the top of her thigh—"even the boats don't go." They walked a block on the quai Branly, under canopied trees with benches beneath. He could still glimpse the Eiffel Tower behind them. Odile glanced at a notepaper from her purse, turned a corner, and led him into a small street-front office. A long crack in the window was held fast with brown tape; brass bells jangled as they opened the door.

Two American soldiers leaned against one wall, smoking filterless cigarettes. A bald man with gold-rimmed glasses sat behind a scarred oak desk. Howard could not believe his luck when he read the sign; Odile had taken him to another walking tour, all right, but not of any dumb bridge, not of a cemetery again. "*Deux billets?*" the man asked, and swept Odile's notes and coins into a cashbox. Then the brass bells jangled, and a boy in knickerbockers from Howard's American school walked in, accompanied by a woman whose hat bore a tilted clutch of violets and whose hands were sheathed in embroidered white gloves. Roger Bullock was two grades ahead, presumably thirteen—a minor god, with neat dark hair except for one unruly hank that fell onto his forehead. Howard knew Roger only by sight from assemblies and chapel, and standing next to him in his short pants, Howard felt absurdly young, and small. The older boy was taller than his mother—he'd clearly had his growth spurt—and his topaz gaze ranged, with oblivion, over Howard's head, as he studied everyone else in the room. Finally, Roger deigned to notice him, and curtly nodded. Howard took this as permission to mutely wave.

A man in coveralls and rubber boots clomped in from a door behind the desk, his face long and shining, his mustache celebratory, upturned. He looked around. "*Français? Anglais?* English?" English, the soldiers said, and no one objected. "My name is Monsieur Aubert. I am an engineer in the sanitation system. Follow me, please. You will need *vêtements de protection.*"

Howard experienced a floating bliss. They were going to walk underground through the sewers of Paris and get spattered with *shit*. Even better than the Catacombs, where he and Odile had looked at millions of stacked skulls in dark and dripping silence, the bones of dead people mosaicked into radiant designs. He glanced at Roger, whose studious face gave away neither loathing nor excitement. It dawned on Howard that he was witnessing a model of how to be in this world. He must show no enthusiasm, he decided, and stilled his face, though he sensed Odile watching him, smiling and hopeful.

Their little crowd shuffled into a second chamber with faded sage-green walls and two long benches where they could sit and thrust their arms into the oilcloth raincoats that Monsieur Aubert pulled from two lockers.

Odile slipped into hers easily as if it were the latest style from Le Bon Marché. Mrs. Bullock looked down at hers with dismay as if trying to keep it from her skin, then fastened its metal toggles with elegant, persnickety fingers. It hung about her, flapping at her knees, making her look ridiculous. Did she know that her son was a young Apollo, that he would be an object of beauty even in the dankest depths of Paris? Howard enthusiastically jammed his socks into the rubber boots. This, he thought with glee, is going to stink, and the smell is going to stick. This made him think about needing a bath, and about the chance of Odile nipping in to wash his hair, getting herself wet in the process—something that both mortified and excited him, something that would never, ever happen to the older boy.

Monsieur Aubert led them down uncountable steps, concrete at first and then stone. They walked single file in semidarkness, the flights set apart by passages in which bare bulbs dimly lit the way. At moments Howard felt his shoulder brushed by the fingertips of *la nounou*. In his mind he savored Roger's mother's disgust; he couldn't wait to see her spattered with whatever dark matter splashed out of the sewers.

But once they had passed through the room of measurements with its banks of strange instruments, they came to a stop at the platform of what resembled a low, half-lit, vaulted Métro station. Here the sewage ran not in an open medieval gutter, as Howard had hoped, but in a deep and narrow greenish canal sunken alongside the platform, as train tracks might have been. Howard sniffed deeply. The odor was distantly noxious, barely fecal. It had been, Monsieur Aubert told them, through a good deal of treatment already. Tracing the arch of the ceiling with his gaze, Howard felt himself installed far below the sidewalks of Paris, the tapping heels of passersby a mile overhead, as if he and Odile were in a buried land of nightmares with a thousand steps to ascend before they could wake. Anything could happen down here, he thought, if you were dreaming, and anything might be happening up above in real life without your knowledge: riots, wars, the dissolution of Buddy Royal, the shopping seizures of Lala Royal in her froth of organza and silk.

Monsieur Aubert gathered them close and recited from Victor Hugo: "'Paris has beneath it another Paris; a Paris of sewers; which has its streets, its crossroads, its squares, its blind alleys, its arteries, and its circulation, which is of mire and minus the human form.'"

Howard saw that Odile appeared to be in a reverie, while a look of revulsion had sharpened the face of Roger's mother. So rewarding, watching her. And it was not only the soldiers who glanced at Odile but Roger, too. It made Howard proud, for she was his.

Monsieur Aubert ushered them along the platform and into a small wooden boat with slack chains bolted to the front. The chains were held by two men in long white coats and high rubber boots. Roger's mother crossed her arms and stood her ground while Monsieur Aubert talked of the earliest sewers that drained into open air, of how Louis Pasteur lost three children to typhoid, an irony, he said, and of how under Napoleon III, a sewer network of six hundred kilometers was finally constructed beneath Paris. "Every building had to be individually connected to it," the guide said, just as Howard realized that his schoolmate had materialized beside him in the boat.

"I thought we might see a dead dog in there." Roger sounded bored.

"Or a body," Howard suggested, and was rewarded with a laugh.

Monsieur Aubert offered Roger's mother his arm and, after assuring her of one thing after another, was able to guide her to a seat in the boat. The men holding the chains leaned forward into a trudge, tugging, and the boat began to inch along. *In the stinky soup*, thought Howard with deep joy. This was a thing he would nurture in his heart and never discuss at home.

"If you lived in Paris before the Middle Ages," Monsieur Aubert said, bringing him back to the moment, "you collected your drinking water in buckets from the Seine, and then you poured your wastewater onto the unpaved streets, where it drained back into that same river." Howard found this morbidly satisfying. He noticed Odile smiling, Roger's mother cutting her eyes at their guide, Roger staring into the murk as if seeking his reflection. The boat slipped beneath glass-robed lights whose shadows, Howard saw, were the very color of that ancient wastewater and lay sallow beneath everyone's eyes, draining their beauty.

Alongside, on the platforms, the men in their white coats lunged forward with their chains. The boat slid in the unspeakable liquid, and overhead the arched ceilings loomed, dark as thunderclouds and sliding by just as slow.

"Is that your sister?" murmured Roger, his gaze on Odile. Her

· LA NOUNOU ·

lips bore a Mona Lisa smile that Howard recognized but did not understand, her eyes a strange and heavy-lidded pleasure. Did she, too, feel that she was in a dream down under the actual Paris—or was she simultaneously awake in the actual Paris and skimming along down below in this subterranean copy, with its arteries and its mire?

He waited for an answer to float to the surface of the sewage as they glided along. "She is a friend of my mother's," he finally said. His mother was walking atop them even now, her heels clicking unheard overhead, her shopping bags swaying above the muck.

"She's a dish," Roger said ardently.

"She has a steady," said Howard just as fiercely.

"What's she doing with you?"

Howard looked at the canal again. What *was* she doing with him? He guessed Odile was waiting for some reaction, day after day, that he didn't know how to cough up. Roger was right, she was a dish, but she was *his* dish, even if he didn't know what to do with her.

When they climbed out of the boat, they were at a different platform, and Roger's mother came over and said, "Introduce me to your friend, Roger."

The older boy laughed in his nose. "Remind me your name." His voice was low, like a man's, and Howard felt young and jealous.

Introductions were made. "Why don't you and your babysitter join us for lunch at La Tour d'Argent." Mrs. Bullock tucked her neatly waved and indented hair behind her ears as if they were not still on the sewer platform but in Le Bon Marché. "It has lovely views of the Seine."

Howard saw the Seine every morning from his bedroom window; he did not care about the Seine. "She's not my babysitter," he said dully. It sounded like the grievance it was, and he had to backpedal and thank Mrs. Bullock. To Odile he said, "I told them you're a friend." She had been chatting with one of the soldiers. Howard envied the man his rifle, long and polished, with that deadly bore and the projectiles it spat. He imagined himself in the woods with his father, just the two of them and a pair of rifles like that, the bushes full of grouse or whatever they had in France, and his father would give him the time of day for something other than music. His father still had him training on classical piano before he would teach him jazz. Howard practiced two hours a day, Mozart, Chopin, Shostakovich, then played popular tunes or the jazz standards from his father's sheet music if the downstairs neighbor, a bachelor named Monsieur Prisant, was not tired of listening and ready to send him upstairs. "Autumn Leaves." "Take the 'A' Train."

Now the other soldier was running his hands over a wooden sphere almost the size of an armchair. It was a *cleaning ball*, mounted on a stand. Howard had kept half an ear tuned to Monsieur Aubert, especially after the pleasure of *slime*. The balls were sent rolling down the spillways to push debris—dead dogs, perhaps bodies—down the line. It galled Howard that they were not to be given a demonstration, that a ball would not be shoved into the water with a great revolting splatter.

"Of course we can go to lunch, if you like," Odile told him. "La Tour d'Argent! I wish you were wearing your best sweater. That handsome person is in your school?" Howard felt perversely young, unhandsome, his sweater stained like a toddler's though he knew it was clean. His *nounou* swirled her skirt and tapped over to greet Mrs. Bullock, who had entirely turned her back on the sewer.

Up on the street, the air felt sweet and clean on Howard's neck. They walked on the cobblestone path of the quai de la Tournelle, the boys scuffing their feet and stopping for a glimpse of the scaffolding high on Notre-Dame, where workmen they couldn't see were rebuilding the wooden spire that had collapsed in the Nazi fire. In the restaurant, Roger's mother made everybody wash their hands. They sat by an enormous window with a sprawling view of the river. Howard wanted to sit by Odile, but she placed herself across from him. Between them on one side sat Roger. Between them on the other sat Roger's mother.

As they read their menus, a waiter poured water, and the women murmured about their choices. Howard began to notice that Odile smiled at Roger often and that Roger stared at Odile. Did Mrs. Bullock see it? She seemed oblivious. But then Odile touched Roger's arm and laughed her tinkling laugh. Before Howard could decide how he felt about that, the waiter arrived, Roger's mother placed orders for everyone, and she and Odile began chatting about Dior's "New Look." Odile loved Mrs. Royal's clothes; she made her own on an old sewing machine.

From the white of his eye, he watched Roger silently. Four plates landed with a flourish: two waiters, impeccable timing. The women were sharing an order of *canard à la presse*. Roger said nothing till after he had confronted his hamburger on brioche. He took a large bite, chewed it thoughtfully, swallowed, and leaned in close to Howard's ear.

"Your babysitter's leg is touching mine," he whispered.

It didn't matter that he was lying. Howard felt defensive and possessive toward Odile. "It's not on purpose," he hissed, gripping his own hamburger. "And she's not my babysitter."

There it was, that little nose laugh again. "I'll bet," murmured Roger.

Mrs. Bullock glanced over. "No whispering at table," she said, and went back to her conversation with Odile.

Howard wasn't certain which statement had been challenged. Not his *nounou*? Or not on purpose? To his relief, Roger said nothing more, so he listened to the women—Mrs. Bullock talking of silks and chiffons and drawing in the air an hourglass shape, Odile discreetly leaving out that her only views of the new Dior and Balmain dresses were when Mrs. Royal unfurled them from boxes delivered to the apartment.

The silence between Roger and him became hard to manage. Howard, nibbling on cornichons, determined to break it. "Don't you wish they'd dropped those cleaning balls into the sewers?" He tried to sound brazen. "I wanted to see the splash."

Roger raised his eyes with a look of infinite patience. "They don't drop them, dummy. They *lower* them." And then he gazed at Odile with a look that seemed to comprise not only longing but also knowing and acknowledgment, qualities so visceral that Howard grasped them in his body though he could not have named them in either language. "She's rubbing my leg," Roger added in a dropped voice.

Howard saw it so clearly in his mind's eye: Odile's stockinged foot nuzzling Roger's brown knickerbockers like a small animal that had picked up an intoxicating scent. How could Odile do it? How could Roger speak of it? "She's *not my babysitter.*" His voice carried across the table. Odile looked up at him, and he cringed.

Odile smiled at Howard first. Then she turned the smile on the older boy.

"I am a friend of the family," she told him prettily. "Just as he says."

Then she winked at Roger.

The wink demolished Howard. A Judas kiss, it almost brought the liquid to his eyes. Heart-struck, he glanced at Odile, but already she was back in conversation with Mrs. Bullock, being her visibly charming self, a piece of duck speared but forgotten on her fork as she laughed, the laugh like tinkling crystal. He saw Roger watching her intently from under long, lowered eyelashes.

Howard thought of excusing himself to the bathroom to bear his humiliation alone, and a sudden cramp of shame told him this might be a good idea.

But he didn't move. He kept secretly studying Roger and Odile. And after a few more minutes of painful silence, Howard began to feel a shift in his emotions, so strong it was almost physical. He tuned in to see if he could isolate the sensation. It felt as if a tiny steel cleaning ball were rolling through his veins, sweeping away all traces of Odile and leaving a coating of ice in its path. When it had rolled all the way through him and done its work, a clean, cold feeling blanketed his innermost being. He was still angry, yes, but he was purified. By the time the plates had been cleared and four chilled metal dishes of ice cream were served, he no longer felt himself in thrall.

He sat straighter in his chair. He was not Roger's little friend. He would never smile at Odile again.

The two of them took the Métro back to Saint-Germain. As they walked to the apartment, he was keenly aware that his *nounou* was not his sweetheart, that they were not holding hands and never would. But he did smile at her, despite his pledge. It was important to appear as if nothing were wrong. They found his mother home earlier than expected, unpacking a handbag with a bamboo handle in the dining room; and Howard saw Odile glide swiftly to the far side of the table, so quickly he realized she was hiding her illicitly borrowed shoes. His mother's pale hair was upswept in some new way, and she wore unfamiliar emerald glass clip earrings that repeated the hue of her eyes: evidence of a day's shopping and hairdressing. She had a pretty heart-shaped face, her mouth lipsticked like Odile's, and smiling as usual. She didn't look much older than Odile, either, but he knew she had to be.

"Muffin," she said, turning toward him with her arms open.

He inhaled her floral scent and happily told her where they had gone. She pushed him away at arm's length. "Germs! Revolting." She was looking at him, but he had an idea she was talking to Odile. "Better you than me. Take a bath, son."

He hesitated. "I should play the piano. And it wasn't germy."

"It wasn't," said Odile, hesitantly. "It's a tour, Madame, every week, very clean. Lots of people did it."

He saw the look his mother flashed Odile. "I'm sure he enjoyed it," she said coolly, and to Howard, "Play the piano tomorrow. You need a bath."

He and Odile retreated to the back of the apartment, Odile to return the shoes, he knew, and to strip off the brassiere for all he cared, though that might have been something to see. He took his bathrobe to the toilet near his bedroom and locked the door against Odile while he ran the tub. A French tub with a spray shower—he generally made a mess of things washing his hair, and Odile often came in unbidden to help him do it. Not today she wouldn't. Once she'd taught him how to swear—*putain de merde, petit con!* Last week she had asked him questions about his body—Did he ever touch himself? To which he had stupidly replied: Where? And did he know that all boys touched themselves? No, he did not know that, nor was he sure why they would, though he might investigate.

He sank into the tub and, using the lavender soap that his mother favored, began to scrub off whatever invisible germs had clung to him. In his mind, his fingers ran over the keyboard, practicing the Liszt, and in his mind, it sounded perfect. He felt lighthearted taking the day off. When the tentative knock came, he lay all the way back in the water so that his hair streamed, his ears filled, and he could not hear her words.

In his room, he dressed with the door closed, ignoring a second knock, and when Odile left for the day he was still there on his bed, reading *The Secret Panel*. His mother coaxed him out after Cook had set the table. With his father playing trombone till early morning, it was just the two of them at dinner.

He let her inspect his fingernails, then they sat. Even without Buddy they ate in the formal dining room. Cook came out perspiring with a platter of peculiarly small birds surrounded by shiny Vichy carrots and green beans with almonds. It was irritating having to cut the meat from little birds—why didn't Paris have pizzerias like New York? If they were in New York, his father would be home more in the daytime. Howard would have the grand piano, showers would be normal, there would be no traitorous *nounou*.

"Tell me about your strange tour," his mother said. "Just don't say anything revolting at the table." Cook easily dealt a bird from a silver spatula onto each plate, and Howard knew he would have to plead before he could use his fingers. He was no fan of green beans, either, though the glistening carrots were cooked in sugar water and tasted all right.

He thought about Odile's foot caressing Roger's leg, about how, like a little cat, it had chosen Roger's leg to rub against over his own. "Victor Hugo wrote about the sewers like they were avenues and streets," he said.

"It sounds educational. And was it awful, could you stand to see it?" His mother worked her knife and fork like surgical tools, expertly removing wedges of flesh. When he tried it, the entire little drumstick came off, begging to be sucked dry.

He told her about the green canals, the cleaning balls, the tour with his schoolmate and the two soldiers. And then he blurted it.

"Odile was flirting with the soldiers." His mother lowered her fork and looked at him levelly. "We went to lunch with them," he said, barreling on. "Odile had champagne. We both did."

Why lie? He had no shortage of truths if he wanted to get her fired, and he did want to get her fired. What Odile had done with Roger at la Tour d'Argent was surely wicked; he could have told her that. What Odile did with *him* was worse than that, but some things could never be said out loud.

"You must be joking," his mother said. "*Odile?* Has she acted like this before?"

Something told Howard that the best weapon his eleven-year-old self possessed was silence. And so he hesitated, inviting his mother to press him. "Has she? You have to tell me, Howard. This could be nothing or it could be serious."

"I saw her kissing one of them," he said quietly, addressing his plate. He chose that moment to pick up the drumstick. His mother let it go. "Like in the movies. I think she was a little drunk."

"Oh, for Pete's sake." His mother sighed heavily and began eating again. Did she even believe him? Cook had poured her a glass of the Sancerre she liked and she took a sip. "Tipsy isn't the end of the world, I suppose. Neither is kissing. Still. I don't like it. I don't like it one bit. What else? Don't hold back."

"She goes into your closet."

"You mean she looks?"

He acted like he couldn't meet his mother's eyes. "She wears your clothes," he finally muttered. He chewed his lip. "This morning she took a bath in your tub and put on your robe." The word *robe* sounded more than intimate in his mouth; it sounded obscene, because the robe belonged to his mother, who pulled the lapels so conservatively close. "She wore . . . she wore your . . ."

"Oh my heavens," his mother said, her eyes wide. "My *what*?"

"Balconette," he managed with apparent difficulty.

"Oh my *God*." She pushed her chair back and stiffly stood. "How do you know?" She waited. "Did you *see*?" He felt again the tiny steel ball coursing through his anatomy, turning his heart into a series of hardened passages through which the green-gray blood moved sluggishly. Then he nodded. "Is there more, Howard?"

He let his head droop so that his mother might read into it the shame of putting the unspeakable into words. Finally, because she had not said anything about firing Odile, he whispered: "She let Daddy see it, too."

He expected another *Oh my heavens*. Instead, his mother took her seat again, moving slowly. When Howard raised his head to look at her, he saw that she sat like a statue and that her face was wet. Had he caused her to cry? His stomach contracted into something the size of a bean. His mother was weeping because of his lie—how could this be fixed; how could such a thing be retracted?

"What did Daddy do?" she whispered. "What did they do?"

· LA NOUNOU ·

He blinked at her. He hadn't thought this far. He was causing damage he hadn't anticipated. "Nothing," he said. "They didn't do anything. I'm probably wrong. I think she had her back turned when he walked into the room."

"But Daddy was in our bedroom while Odile was—" His mother stopped, apparently unable to say *undressed*. *Déshabillée*, he thought crazily.

"Wait," he said. "I know I'm wrong. She was wearing her dress." He sounded frantic. This was all wrong. Had he learned nothing from Roger's casual and cruel splendor? From having his heart scrubbed clean in the sewers?

His mother looked at him without pretending she wasn't crying. A drop gleamed at the end of her nose. He wanted to fetch her handkerchief. "You can't fix this, sweetie," she said. "Don't try."

But he did try, though he might be punished for the admission. "It wasn't true, what I said about Daddy. I just wanted to get her fired."

To his surprise, she didn't ask why. Instead she gazed at him with an unalterable sadness that seemed to well up from a tunnel as deep as the sewers of Paris, a tunnel with crossings and blind alleys and arteries, all of them buried far beneath her tapping heels as she strolled about the city. Did everyone have access to that fathomless system? She had always just been *mother* to him, a kindly woman who nuzzled him and bought him the latest Hardy Boys from Brentano's, who shopped and indulged his truant father, and who occasionally took him to the clubs to hear his father blow the trombone. Now he gathered with a sick fascination that she had a life of the emotions, and that if she did, that probably meant everybody else did, too, and that he was not the *I* at the center of the world.

But it was not a moment that would stay with him.

"Well, muffin, you certainly did get her fired," his mother said, her hands clasped and comforting each other at her chest. "Do you think you can survive a few days alone till I find you another *nounou*?"

But there could be no other, he wanted to say, not in all of Paris—there would be no woman in his life again who would wring from him a sense of longing, knowing, and acknowledgment all at once. She had turned to him on a velvet stool, one tooth sunk into a promising scarlet lip. *I will take you someplace from a nightmare.* How many girls would ever bring him to the land of dreamers, to a living city far beneath the living city, would promise such excitement, or know him so well?

LIST OF ALL POSSIBLE DESIRES

1958

Laurette Barbanel creases her lovely new paychecks so hard they nearly tear and stares at the model sashaying through Chemical Bank. The model wears heels like paring knives. She wears a mink stole that she sensually nuzzles, beaming at the women lined up for the tellers.

Laurette's teller whispers, as if disclosing a bank secret: "No one wants a toaster after seeing *her*."

These are Laurette's choices if she opens her passbook account at Chemical—a toaster, a cigarette lighter (engraved), or a raffle ticket for the mink. She has been shopping, bank to bank, for a premium that will make her feel like a winner, a real *nonpareil*.

By her side, the woman in the wheelchair begins to stir. The woman is shockingly pretty in the Aryan way, except for a sag on the right side of her face. Mrs. Kleid is Laurette's charge from eight in the morning till six at night and she is a delicate, broken vase. Her left arm, the good one, makes the undersea movements of a lazily flapping skate, which tells Laurette she is preparing from deep inside to boom out her single, solitary word.

"Hush now," says Laurette warmly, stroking Mrs. Kleid's hair. She likes strangers to think she's a loving and competent daughter when in fact to her own father she, Laurette, is an old maid and a *shtuken nisht in hartz*, a stab in the heart. Mrs. Kleid bats Laurette with a vaguely swaying arm. The right hand, the dead one, dutifully rests. Bruises like fat pansies purple her soft white flesh, and Laurette believes it's from being lifted out of that chair by hands more powerful than her own.

"Darling, hush," says Laurette, her voice self-consciously loud.

But once the Word forms in the folds of Mrs. Kleid's brain, it cannot be stopped; and here it comes, belted out on the exhale like an umpire's call.

"*Wunderbar!*" cries Mrs. Kleid. Heads swivel. Laurette knows this much: Mrs. Kleid is Austrian by birth, and the Word in her mouth means *marvelous*.

The teller, nametagged Barbara H., stares down at the wheelchair from behind the marble counter. A small child asks a loud question. People edge away. Laurette looks around at the stunned faces, then at the beautiful, helpless Mrs. Kleid.

"It's her lunchtime," says Laurette, flushing and nodding to the people in line.

"Wunderbar," murmurs Mrs. Kleid, leaning into Laurette's hand. But after three solid weeks of work, Laurette still cannot decipher the meaning of the *wunderbar*s.

"Is it for you or—" says Barbara H. a little brusquely, lifting her chin. She delicately coughs. "You want to get her the raffle ticket for the mink or—?"

But Laurette and her twin sister, Linda, already have furs, thanks to their father the furrier. Laurette has a cloth coat with a mink collar and cuffs; Linda's is all sable, with her monogram on the silk lining. But then Linda got pregnant with Rainey and ran off with that *farkakte goy*, a jazz pianist named Howard Royal, a man whose mother traces her lineage back to a ship and not the kind you rode in steerage. Linda insisted on trading coats with Laurette before she left, which is only one reason Laurette loves Linda to death. After Howard happened, their father made the family sit shiva for Linda so that now she is dead to them. He insists their mother write *Return to sender* on Linda's letters, hang up when Linda calls, and not coo to her granddaughter on the phone. But Laurette, watching her mother hide Linda's letters and read them with visible longing, is swamped with envy.

"Wunderbar," announces Mrs. Kleid, and Laurette, startled, thinks it sounds like a *potty* wunderbar. Behind her in line, she hears another cough and a woman whispering loudly. *How complicated can it be?*

"These premiums fly out," sings Barbara H., and Laurette knows it's true, that anything you love today could fly away tomorrow. Her own sister, gone with a stroke of their father's judgment. Mrs. Kleid's speech, gone with a stroke in the brain just six weeks ago. Laurette skims her three creased checks off the counter, mortified, for if Laurette has learned anything from this job it's that time is precious. Mrs. Kleid is only forty-one and she's had that stroke. Laurette was just a girl when she failed out of Brooklyn College with no fiancé to show for her father's investment, and two years later she is still at home, with no prospects except for babysitting Mrs. Kleid.

Worse, she now understands that her own brain, too, could be ticking like a cartoon bomb. The stroke deprived Mrs. Kleid of all her words except one that clings from years ago, so when Mrs. Kleid has a craving, or a need, she announces *Wunderbar!* and Laurette, who can never decide what she truly wants her own self, runs down the list of all possible desires: chocolate, perhaps, or potty, or a new record on the phonograph, or a forbidden glass of sherry (Laurette's idea), or a turn outside in the wheelchair, or five minutes of staggering through the apartment with Laurette propping up her bad side.

Laurette shoves the three checks, inked with Mr. Kleid's gold fountain pen, down into her purse and backs away, pulling the wheelchair with her. She's bolted from two other banks and their offerings so far—clocks, cleaver sets, a raffle for a color TV, a coin bank shaped like a Hoover vacuum. Laurette's whole problem is she can't tell what she's yearning for—some object that will make her whole, perhaps even in her father's eyes—so she grasps at all kinds of things. While Mrs. Kleid's problem is that she knows exactly what she wants and cannot say it.

"Try the auto-visor kit," the teller sings out, sucking all the oxygen from the marble-clad bank.

Laurette, feeling panicked and stupid, shoves the wheelchair toward the doors. Just as she turns back to call *sorry*, she hears a shriek and feels the wheelchair ram into something simultaneously hard and soft.

"Damn it!" cries the model, which will get her fired despite her injuries. She is on the floor clutching a bleeding ankle, her fur stole trailing onto the terrazzo, and a high-heeled pump languishes several yards away near the doors. The run in her stocking is a bloody ladder. Two bank officers rush over to pull her up.

Laurette must apologize. But first, that pretty pump! Its shank is arched, the toe box provocatively swollen—this shoe radiates confidence. She rarely gets signals from the same kind of object twice, and she's never been spoken to by a shoe.

She rolls Mrs. Kleid rapidly forward, bends, and picks up the black stiletto. The model, still making high-pitched utterances, is focused on her ankle. The bank men are focused on the model.

"Dear God, forgive me," murmurs Laurette, when what she means is *wunderbar*. She tucks the shoe into Mrs. Kleid's coat, pushes the chair briskly to the bank entrance, tugs at the door with twice her natural strength, and struggles out into the soft, windblown snow.

Panting, she races the wheelchair to the corner and stands there, stopped by the light, careful not to step off the curb yet—the wheelchair sticks out so far. This was something she learned, to her shame, from a woman on a street corner who scolded her one day for putting her charge at risk. Now Laurette turns to look: Though no one from the bank pursues her, she wants to jaywalk, wants to run—but she can't have her darling clipped by a cab.

EARLY THAT EVENING, she keeps up her mission of teaching Mrs. Kleid to feed herself. She tucks a spoon into the poor woman's fist and guides her right arm, shapely and slender, from the plate to the little bird mouth.

Her mother used to say that: *Open the little bird mouth.* Her mother's mouth always falls open when she has a fit—a fit, like in those Russian novels. What she has, *epilepsy,* you don't say aloud any more than you utter *cancer.* When Laurette was little, she thought each fit was her mother dying. Then came the resurrection, but first, the death. In this manner, Laurette was orphaned more times than she could count. And wasn't she searching for the perfect thing even then?

Mr. Kleid stands behind his chair, sucking in smoke beneath those cutlass cheekbones of his, casting a blue gaze at the dinner Laurette has set out for him and watching her feed his wife. "You're a good kid," he says, which means *there's no hope,* or something else. "Have a smoke."

Laurette doesn't dare smoke around her father. She accepts the cigarette.

Every evening, at 5:25 P.M., Mrs. Kleid greets her husband

with wide eyes the washed blue of sea glass. "Are you my sweetest lemon bar?" he says. Every night a different pastry. "Are you my most delicious strudel?" Mrs. Kleid does not say *wunderbar*. Mr. Kleid sets his briefcase on a chair, bends to her, and cups her thin, half-drooping, half-elegant face; he smiles at her like a man about to cry, and from this Laurette deduces love. She watches, fascinated, as he smells his wife's hair, which Laurette has perfumed and brushed one hundred times and coiled up with bobby pins. Mrs. Kleid is wearing lipstick, too. Night after night, it is like readying a bride. Because Mrs. Kleid is above all still a wife.

"And you always put her in something nice," says Mr. Kleid. "Those lavender underthings. Pretty." Laurette flushes; she does not want to discuss underthings with anyone, least of all him. She knows from the magazines and from her sister that a man wants his wife dressed up that way, and so she always slips Mrs. Kleid's stockinged feet into high heels that make her slim ankles look pert. But what about the bruises inside Mrs. Kleid's pale, slender thighs? What do the magazines say about those?

"Go home already," says Mr. Kleid, and Laurette's mind flashes onto her room in her family's apartment three floors down and onto the model's shoe, now in her purse, which she will move around like a statuette till she places it correctly, on her nightstand or her matching white bureau, in accordance with its powers. Mr. Kleid lights another cigarette and stabs out the first. "I'll take over," he says. "Thank you."

"Wunderbar," whispers Mrs. Kleid, and from the list of desires Laurette intuits: *Don't leave.*

. . .

THE NEXT MORNING is eventful because the Kleids' son, David, a disappointment to his father, will arrive from Florida after driving for three days. He hasn't seen his mother since he came home last Christmas, ten months before the stroke. Mr. Kleid checks his watch frequently while he waits for the visitor. He's missing work for this, and his irritation makes Laurette jumpy, as if she were the cause of the annoyance. When David finally rings, Mr. Kleid opens the door wide and gestures him inside.

"My son," he says with exaggerated warmth. "Down out of the trees and back into civilization."

Laurette knows that David Kleid is an actual beatnik, that he is *down out of the trees* because he lives in a treehouse. He built it himself—cutting up two telephone poles for supports—in a live oak that overhangs the Suwannee. Later he tells them it's a slow-moving blackwater river. Privately, Mr. Kleid says to Laurette with a note of disdain, "When the river rises, he gets to the ladder by *canoe*, for Chrissake."

David Kleid is lean and tanned, with exuberant facial hair, and he carries a canvas army pack messy with pockets. "Hey, Pop," he says when he walks in, but Laurette sees his gaze slide right past his father, and lock onto the woman in the chair. He utterly fails to register Laurette, who is positioned behind Mrs. Kleid, hands resting on the thin shoulders, trying to radiate loving attentiveness.

"*Mother*," breathes David Kleid, striding over. He drops his pack and genuflects.

"Filial piety," says Mr. Kleid.

His wife's good arm floats toward her son's hair. "Wunderbar," she murmurs.

"My God," says David. He leans his forehead against her knees. "Mother, I'm so sorry."

"Look at your son, dear." Mr. Kleid walks to the little pietà so that Laurette steps away, and strokes the nape of his wife's long neck. "Six weeks after the blessed event, but at least he's manifested himself." He jabs a cuff link through a thickness of buttonholes.

Laurette agrees secretly that six weeks might be forever. But she hears David whisper, "I came as soon as I could afford it." Surely that's not lack of love—he has pressed his mother's limp right hand to his face. Laurette imagines that David will suddenly look up and, in a thunderbolt, perceive *her* own inner beauty—though David shows no sign of seeing her at all.

"I'm going to work," says Mr. Kleid. "David, don't wear your mother out. No climbing the darn Statue of Liberty. Tonight you can tell us more about that tree of yours." And to his wife: "Don't go encouraging him with that *word*."

He steps through the front door, then turns and beckons Laurette. She walks over, wondering if he wants his shirts picked up early.

"My wife keeps falling off the bed," he says in a low voice. "If you see bruises." He looks back at Mrs. Kleid. "My little zwieback," he says ruefully. And again to Laurette, who marvels, because who falls off a bed with her legs spread? "You want to wash her better down there."

Laurette stammers. She hasn't soaped up Mrs. Kleid's *shmundie*, exactly, nor her *tuchus*, because it feels like such a trespass, but if this is a desire of Mr. Kleid's then it must be tended to. She wonders if his words might have reached and penetrated Mrs. Kleid's brain, an organ Laurette envisions as a snarl of wax and dental floss. Her own brain she imagines in a liquid state, swashing about as she searches for her object of desire. She believes if she were to be caught at this search, she would be forcibly stopped: perhaps by a stroke of her own, or even a forcible lobotomy, because it wasn't just Rosemary Kennedy that happened to. There is that Ohio fellow who performed twenty-five in one day, and another day he held an ice pick in each hand and did two, together, and this is supposed to be *wunderbar*. Laurette struggles to act like a person who never picks up bottle caps in the park, because who were these patients and what was their search?

That first afternoon of his visit, David and Laurette take Mrs. Kleid to see *Some Like It Hot*—his choice. Because of the wheelchair, they are relegated to the back row. Laurette fingers the soft mohair on her seat and pretends that the movie is a date and that David, holding his mother's hand, is merely distracted. Not a single *wunderbar* is uttered. Later that afternoon, as Laurette undresses Mrs. Kleid for a bath, that sea-glass gaze starts in on her. She unhooks the brassiere and pauses. Other women's breasts still have the power to shock, except for Linda's, her sister's, and even then. Linda is bountiful, and also shameless, because she is single and having intercourse with an uncircumcised musician named Howard who has intercourse with other women, too, sometimes at the same time he has it with Linda. How this might be accomplished is beyond Laurette.

This is when she sees it, before the pink bloomers come down: two new bruises, like plums, on Mrs. Kleid's inner thighs. They look like they were made with teeth.

What is she to do about this? How is she to make it stop? Mrs. Kleid looks at her with bright interest and grips the arms of her wheelchair as if it might otherwise take flight.

Straining, Laurette helps seat her—a slim thing, she can't weigh more than a hundred pounds—on the edge of the tub, then eases her into the water. She gently washes her hair, rinsing it with a plastic cup, then soaps up a washcloth, saving the intimate bits for the end. Bruises glare at her like eyes, and she sees angry red marks that might be from pinches. "Excuse me," she says, then rubs the cloth right in Mrs. Kleid's crotch, head turned so their eyes don't meet. She re-soaps and reaches further beneath to do her bottom, the white cloth coming away with a little smear.

"Now we're spiffy," declares Laurette, wondering what to do with the telltale cloth. What if David sees it? Will he think she has failed to wipe his mother properly? In the end, she balls it up tight and tucks it into a tiled corner above the tub, leaving it for the maid.

In the bedroom, she chooses a cashmere sweater for Mrs. Kleid, and a narrow skirt, because who would make bruises on a living doll? She pushes her charge's sleeves up so some of the bruises show. "Come join us," she calls when she has settled

Mrs. Kleid in the living room. David emerges from his boyhood bedroom. Again he genuflects before his mother. Mrs. Kleid trains those searchlight eyes on him, and Laurette withdraws to the windows, giving them some room.

When David rises, he sits on the sofa and cups his mother's face like a chalice. When will he do this to Laurette? His eyes are like his mother's, she thinks, tunnels of sky. She pinpoints exactly when he registers the purple thumbprints on his mother's arms. He frowns, turns his mother's arm over, then examines the other one, similarly afflicted.

"How'd she get these?" he demands.

Laurette bites her lip. "I can't say."

"If you're rough with her," David says fiercely, "I'll have you fired."

"I would *never*." Just being accused makes Laurette flush with shame. "I love your mother."

"Oh God, don't tell me," says David. "It's *him*." He strokes a bruise with a fingertip. "Does he hurt you?" he asks his mother, and to Laurette: "He always had a short fuse and a nasty edge, but I've never seen him hit her."

"Wunderbar." Mrs. Kleid looks at each of them with a face half wilted and half sublime. Her good hand floats up to David's curls. He makes a strangled sound.

"She's locked inside herself," volunteers Laurette. She's wearing a pair of Mrs. Kleid's heels; hopefully David can't discern it. From the shoes she gleans a ladylike power, and Mrs. Kleid's silence feels like assent.

David leans toward her, intent. "Do *you* think my father did this?"

Laurette takes a sharp breath and says, "Maybe you should ask him."

"Believe me, I will."

How many inches of leg above the knee is a woman's grown son permitted to observe? With David frowning, she pushes up Mrs. Kleid's dark pink skirt. Its silk lining hisses across the nylon stockings, going higher still past the garter, till bruises bloom in plain sight.

"Never again," says David Kleid, "do you hear me?" and then, "Make her decent, please."

On his second day home, he takes his mother and Laurette in a Checker cab to ride the Staten Island Ferry. He wants his mother to see the skyline come and go, see the river ripple. At the curb, David plants a foot on the chair and tilts it up. He has a rugged frame and makes the work seem effortless, and with his deep tan, he looks alien in the gently swirling snow. Mrs. Kleid glances up at him with yearning eyes, and Laurette offers to take over the pushing so he can walk alongside, hold his mother's gloved hand, and talk to her about the Suwannee River gliding smoothly past beneath his tree.

But as they board he falls back to keep pace with Laurette. He tells her: "I talked to him last night. My father. I said if he doesn't stop hurting my mother, I'll come back up north and kill him." He nods at Laurette sagely. "It won't happen again."

Is he really that naive? Behind all his pastry, Mr. Kleid is a bulldog. "Take her home with you," she begs David with sudden urgency, because this morning she found a new bruise above Mrs.

Kleid's wrist. It's hidden by her watch, which Laurette winds every day and slips on along with the clip-on earrings.

David gives a dark laugh. "A rope ladder sways like crazy. I need two hands to hold on."

"How about just up, just once?"

"Laurette, I'm a wilderness guide," says David. "I barely make enough to eat. I disappear for days at a time."

The wind strengthens; cottony clouds turn the color of iron. Their little group retreats to the innards of the ferry, where they buy hot chocolate in paper cups.

"I love you, Ma," says David, and drapes his arms around her.

MR. KLEID OPENS the front door that evening but doesn't come right in. First he hands a cake box by its string to Laurette, then peels off his wet black rubber galoshes, bending up one long leg and then the other like an egret. Finally he steps inside. "Greetings, my errant son." He wallops David on the back with something vaguely resembling fatherly affection. *Don't stagger*, Laurette prays. David doesn't stagger. "Three years of Princeton down the drain," Mr. Kleid says cheerfully. Laurette sees the tightening in David's jaw. She pours Mr. Kleid his two fingers of Johnnie Walker Black, and he sits at the table and drinks down the first finger.

"Hello, my little rhubarb tart," he says when he has swallowed it down.

Mrs. Kleid floats her good hand toward David. Mr. Kleid studies her, then tells Laurette, "I think she needs a pre-dinner nap."

David stays a third day, and on his fourth morning, as he prepares to leave, the tears stand out in his eyes. Laurette sees him speak to his father in a low voice before he leaves; she sees his father wave him away. Maybe it's worked, though, his threat, because when Laurette dresses Mrs. Kleid for the day, she sees not a single new bruise. She has a vague understanding that perhaps he can't help it, the way some mothers shriek back at screaming babies when it gets to be too much. She wants to ask Mrs. Kleid, Why do you cry out that single word, why make yourself complicit?

David pulls Laurette aside as he packs. Almost pleading: "I'm asking you to protect her."

"Don't say that," begs Laurette, but he's choked up, jamming his toothbrush into the pack.

Over the next few days, the old bruises start to turn green and fade, and no new ones appear. But four days after David leaves, Laurette finds a purple bruise flowering near the left breast. Her heart bangs as she imagines a confrontation with Mr. Kleid, an encounter she would surely lose.

Silently she serves him breakfast of two seven-minute eggs and toast. She sits at the table while he stands behind his chair, tying his tie, leaning over to manage bites of the egg. She'll boil two more for his wife when he's gone. "Mrs. Kleid is getting hurt," she says in a sudden rush, cracking open their silence. "A lot." Then, in a panic as he stares at her, "She needs to see a doctor. Something is wrong with her." How did she veer off target like this? Nothing is wrong with Mrs. Kleid except her one shimmering word.

Mr. Kleid's gaze bores into her forehead.

"Maybe she has a vitamin deficiency," Laurette says, praying *Don't get angry.*

His wife, wide-eyed, shifts her watery blue gaze from one to the other.

"You're darn tootin' something is *wrong* with her," Mr. Kleid says amiably.

"I'd take her," offers Laurette. "To a doctor. I think she bruises when you move her."

Mr. Kleid shakes his head indulgently. Laurette says, "Maybe some medication?" Help shmelp, she thinks. There is no escape for Mrs. Kleid.

"I'll put it under advisement," says Mr. Kleid in a dry tone, tugging at the knot in his tie. "Here, have a cigarette."

He must not think about it very hard, because two mornings later, Laurette sees a new bruise on her charge's slender thigh.

What do they expect of her, these people? "Mr. Kleid," she begins at breakfast, but he is already late, reaching for his hat and gloves. "Wait." She slithers between him and the front door, propelled, no doubt, by the powerful black patent heels she has borrowed from Mrs. Kleid's closet and slipped onto her own feet. Mr. Kleid smiles, and the smile says, You are trying my patience. "I'm supposed to call David." Her voice quavers. David has no phone, and in emergencies she can only call a nearby diner where he gets his mail, and leave a tangled message for him with the cashier.

Mr. Kleid studies her hard. "Yes, call the tree dweller," he finally drawls.

"Or the police." Laurette is whispering now.

Mr. Kleid's sigh is heavy. "Laurette," he says, "you smoke my cigarettes—who's to say *you* didn't bruise her? I run a sales department employing sixty-five men. You're a babysitter." Unable to meet his eyes, she watches his mouth move. "Little girl," he says gently, "some men would stick their wife in an institution. I don't do that. I'm a good provider. But oh sweet Jesus I do hate that word of hers."

At home that night, Laurette gets up from dinner to answer the hallway phone. It's her sister, with a musical racket in the background. That must be jazz. Her father watches sidelong from the table. Laurette says happily, "Mrs. Rudnick. How are you?"

"High as a freakin' kite." Linda's voice is languid, a blackwater river. "How you doing, babe? You all at dinner?"

"Yes, Mrs. Rudnick." Laurette wants to ask her: Do you take a lot of drugs? Do you have a lot of intercourse? Is it fun, your life? Instead she sidles from the hallway into the maid's room and closes the door on the curly cord. "Linda," she hisses into the phone. "I need you to tell me what to do."

A knock at the door and an elaborate falsetto: "Is that for me?" The ruse of Mrs. Rudnick is already painfully thin.

"Soon," calls Laurette. She hears the shifting of her mother's weight. "*Soon*," she repeats, and stretches the cord to the narrow bed, where she slumps.

"What's eating you, babe?" says Linda, and Laurette sees her sister settled like a contented cat.

"The people I work for," says Laurette. "I think he's hurting her. The wife. He leaves bruises on her."

Linda makes a thoughtful noise. "Maybe he's just a great lay."

"Not everything is out of the gutter," says Laurette coldly. "She can't walk or talk. Do I call the police?"

"Babe, babe, babe," says Linda dreamily. "It's a gift to feel the pain of others."

Another knock at the door. Their mother is like a woman parted from her lover, straining for the banished daughter.

"The police would only roll their eyes," says Linda in her river voice. "You marry a woman, you're pretty much allowed to beat her up and rape her. Isn't that something? You confront the man, he'll just promise to stop."

The next day, a pearly sky blesses everything with heavier snow. The snow clings to parked cars and fluted metal trash cans and packs down in the park, so when Laurette, wearing thick socks and rubber boots, wheels Mrs. Kleid out of the building at ten o'clock in the morning, sledders dot the steep hill on Riverside Drive.

We could almost do that, she thinks ruefully, pile onto my old Flexible Flyer and race downhill. Her mind completes the thought: *into traffic*. The vividness of this savage mercy shocks her, as if she could harm Eleanor Kleid with just the power of her mind. Cruel, to even think such a thing.

She pushes the wheelchair across little Riverside Drive and eases it, laboriously and gingerly, down the shallow steps to big Riverside Drive, where cars hiss through the slush, spraying it. There she presses the button, waits for the light. Across the wide boulevard, the oak trees lining the park are all stripped bare, and Laurette, longing for the lost bright canopy of leaves, tells herself the trees aren't dead, just resting.

Two blocks south, the number 5 bus heaves away from its stop and picks up speed.

She strokes Mrs. Kleid's hair with a frosty mittened hand. And because anyone might be this absent-minded, she takes a large step toward the curb. "Imagine, darling," she croons, the chair still moving but still half on the sidewalk. "You'd never have to see him again."

EMBOUCHURE

1970

"Nothing you will see tonight is normal," said Elihu's mother.

It was the first exciting thing she'd ever said. "Hold the railing or you'll trip," she added. They were climbing the front steps of the townhouse on West Tenth Street. "I love my sister, but this is not how a person should live."

Why wasn't it? Piano leaked from the windows, the notes insouciant. Breath went in one end of a trumpet and pure joy came out the other. If he owned such a thing, shining and insolent, his mother would confiscate it.

She pressed the doorbell. She wore lime-green pants and a matching jacket, a walking parrot. She had not left their own apartment in a long time. Twice, on the subway, she had tried to hold his hand.

His cousin Rainey opened the door, shrieked "Aunt Laurette," and flung herself into his mother's arms. She gripped a record album, open end down, and he watched it fly around his mother's back. Her eyes were alive, and she looked like their super Ardelio's daughter, who had a baby—but that was silly, Rainey was twelve. Her album cover read *Stand!* He was already standing there, but this was probably not the message that Sly and the Family Stone, whoever this was, meant to convey. At home, Elihu's grandparents played Broadway-musical records like *Oklahoma!* and *The Boy Friend*. She let go of his mother and stared at Elihu from across the threshold, from a different planet, from a Thanksgiving and a half ago.

In the foyer, Elihu looked up the staircase. He remembered secret rooms, high floors, places to hide. He had been nine then. Uncle Howard had played the piano and kissed some ladies, and Aunt Linda laughed. People lit lumpy, fragrant cigarettes right at the dining table and passed them around. A pale man with long white hair offered to let him blow into the trumpet, but his mother looked at where the man's mouth had been and said, Thank you, no.

Then they stayed away for a long time.

He watched his mother's gaze bind to Rainey's chest. "Sweet pea," she said. "You *grew*."

The piano stopped. The trumpet stopped. People laughed in the parlor. His Uncle Howard appeared with his arm around a lady who was not Aunt Linda. The lady sang out her name, *Radmila*, and offered to get them drinks.

Her pockets were longer than her shorts.

"Maybe a Tab," said Elihu's mother. "I'm Laurette. I'm the crazy sister."

"I never said *crazy*." Uncle Howard unslung his arm from Radmila and hugged Elihu's mother hard. Elihu watched her hand float up. It quivered in midair. Then it gave up and patted Uncle Howard's back.

"Clutterhound, maybe," said Uncle Howard cheerfully. He released her. "Call me a bastard, I'll own up to it," he said.

"*Howard*," said his mother.

"Sue me," he said, then presented Elihu with a large, long-fingered hand.

Elihu took it and found himself trapped in the handshake.

"What are you giving me?" said Uncle Howard. "A baby bird? Crush it, son. Be a man. Welcome to the house of laughter and song."

Rainey dropped the album on the foyer bench. "So who do you like better," she asked Elihu, "Roger Daltrey—"

She was just standing there, but she had a fearsome way of just standing there, like a snake gliding up a pole. His mother was right: Something had turned her into a woman. And however he might squeeze his uncle's hand back, he was going to remain a stalk of wheat. Wheat was the third-largest crop in the United States. He would always look like a stalk of wheat. He would look like wheat in four months when he turned twelve, and if he didn't get killed in junior high, he would look like wheat when he grew up. He knew it, and Uncle Howard, who squeezed his hand even tighter, knew it and didn't like it.

"—or Pete Townshend?" said Rainey. "Tina and I are having an argument."

"Over what?" said Elihu. He didn't know who Tina was.

Uncle Howard laughed and dropped his hand, finally. "Tell Tina to get me a drink," he told Radmila as he walked into the parlor and sat down in a deep chair. "An elixir of beauty and youth."

Radmila said to Elihu, "Tina is a *little girl*." She clopped away on shoes like wooden blocks.

His mother shouted up the stairs, "Linda!" She began climbing. Rainey bounded after her. Halfway up, his mother turned and said firmly, "Elihu. Come with."

But in the parlor, he saw, the pale man was watching him.

Indeed, he seemed to be waiting for him, sprawled on the sofa with his trumpet. Uncle Howard leaned forward in his armchair, knees wide, watching Elihu with obvious amusement.

"*Elihu*," said his mother.

"Crush it, son," Uncle Howard said softly.

Elihu experienced a tiny explosion in his brain. He walked over to the pale man. "I remember you," he said. "You're albino."

"One of my many talents," said the man. "I remember you. You asked if anyone played chess."

Uncle Howard laughed. Across the parlor a red-haired girl lit a cigarette, the same kind from Thanksgiving.

The trumpet glittered and coiled. "Can I try it?" said Elihu.

"Can you *blow* it," said the man. "Let's find out. Seal your lips. Say *mmm*." He waited while Elihu did this. "Now keep your lips together and blow out hard, like this."

The man made a kissy face and then a fantastic, terrible fart sound.

Elihu glanced at Uncle Howard to see if he was in on this mean joke, the idea that Elihu was supposed to make this sound himself. But Uncle Howard was distracted. Radmila had walked in with his drink, and Uncle Howard was pulling her down to him by the hair.

From upstairs Rainey shouted, "Elihu! We can't order pizza without you!"

"I have to go," said Elihu. He would not be humiliated by a mouth fart. But he did not move.

"When you do that into the mouthpiece," the man said patiently, "you make music. But first you have to teach your mouth to do it."

It didn't sound like a trick.

"Harder than you think," said Uncle Howard, while Radmila sat on his lap and picked his fingers from her hair.

Elihu compressed his lips. What he blew out was spit and air. No one laughed.

"Developing your embouchure takes time," said the pale man. He did not explain. "Relax your lips," he said. He did not explain that, either. But Elihu erupted, finally, in a mouth fart.

It was, for about three seconds, a fantastic, terrible mouth fart. No one applauded. This seemed to be serious business in this house. Radmila's smile was a lovely, crooked line.

The man placed in Elihu's hands a gleaming machine that might as well produce chocolates as music, so mysterious were its tubes and curves.

"Bell," said the man, touching it. "Valves. Mouthpiece. Okay? Give me your left hand. Hold it around the valves. Relax those fingers, child. Thumb here, next three fingers around this curve. This one through the ring. Move it. That's the third valve slide. Pinkie here."

Elihu took a breath and raised the trumpet. It might have been a goblet and he might have been a thirsty child.

"Whoa," said the man. He tipped the trumpet back down.

"This is Gordy Vine, son," Uncle Howard said, watching. "I expect you to remember his name."

Mr. Vine took Elihu's right hand. "These three fingertips cover the valves. Pinkie here. Thumb here. Now just feel yourself with the instrument. Take a deep breath. Let it out. Feel the difference? Let those shoulders go. Man oh man. Who knotted you up?"

"Guess," said Uncle Howard.

Radmila ambled over to Mr. Vine and held the cigarette to his lips.

"Elihu," Rainey shouted down the stairs, "you better like mushrooms."

If they served mushrooms in this house, he would like mushrooms.

The girl held the cigarette out to Elihu and arched her blond eyebrows.

"Later," said Mr. Vine. "Lick your lips. Seal them." His finger landed at the corner of Elihu's mouth. "Stay tight *here*," said Mr. Vine, "but try to release the middle. *Now* raise the trumpet. *Blow.*"

Elihu blew. The trumpet made an exasperated sigh.

"Steady air," said Mr. Vine. "You want steady air."

The girl offered the cigarette to Uncle Howard, who sucked on it right from her fingers and held his breath.

Elihu understood that he should not wait for his brain to process *steady air*, that if he placed his faith in this nearly white man and did what he was told, the trumpet might transform the revolting product of his puny body, the mouth fart, into something clarion and burnished and pure.

He inhaled sharply and blew.

Uncle Howard, still holding in the smoke, said in a croaky voice: "Whaddaya know."

HE FOUND THEM eating pizza on the blue bed in the blue room and playing cards: his mother, Aunt Linda, Rainey, and a girl with caramel hair, Tina, he guessed.

When Aunt Linda scrambled off the bed to hug him, her ashtray spilled ash on her pizza. Rainey laughed.

Aunt Linda smelled of flowers. "It's not fair," she said. "He gets all the blond." She stroked his hair out in little tufts. "Sweet pea, we never see you. Laurette, he can't ride the bus?"

"There are creeps on the bus," his mother said.

"There are creeps everywhere," said Aunt Linda. Her voice was exactly like his mother's, but happier. "Rainey rides the subway already. I swear this household runs on pizza. Let's take it up to the roof."

Rainey and Tina exchanged a look, and in the look Elihu saw the engineering schematic for the evening.

"Air would be lovely," said his mother. She unfolded herself. Her feet were bare. Maybe Aunt Linda had told *her* to relax.

"No, thank you," said Elihu. He would stay in this good room and read the posters, which had lots of agitated text and pictures of horns and piano keys. One showed a close-up of a Black man blowing hard into some kind of horn with the mysterious word SOULTRANE. Another one showed many candy-colored circles with holes in the middle, like for a phonograph.

"Why?" Tina ran the tip of her tongue along her teeth. She was taller and she stood too close. "You scared of heights?"

Rainey edged up to the nightstand and tugged the drawer open. Elihu watched her hand dip into the drawer and extract a pack of cigarettes.

"Or you scared of us?" Tina's voice was poured honey. It didn't go with the words.

Meanwhile, Aunt Linda lifted the edge of the mattress and slid money far beneath. "Thanks," she said to Laurette. The women caught him watching. His mother placed her hands on his cheeks and sharply turned his head away.

Rainey came up beside him. "He's always scared," she said. "Double dare you."

His mother and Aunt Linda moved into the hall. His mother carried her Coke and Aunt Linda's wine, and Aunt Linda held the pizza boxes. "All I could get," he heard his mother murmur.

"Hey, it's fifty bucks," Aunt Linda said. "Thanks." The sisters ascended toward the roof, their bare feet glowing. "Ticket out of here," he heard his aunt say, and the women's feet flashed out of sight.

THE ROOF WAS the moon with lawn chairs.

He scuffed along the scumbly black surface. His mother and Aunt Linda dragged two chairs together so they touched. Rainey and Tina whispered near the doorway.

"Watch the parapet," called his mother. "Sweet pea, that's far enough." The world lay everywhere, inky and glittering. Buildings of every height stood bravely in their places. No one made *them* line up by size.

Down on West Tenth Street, the cloth-covered people were convincingly real. They were not like the moving entities far below his grandparents' windows. These were crushable. If Uncle Howard wanted to crush things, here they were.

"El-i-hu," Rainey sang. He turned. She and Tina lounged in the doorway to the stairs. Aunt Linda's head rested on his mother's shoulder, and his mother was fanning away smoke, but peacefully.

He let Rainey and Tina lead him away from the mothers, out of sight, behind the little hut with the stairway door.

"Sit *down*, Elihu." Rainey's voice was velvety but not nice. He sat. "Elly-belly," she crooned. *Stand!* It was not advice he could take right now. Rainey and Tina each lit a Kool cigarette, their long hair dangerously near the match, their hands touching in a tender cup. Then Rainey whacked the pack on her knee and a cigarette shot partway out. She extended it.

"Afraid, Elly-Belly?" said Tina.

"Yes," he said.

"Jesus H. Christ," said Rainey.

"Don't call me that," said Tina.

"Quit it," said Rainey. "That's my father's line." A knife shot out of her eye, but Tina, he noticed, seemed not to feel it.

One of the mothers called out, "You kids all right? There's still pizza."

Rainey shoved the pack at him. "Smoke," she said. "It'll put hair on your chest." She and Tina cracked up.

"I bet you're scared to kiss a girl," Tina said.

"No," he said. This, too, was true. Kissing a girl was not scary, exactly. Disgusting, maybe. And this was a function of something deep inside, something that would persist, something, also, that he knew his uncle could perceive.

Tina planted her palms on the tar paper and leaned toward him so her chest stuck out. "Show me," she said.

"Yeah, show her," said Rainey. "'Cause you look scared."

Tina licked her teeth. Her mouth was a Venus flytrap.

If he ran, there could be no stopping. He would have to run past the mothers, down the stairs, past his uncle and Mr. Vine, east on West Tenth, uptown on Sixth, left around Central Park, north on Broadway, west on 100th, downhill and into his building and rudely past Ray with no explanation, up five flights, past his grandparents and into his own room, *slam*. And then?

"I can't," he said. "Kissing is private."

Tina made a noise in her nose. "Not in this house," she said.

"Oh, come on. Rainey's parents are all *I Am Curious Yellow*. No one cares."

Rainey waved her cigarette and said, "Kiss her or we'll drop you over the roof."

They could do it.

He said, "My father is teaching me kung fu."

A whirl of smoke found his face. "Oh, right," said Rainey. "Everyone knows about your dad."

But that was not possible. His mother never spoke about his father, ever. No one knew anything about Elihu's father except Elihu, who had it all worked out, including: hair color, eye color, hometown, career, unassailable reason for departure, the day of their eventual reunion, and the rest of their lives together.

"Your dad took *one look* at you." Rainey exhaled a Saturn ring. Her hair dipped forward. From behind it, she said, "My father was right about you." Elihu waited. Sometimes, if you waited, they got bored.

Rainey said, as if murmuring to someone else, "Little faggot."

"Kiddos," one of the mothers sang out. "Last slice with pepperoni," and then the other called, "Elihu? Sweet pea, you want to join us?"

Tina laughed. "Look, he's scared to defend himself."

Jab. Right hook. Grandpa Marty kept trying to teach him those. It turned out that what the body wanted was to curl like a poked caterpillar and take its blows.

"I know," said Rainey. "Let's go to my room and play the Who."

"I don't know how," said Elihu.

"Oh," said Tina, "trust me. We'll show you."

RAINEY PRODDED HIM to her pink rug, to sit. Tina split open a blue album like a book, and placed a record called *Tommy* on Rainey's stereo. He watched her carefully, even reverently, set down the needle as if some sacrificial ritual had begun.

The speakers hissed. Then music yanked at his body. He was a marionette. It *danced* him. The girls looked down at him with light in their faces, and he davened to something sovereign and dark.

"Ooh, he likes it," said Tina, and Elihu came to himself, and froze.

"We have a joke for you." Rainey knelt on the rug, moving in that snaky way.

"It's a test," Tina said. "If you don't get this, you are *definitely* what Howard says."

But he was not going to pass the test.

Rainey licked her lips. "Ready?" He was not ready. "Two monkeys sat in a bathtub," she said. "One said, 'Pass the soap.' The other said, 'No soap, radio.'"

He looked at her radiant, expectant face. That was it? That was a joke? He reached out to her bookshelf and picked up a tiny plastic creature. Its ugly face had a sweetness, and from its head flowed a fantastic length of soft orange hair.

"Un. Be. Lievable," said Tina in three distinct sentences. "Rain? He doesn't get it."

"You need to hear it again?" said Rainey. "'Cause I can say it ve-ry slow-ly."

"No," said Elihu, stroking the creature's hair. A new song came on the stereo. The voice had an intimate rage he had never heard before.

Tina said, "That's Roger Daltrey," and he remembered now: an argument. He liked Roger Daltrey.

"I've told this joke to fourteen kids," Rainey said, "and everyone got it but you."

If he stood up and walked to the door, would they stop him?

"Oh, hell," said Rainey. She tipped gracefully to one side, a tulip, and he felt something heavy slip from her. "Let's tell him."

Tina touched his knee. "You passed," she said. "There is no joke. If someone says 'I get it,' it's peer pressure." She took her hand back but still he felt it.

"Everyone says they get it," said Rainey. "Like every single one. Except you."

"Okay," he said. Maybe they'd let him get up now. He stood. They didn't stop him. He walked to a pink table that wore a skirt, set down the plastic creature with the orange hair, and picked up a small glass bottle.

"That's Lala's," said Rainey. "My grandmother's. I get them when there's just a little left. Sniff." She sounded like a whole new cousin. The bottle said *White Shoulders*. He sniffed. It smelled of violin music and pretty teachers and buildings lit up at night.

"We could put a dab behind your ear," said Tina. She got to

her feet and walked over. "He has no idea how gorgeous he is," she said. "We could even do makeup. Just the teeniest bit."

He knew what Uncle Howard would think of that.

"You'd be beautiful, Elihu," Rainey said. "You already are, but more."

On the table he saw lipsticks and a compact, items his mother and grandmother seemed to fish for in their purses every fifteen minutes, and little containers that said *Love*. "If you don't like it," said Rainey, "it comes right off."

"We're really good," said Tina.

His tongue stuck to his mouth inside so that he couldn't answer.

"*Yes*," said Rainey, addressing the ceiling. She pulled out a little stool, which wore a pink skirt like the table.

He sat. He closed his eyes. He was ready to eat mushrooms now. He felt and heard the girls moving around him, clicking things onto the glass top, leaning into him with a thigh, an arm, touching his face, murmuring in another language, the language of girls. *Cream blush*, he heard, and *Pass me the blue* and *Gloss, right?* and then Rainey told him to open his eyes but look down, and something stroked his eyelashes.

"Look at you," said Rainey. "Twiggy's little sister."

He opened his eyes. A girl looked back at him. She had his hair, blond, and his eyes, blue. But these were girl eyes, dark rimmed and long lashed. She had his cheekbones, but very pink, and his mouth, also shiny and girl pink.

But Elihu was not a girl! He thought he might vomit. "No," he said.

"You're beautiful," said Rainey. "Most girls would kill to look like you."

"I would," said Tina. But she was already perfect. She had cat eyes, and gold in her hair.

"Take it off," he said. He had no idea what this might involve, the removal of a face.

"But we did a nice job, right?" said Rainey.

He rubbed at his eye and his knuckles smeared blue.

He wanted to be a boy again—but soft. A boy, but pretty. He wanted to move like a snake while standing still.

Rainey held up a cotton ball like a prize. "Just say you look pretty," she said, "and I'll take it off."

The door to her room opened.

For a moment the grown-ups remained in the hall, laughing. Then his mother walked in with Uncle Howard. They were kidding with each other, and then not.

"Jesus Christ, don't knock or anything," said Rainey.

"Elihu?" said his mother.

Uncle Howard said, "Better turn the music off."

"*Elihu?*" said his mother.

Rainey silenced the stereo. "It was my idea," she said.

"But I did it," said Tina. "I made him up."

Aunt Linda leaned in the doorway. "A game," she said cheerfully.

Uncle Howard said, "Laurette, let's give him time to get ready."

"What ready?" his mother said. She was a crazy sister, a clutterhound, a thirty-three-year-old spinster with no husband or job who lived with her parents and her bastard son. She was no one to be afraid of. Yet Elihu was afraid.

His mother said, "It's eleven o'clock at night, he should be ready. What have you done to yourself, Elihu?"

"Laurette," said Uncle Howard. "Come with me."

Aunt Linda said, "Sweet pea, they were just playing. Why don't you let me—"

"Don't try to fix this," his mother said. "This would only happen in your house." She came over and inspected his face. Her irises were brown. His irises were blue, but she never commented on that. "Who are you?" she said. "I walked in with a son. You think I'm going home with a daughter?"

"*Laurette*," said Uncle Howard, and Elihu knew now what his grandfather had meant. That time those boys bloodied him up, walking home from Hebrew school, he had not fought back, and at dinner his grandfather looked down at his plate and said *feygele*, and his mother rose from her chair and gripped the table, and Grandma Sophie had said, Mart. You don't know.

"I made him do it," said Rainey.

"Excuse me," his mother snapped. "He's a boy. You're a girl. You can't *make* him do anything. I have news for you, sweet pea. In life it's the other way around."

Rainey didn't answer, but Elihu saw light flare in her eyes, and he sensed that the light would be her ticket out of there.

Then Aunt Linda tugged his mother out of the room, and the door closed hard. Uncle Howard was with him now, talking quietly. He felt, to his amazement, Rainey braiding her fingers with his.

"Look at me," Uncle Howard said.

Elihu watched instead Tina's toes, long and elegant, curling into the rug. The nails were painted. They looked like garnets.

"I want you to have a good life, son," Uncle Howard said. "A safe life. Who you are"—he touched Elihu's cheekbone—"is not something to wear on your face. Not yet. It's your secret. You dig?"

Elihu dug.

"You think you can change now?" Uncle Howard said.

The door opened and his mother cried out, "Make him understand, Howard." He heard her say, in a lower voice, "I should have done something, Linda. I should have taken care of it."

Who knotted you up? he thought.

Out in the hall, he heard Aunt Linda say, "Laurette. Don't even *think* that."

Elihu looked at his uncle, finally. He thought he could change now.

Uncle Howard said, "Try not to worry your mother again." He thrust his hand out, and Elihu saw that he was, again, expected to shake.

Here was a little faggot fact: This was not a hand he would ever manage to crush.

But he took it.

THE WISE AND THE HONEST

1971

For three days after he died, Jim Morrison sang in Rainey's room—about girls, thrills, a crystal ship to where, exactly? Knocking got Linda nowhere.

Finally, she readied herself by her daughter's door. In one hand she held a mug of licorice tea. From the other hand dangled all the hair that belonged on her head.

What do you tell a daughter, thirteen, at such a time? That every girl must get dismantled by such a love? Linda nudged the door with her foot.

Her daughter stood tiptoe on a chair, between the windows, reaching up, so that Linda got a flash of the paint-stained soles of her feet. In one hand Rainey held an emerald-tipped brush, in the other a cigarette.

Broken sunlight filtered through that stupid dying elm out back and fell across her daughter's skin like torn lace.

Linda set the tea on the sill by the chair and stepped back. Rainey was painting a tree of life. She had centered its trunk between the room's two windows. Animals smaller than Linda's hand balanced with grace on heart-shaped leaves, some painted, some still lightly sketched in pencil. You could see the *weight* of each creature—the shadowed green sleeve of leaf from which a caterpillar reared, the startled shadow of a sweet kangaroo. An armadillo crept along the baseboard—didn't they carry rabies?

Linda lowered the volume on the stereo. "You can't mourn in here forever, sweet pea," she said, and that was her first mistake.

Rainey swiveled. Her narrow gaze flicked first to the hair that streamed, luxurious and sensual, from Linda's fingers, then to her mother's bare head.

Linda's scalp ignited.

No one could explain to her why her own, real hair had taken a hike. The first clump had washed out several years ago with a lather of Lemon Up. The hairs did not want to leave Linda any more than Linda wanted to surrender them. They clung to her shoulders and flank. They swirled her initials on the shower tiles.

Rainey exhaled a wand of smoke. "Beauty is dead," she said.

Linda understood this to mean that Morrison, that lush, thin boy who was half Jagger and half Jesus, still belonged in some way to his girlfriend, Pamela Courson, whom Rainey loathed like a rival. So Linda kept her counsel on Courson, but Christ Jesus, what she wouldn't trade to be Neil Young's Cinnamon Girl while running her very own fashion boutique, like Morrison gave Courson? Anything. She'd trade anything. And anyhow, her daughter was so wrong.

"Sweet pea," said Linda, "beauty is everywhere."

Beauty lay as near as their own basement. Beauty was Linda's suitcase, packed and stashed under that nasty heap of duffel bags near the boiler. Beauty was a bus ticket to Denver for 5 A.M. tomorrow, tucked in the blue satin lining with a hundred dollars from her mom and fifty from her sister, Laurette, and a packet of letters from a man named Ask Du Plessis who existed in a whole other dimension of kindness than Linda's husband.

Her daughter reached up and stroked a leaf stem into existence. An antelope, sketched in pencil, stood on the leaf, distending it with its fairy weight. "You know," mused Linda, "the Kabbalah's got a tree of life, but with mystical spheres instead of leaves."

She had saved the first clumps of hair in a baggie. The doctor wasn't interested. He gave her a big-name diagnosis for Your Hair Got Bored Of You. Two words, both pretty. She promptly forgot them. *Bald* and *ugly*, she told the doctor, those would do fine.

"This isn't mystical." Rainey drew on her cigarette, then filled in part of the leaf. "It's from the Persian carpet in the store window on Fourteenth Street."

Linda studied the tree. She had something to say about divine energy and limitless light, but she simply said, "You've been holed up here for days. Come take a walk."

No response. She looked around the room, struggling for purchase. On the wall over the bureau, her daughter had painted a lamp with knowing eyes; over the dressing table, a flying horse. And levitating over the pillow of her daughter's bed, either guarding or grieving, was a painted four-armed girl goddess, sitting lotus-style and bleeding from the tips of all twenty fingernails: What was that?

Desperate, Linda spotted *The Last Whole Earth Catalog* on a cache of dropped clothes. "How's Divine Right?" she said. Divine Right was a man on a journey. The story was serialized. You had to buy each *Whole Earth Catalog* to read it. In fact, Divine Right was making a journey by bus, too, a VW bus—wasn't the bus *narrating*?

Her daughter got down from the chair. Linda admired how even that loose, thick braid seemed to move with a mind of its own as Rainey knelt to swap paintbrushes. She traded emerald for jade, rose, hesitated, and angled a look at the hair Linda held.

"Dad hates it when you take that off," she said, then climbed back up.

That was Veruschka, the prettiest Linda owned. Veruschka was long, almost riotous, luxuriant and dirty blond, made with actual hair from some actual chick's head. But the itching was torture. Linda kept dislodging it to scratch. She was *supposed* to take it off sometimes, let the scalp breathe.

Howard didn't like watching Linda's scalp breathe.

He had fallen in love with Linda and Linda's real, original hair inseparably. He would toy with the tangles, plumb the nape of her neck with his thumbs till she groaned with pleasure, and kiss her temples. He would lift the locks and let them spill, entranced as a boy playing with mercury. Back in high school, Laurette rolled her hair around Minute Maid cans at night, while Linda finger-fluffed hers before school so it spelled out certain things very clearly, if invisibly, around her head, like S E X and D R I N K I N G. Her father railed about it every morning.

Linda hung in her daughter's doorway, feeling ignored in a bruised sort of way.

"Come out, and I'll wear it," she said. "There's something I have to tell you."

Rainey lifted one knee, tipped her ash onto the thigh of her jeans, and rubbed it in. Linda understood this to mean that new hip-huggers were being aged.

"C'mon, a mother-daughter walk," said Linda. God, she sounded needy. She wanted to call her own mother and cry, but if her father answered he'd hang up and Linda would feel worse. She and her mother had to sneak-meet at Gristedes once a week.

Ask had written: *When home is a place you carry inside, no one can evict you.*

"Pretty please." Linda jammed her mother's emerald-cut diamond ring into her other palm, then dipped a fingertip into the rectangular dent. Bitter Creek was as alien to Linda—whose parents had taken her and her sister only to Jerusalem and Jones Beach—as the moon. If something bad happened to her out there, that ring was a car, it was six months' rent; it was a ticket out of there, it was a ticket home.

Rainey said, "Tina and I are *officially* in mourning. We're wearing black for a year." She had on, indeed, a black T-shirt, but regular jeans. Since when did her daughter own black anything? And who would scrub the ring of black Rit dye that would probably manifest in her sink? Disheartened, Linda looked again at the antelope. It had such sweetness in its stance that she was moved.

And this, too, was beauty: a weeping gray lady in the dairy aisle of Gristedes, tugging off her own engagement ring, a two-carat diamond in a three-stone setting, and giving it to her bald, fucked-up, disowned daughter who was, once again, running away from home.

Jim Morrison was singing about a blue bus. It's calling us, he sang, and Linda thought, You got that right, sweet pea, only the bus that's calling me is silver and red: Trailways. She was studying the tree of life, how Rainey had notched the bark with bits of silvery light, when the piano banged discordantly to a stop downstairs. Then came a disgruntled silence, broken by Howard's shout: "Yo. Linda. Think we could get some *god damn lunch*?"

"Huh," said Linda, as if lunch were a quaint and novel idea, as if it were not her job to make it materialize by three in the afternoon for any musicians playing that day, then collect the dishes, then throw in the laundry and get a start on dinner. She wasn't complaining. Was she complaining? She was thirty-five, less than halfway along the highway of life—she was lucky. She was alive. She had a beautiful child, her health, her teeth if not her hair, a roof over her pretty head.

Rainey shot her a questioning look.

"What?" said Linda musically. For she had made her last

salami sandwich ever. She had made enough salami and cheese sandwiches to pave the planet, and not just for her husband and his best friend, trumpet player, charity case Gordy, who God forbid should pay some rent, but for Howard's talented, pretty acolytes. Acolytes did not make sandwiches. They did not clear. After meals they stubbed their smokes into their plates and went back into orbit around Howard in the parlor, playing flute, violin, she could barely keep track. She'd rather be sewing clothes. Jesus, Linda, stop suffering, Howard said. They're *artists*.

Suffering is a crucible that helps make us wise.

That was Ask quoting Ram Dass, or misquoting, she could never be sure with him. And Linda agreed, after she asked what a crucible was, but she had written back boldly, I *think suffering is a crucible that helps make us wives*. Then Ask blew her mind. *Well, Ms. Linda Royal*, he wrote, *you just nailed a major American social and economic problem going back centuries with one ironic line—pow.*

Pow? Had Howard ever listened to Linda and thought *pow?*

She looked jealously at her daughter. Howard would see Rainey every morning after Linda left, eating breakfast cereal or calling Tina like it was no big deal.

Memorize me, Rainey. I'm about to disappear. But she couldn't get the ESP phone to ring, so all she said was "Just to the Arch."

In the park: that's where she'd tell her. Squinting up at the words of George Washington, engraved so clear he might as well be standing there, hands in his Colonial pockets, going, *Let us raise a standard to which the wise and honest can repair.*

She had a plan for telling her, too. The plan got as far as this line: Your father drains a drop of my blood every day with his casual cruelty. And beyond that? Every time she saw her daughter's face in her mind, it bore an entirely different expression.

Howard bellowed again. "Yo. Babe."

Linda tipped her head toward the waiting staircase. "Yo. Busy," she shouted.

The house crackled with an astonished silence. "Go, Gloria Steinem," Rainey said, and returned to the delicate veinwork on the leaf on which the antelope stood.

"Rainey," said Linda. "I can't tell you what I need to tell you in this house."

"Yeah, but—" Her daughter fell into the absorption of a watchmaker. Linda watched the brush move in incremental ticks, like the second hand on her Timex. Then a slow, audible exhalation. "I can't leave 'cause Tina's on her way."

Tina, the alter ego. On the subway from the grandmother's in Spanish Harlem. Linda was beaten. "Well, aren't we all just walking each other home? Or something like that." It came out way too cheerful. Linda doing Ram Dass was nothing like Ask doing him, looking into that jewel box of quotes and extracting the perfect solitaire.

And you know what? Fuck it. She'd slip into her daughter's room just before dawn. The house would be asleep. Her suitcase would do half the talking. When Linda left, Rainey would still be in bed, rubbing her eyes, wondering if it had been a dream.

Surgical.

· THE WISE AND THE HONEST ·

A pair of silver earrings, shaped like clefs, lay on Rainey's bureau. It was so easy to cup her palm there, to slide the earrings out of Rainey's old life, which contained a mother, and into Linda's new life in the mountains a hundred miles from Denver, where, she imagined, the air was so credulous a blue she would awake each morning forgiven.

IT WAS TWO o'clock in the morning, and upstairs, in the parlor, people were playing the kind of loud, live music that thirteen years ago her infant daughter had learned to sleep through. But at the bottom of the basement stairs, where Linda groped in the air, the sound reached her as if through cotton wool, thanks to the muting of wooden rafters.

She pulled the string. A solitary bulb wept yellow light. At the back of the cellar, her fawn suitcase glowed beneath duffel bags gone stiff with grime and life experience.

"Ticket out of here," she said aloud, as a thin, pure clarinet leaked through the beams and insulation.

Where had Howard stashed his mother's jewels? *Unblind my eyes*, she prayed, and the basement shewed unto her its grand decay. She saw a water bug burble from a wall. She saw sheet music flaking on a shelf. She saw paint cans necklaced in rust, drying from the inside out.

Last summer, when the ambulette men carried Lala Royal away, Howard had wrapped up his mother's jewelry and brought it down here. All those acolytes getting into things, he said. A ring had already disappeared. Lala couldn't walk after the first stroke and she couldn't hold her pee after the second, so he moved her into a Home. Don't, begged Linda. She missed her own mother every day, and she had attached herself to this sweet, spacey cloth mother who loved her back without quite perceiving her. Linda pleading, I'll change her diapers, I'll feed her dinner. Rainey blocking the front door. Howard saying, Ma, for God's sake, don't be like this, I'll see you every Sunday. But Lala turned her face from him, and every Sunday was a load of crap, and after the ambulette left Howard yanked his mother's dresses and shoes from her closets, shouting things Linda could not believe a man would say about his mother, and hurled them into the hall and down the stairs. How could she, Linda, have been his helpmeet then, when he would not let her near? Howard sent an acolyte to dump the clothes on the curb, and Rainey barged out and picked those slim, elegant, old-lady things out of the gutter before scavengers could descend. They were down here now, boxed up and mislabeled on purpose, stashed in the utility room.

Pretty soon, Linda's clothes would be down here, too, and it would be her daughter's secret job to transport them: hidden, mislabeled, safe from Howard's rage.

She undertook the filthy concrete floor in her bare feet like a cat traversing a puddle. This place was full of goddamn beauty. She had helped Howard wrap his mother's jewelry in torn-out pages of *DownBeat*. Beauty was a watch with a rind of diamonds. Beauty was a rare faceted painite like a champagne grape, poised impertinently on its prongs.

In Lala's portrait upstairs, these things lay warm on her skin: her eyes young and mischievous, sadness sealed in her mouth.

Nearly everything would be their daughter's when she turned twenty-five. First, the jewels, which Rainey had played dress-up with as a little girl. Second, the house. And third, the trust. Her daughter had never asked about any of it. She didn't see it speeding toward her down the years like a comet, shedding money from its tail. And Linda wasn't supposed to tell.

How much was in the trust depended on Howard's mood. *Plenty* or *We won't starve* or *Don't you believe me?* The lawyer had said, in front of Linda: If it's spending in support of your daughter's household, it's fine. Howard was spending on the household, all right—six people, eight people, give or take, mostly female people playing all kinds of music and having all kinds of sex and letting Howard pay for all the rocky road and meat loaf to fill a couple of bathtubs a week, never mind the wine and pot and beer and coke and reeds and guitar strings and concert tickets and two-drink minimums and visits from the piano tuner.

Besides her daughter, nothing in this house belonged to Linda, and nothing was what she planned to take.

The shovel leaned by the sidewalk salt. She carried it to the boiler, dropped to her knees, and poked it underneath. On the concrete floor it made a sound like a taxi colliding with a bus. After some scraping, she had amassed only a dune of tarry dirt.

She rose, dusted herself off somewhat, and looked around.

A shadowy movement caught her eye, and something rustled,

ghostly, by the dryer. Linda yelped, wielding the shovel. But the ghost was only a girl: Gemma, weeping.

Howard didn't like to see girls cry.

"Scare the shit out of me, why don't you," said Linda.

Gemma stood beneath a cloud, an Afro of such enormity and atmospheric delicacy that Linda wanted to pillow her face in it, though she knew that would be rude. Howard pillowed all the time. Howard had found Gemma in the Times Square subway, playing a ribbony electric violin. Her other instrument was her throat; she scatted with a buttery voice.

"I need to be alone down here," said Linda, "if you don't mind."

That was her second mistake. Something girded in Gemma's gaze, and Linda felt herself slowly scrutinized, her filthy arms, her dirty feet.

"What are you burying?" Gemma's eyes were drying. She had a clipped English accent that Howard used to love.

Linda weighed the shovel. She wore the very armament of the world's most powerful model—Veruschka—who had made the cover of all four *Vogue*s: American, Italian, British, and French. Who had made ten thousand dollars a *day* with that hair. Whose father had tried to kill Hitler, for Chrissake. Linda's own father would have loved that, the Hitler thing, but Linda was dead to her father, not capital-*D* dead, but sitting-shiva dead. He had covered the mirrors right in front of her.

She hiked the shovel instructively toward the stairs. "Ciao, bella."

Gemma sagged. Snail tracks peeked from her nose. "Howard doesn't love me."

Linda found she had so many things to say she had to boss them into line.

Howard loved Howard, first. Howard loved Rainey, in his way. And? There was no *and*. He had goaded Gemma into working harder and singing better, and while she was soaring, he'd sucked her dry. That was the point of Operation Acolyte.

"Join the club," said Linda. Gemma's eyelids brimmed. Encouraged, Linda went on. "The Howard Doesn't Love Me Club. I'll get you a membership card," and Gemma began to cry. "Embossed!" said Linda brightly.

Ask had written: *It's not what you look at that matters, it's what you see: Thoreau.* Ask did not give one flying fuck that she was bald. So he was entitled to the detriments of his own particular body, specifically, as he wrote with neither embarrassment nor embellishment, that he had three fused vertebrae in his neck and could not turn his head, and that he was old—fifty-one.

Linda didn't want Howard to find that one out, ever. He would laugh his ass off.

Gemma said, "But you're his *wife*."

Then her gaze shot to Linda's ankles, and she screamed and launched herself onto the dryer, emitting psycho shrieks.

Linda looked down. It took a split, blissful second to grok that the thing rippling past her was a rat. But Linda had a low freak-out reflex. She stood and watched Gemma on the dryer yelling for help as the rat wound disinterestedly past her toes and skittered toward the boiler.

A moment passed. Then footsteps and yelling commenced overhead. The rat had just finished streaming under the duffel bags when Howard charged into the basement, stirring the air with that stupid snubby revolver he kept in the file cabinet.

Gemma, up on the dryer, cried out in pulses.

Linda, amused, watched Howard assess the situation. On his T-shirt, which he planned to die and be buried in, Satchmo looked heavenward, struck by joy. Howard, struck by irritation, looked at Gemma on the dryer. "Don't make me shoot you," he said.

Gemma, pointing toward the duffel bags, dialed into the sound of a beagle tied to a parking meter. It sounded to Linda like she was barking *rat, rat, rat.*

"Mercy killing?" suggested Linda, and that's when Rainey sauntered downstairs.

She wore a white nightie. Her eyes shone. She sashayed toward them as if they, her parents, were a source of light, and Linda thought: Finally, we staged something of interest to our daughter. "Hey, sweet pea," she said.

Rainey swayed into Linda like a vine finding a stake, and coaxed something brackish from her mother's ostensible hair.

Her daughter's body felt anchoring against her own. Linda smiled at Howard. He had the countenance of a baron, or a duke—a skinny title, not like earl. He could make it rain on other planets just by playing the piano here on Earth. And Linda?

Linda was a little Jewish girl, high school diploma, raised for docility by a man who pounded the dinner table and a woman whose shoulders had gone round under the shouting in the apartment. For a while, after Linda got declared dead at home, she did alterations, but taking in other people's seams just made her sad. Then she modeled for a catalog.

But Howard had married her. From the start his girls had walked her halls, shared their bed. But he'd married *her*.

Rainey hung off Linda, looking hopefully back and forth between her parents.

"Gemma saw a rat," said Linda, and when Gemma covered her own breasts, as if rodents might be leaping at them even now, Linda added cheerfully, drawing it out, "Rrrrat." She felt Rainey's laughter in her own body. It was nice.

"You women," said Howard, "you astonish me." He turned, the gun swinging loosely at his side, and began to walk upstairs.

Gemma looked urgently around the basement, and Linda saw her gaze alight on an offering, and she saw, also, that she was it.

"Hey," called Gemma. Howard ducked and looked back at her. "Linda was digging for something under the furnace."

Linda whispered into Rainey's ear, "It's a boiler."

"Don't talk about my mother," said Rainey.

Howard paused. He stepped back down and stood under the golden weeping bulb. He looked at Linda, at the shovel, at Linda.

Linda said, "I was after the rat, baby." But she had answered a question he hadn't asked.

"She's ly-ing." Gemma drew it out teasingly, like there might be a blow job waiting at the end. "Your wife was all on the floor poking that *shovel* under there." Now that she had everyone's attention, she lowered herself to a seated position and swung her heels, till Howard shot a glance at her booming feet.

"Interesting." He walked over, tipped up Linda's chin, and smiled into her eyes.

Linda's composure had been tested by the best. Her composure had been tested by a pair of tan-slacks-wearing "account executives" who posed her in peephole bras and G-strings for a "catalog." She never saw any damn catalog. *Okay, honey. Show us some thigh. All fours now. Take it off. Yeah, off. Don't be a cunt.*

"Plus I clean out the gunk under there once a year," said Linda, answering another question he hadn't asked, "so it won't run hot. Thank you, Linda. You're welcome, Howard."

Her voice did not waver. She concentrated on the divot her daughter's chin was making in her shoulder, while Howard evaluated the little hill of dirt across the basement.

Finally he told Gemma, "That was *my rehearsal* you interrupted," and stalked toward the stairs.

Gemma cocked her head, about to sing out, and Linda observed how fine an instrument she had become, metering Howard's interest merely from the flare of his eyes. "She said she wanted to be alone down here," crooned Gemma. "She said—"

Howard turned back, his eyebrows peaked. He met Gemma's gaze. She fluttered her lashes and slipped into Linda's musing voice. "'—*Ticket out of here.*'"

The stiffening that Linda perceived in her daughter was so subtle it could have hidden in the space between heartbeats.

She beamed at Rainey a mental image. It was a picture of a sock.

Rainey beamed back a telepathic query: *Huh?*

Watch me, Linda commanded her daughter in silence. She concentrated hard. In her mind's eye, she held out to Rainey Lala's jewels, a glimmering heap in the cup of her two palms. Linda focused so hard on the images she was transmitting she realized she had stopped breathing. No matter: With pretty clinks, she funneled the pins and rings and earrings into the sock. *Keep watching*, she silently commanded her daughter, while giving Howard a brilliant smile, and she mentally deposited the sock into the toe of a fringed suede boot, now rigid from rain, that Rainey had shoved into the far-back dusty corner of her closet.

Don't forget, Linda added telepathically, *because at some point your father will storm around saying I made off with these things, and you'll want to remember where they are.*

When she felt her daughter relax against her, Linda hung up the ESP phone and went into action.

"Gemma fakes it," she said, in a tone caught between *bored* and *disgusted*. "Every time." She would know, it was her bed—she was right there. But Howard wasn't listening.

He jerked the gun toward her. Every time he told about buying that gun off the street, the dude got meaner and bigger, and Howard just got cooler, till at some point in the retelling the guy—if there was a guy—started throwing in an eighth of a gram for free. That was his story.

"Ticket to where, my wife?" Howard spoke gently. He stroked her cheek. His pupils were dimes.

Never complain, never explain. Linda's own mother said that. She felt the penlights of Rainey's attention. Howard's muscular fingers wove into her hair, looping it lightly around one fist. Veruschka scritched on her tender scalp.

"Aw, baby. How do I love thee." He pulled her close and sniffed, and she knew he smelled her tea rose oil. In his eyes she saw again the thin French omelets he had once cooked for her, the telling little portraits he used to draw of her on napkins and envelopes, on the backs of sheet music. Howard said, "You cook good. You look good. You make a *fine* shirt."

Then his tongue moved wet and snaky up her face, and she smelled tobacco, peppermint, and far beneath it the odor of sleep.

"Daddy, that is gross." Rainey squirmed back a step. Linda felt Gemma's sticky attention on them all.

"You're still the sexiest woman I know," said Howard. "You're my one true friend. I have always trusted you."

He had never before said that. His gun hand caressed her, and she thought: *My man.* Hidden under the duffels, her suitcase sent out Morse code to her heart. *Unpack me*, it said. *Stay. Make your marriage a standard to which the wise and honest can repair.*

She thought about it. Fifteen years invested. A *child*.

"I never regretted marrying you," said Howard. "You've been my partner."

"Howard," said Gemma. "Why does she want a ticket—"

"Not now," said Howard. Though he held Veruschka taut, the smile he gave Linda conveyed an easy and intimate pleasure.

The doctor, after waving away her baggie of hair, had one more thing to impart. A wig can be sexier than the real thing, he'd confided, before dismissing her. Some husbands love them. And Linda had said, Really? Does your wife wear one?

Still holding Veruschka, Howard lifted her chin with the gun. He was a pianist—she knew his fingers would not slip.

"I should take you to Paris," he said. "Or Madagascar," and Linda closed her eyes. As their daughter's fingertips spidered down a lock of Veruschka that had slipped his grasp, Linda dreamed of Madagascar, where the air, she imagined, was so clarified a pink she would awake every morning beloved.

"First class all the way for my bride," said Howard. She leaned into him, tuning out an irritable, hollow drumbeat: Gemma kicking her feet again. "How about this," he said. "You tell me when you find my mother's jewelry, and I'll take you to the Forest of Knives."

Linda bit down hard on her lower lip. The pain shocked her brain, and her brain told her that somewhere she had made a third mistake.

Rainey shoved the gun away from Linda. "Daddy, you can't sell Lala's jewelry."

Gemma watched wide-eyed as if in a movie theater. Make

her go away, Linda wanted to say, but she had no currency now and she knew it.

"Sweet pea," she said. "Rainey's right. We can't sell it." She inhaled sharply. "Tell her what happens when she's twenty-five."

Rainey draped an arm around both of their waists as if they were all one big love bomb. "What happens when I'm twenty-five?" Her breath licorice-sweet.

"I give you the keys to the kingdom," said Howard. "If you're good."

Linda whispered, "Howard, couldn't we put it in a vault till then?"

"We?" He gave her a metallic smile. "There is no we."

"You guys," said Rainey. "What kingdom? What happens when I'm twenty-five?"

Linda understood now that she was already on the bus. That Howard not only had packed her suitcase himself but slid it into the belly of the Trailways.

"What is the Forest of Knives?" Rainey squeezed her father's arm.

Linda said, "You said I was your one true friend." He could have the jewelry if he would repeat it. "You said you trusted me." Had he even *blinked*? "If you love me, there's a we."

Howard stretched his back till something cracked. He looked pleased. "Oho," he said. "So we're playing If You Love Me."

Gemma swung her legs, and the dryer gave two sharp retorts. "Embossed membership card," she sang.

"I'll go first," said Howard. "If you love me"—he looked

thoughtfully up into the rafters—"you won't walk around *my house* looking like a goddamn egg."

"*Daddy?*" Rainey stared at him.

"What is it, baby?" Howard's hand moved.

And for a moment, it could have gone either way, a caress or a smack. Instead, Linda felt cool basement air on her scalp, and then he held her hair, limp and high, like a rat pulled from a trap.

"I mean," he said, "look at you, baby. Why do you make me look at this?"

And the heart of Linda was blacked by the closing of many gates, and their names came back to her from the temple of her childhood, shaming her: the Gate of Ephraim, the Old Gate, the Fish Gate, the Sheep Gate, and the Gate of the Guard.

But the eyes of Linda were opened, and she knew that she was naked.

"You let him *talk* to you like that?" Gemma breathed.

"A luminous egg," said Howard, "but an egg."

Then she felt her daughter struggling to squeeze Veruschka back over her tingling skull. Rainey saying, "Please, Mommy."

But it wasn't a hat. It didn't work that way.

"I moved the jewelry a long time ago," said Howard. "Have fun with that."

And in two minutes his piano came through the ceiling. He was scissoring up "Sister Morphine," cutting it into musical shards.

Linda had dreams like this sometimes. Not before she lost her hair, of course. Before, she'd had naked dreams like everyone else. Then *bald* and *ugly* happened, and in the new dreams, she was back in high school, her body dressed and her head stark naked, and everyone was about to *see*.

THEY WERE STILL in the basement, Linda and her daughter, lying on the abundant laundry heap, aiming smoke rings into each other's smoke rings. Linda's watch had stopped, her bus had left, and the house had gone to bed. Her mind was thinking for itself.

She had not been prepared for Rainey, furious, in her white nightie, hauling her own dusty suitcase from the utility room, saying, You're not leaving *me*.

In the face of her daughter's fire and fury, she had let Rainey unpack her, Linda's, suitcase, latch it, and stash it out of sight as if it would never be called into service again.

Now, cushioned by the musky laundry, Linda said, "I gave birth to you upstairs on that bathroom floor, and I have loved you ever since."

She wanted to tell her daughter the story of the three wishes. She wanted to tell how she, Linda, lay naked on a towel, panting, and how Howard opened the bathroom window so she could hear the Welcome Baby party out back, Elvis Presley singing "Heartbreak Hotel" on a transistor radio.

The midwife had such sympathetic hands. Linda labored with her head in Lala's lap, Gordy standing silently back in the hall, Howard saying, It's only childbirth, babe. Pop it out. And she had chosen to translate: Mother of my firstborn, cherished wife, I will love you unto death.

Her daughter's arm pressed warm against hers. Linda said, "There are things I need to tell you." She did not say, A bus ticket can be traded in, a suitcase repacked. She said, "A body like yours is a source of power. Don't give it away."

"Are you asking if I'm a virgin?"

"You're thirteen," said Linda, "so no, I'm not. I'm trying to tell you that if you go to bed with mascara on, your eyelashes will fall out."

"I'm half a virgin," said Rainey.

Half? Her daughter's body was a sealed envelope, wasn't it? Half a virgin, what was that? Sex, but in the hand? Sex, but in the mouth? Linda imagined her daughter's vagina pure as a Communion cup, though she had never seen one. Sex, but between the breasts? Sex, but in the back? Sex, but with two guys who suddenly got more interested in each other than in you?

On the bathroom floor, nursing her newborn daughter, who was sticky with blood, Linda had said: I want to make a wish for her; and Howard said: I wish her golden ears. Let her play piano. Or clarinet. I'll let her choose.

Now Rainey said, "Aren't you curious *why*?"

Why what? No, she did not remotely want to know why her daughter was half a virgin. In the birthing bathroom, Lala in her silk wrapper leaned dreamily over Linda, an attending angel who might or might not be high on Darvon, Demerol, whatever that doctor kept writing. "God grant her health," said Lala. "Health, Howard, is the greatest gift, not to be squandered."

In the basement, Linda stroked Rainey's hair, so straight it looked ironed, and said, "If a guy says *free love*, tell him to fuck off. Or if he says, 'What are you, frigid?' just run, baby. There's no such thing as frigid or free love."

"Daddy says free love all the time."

Linda twisted off her mother's engagement ring and looked at her daughter's hand—the fingers ink-scarred, nail-bitten, impudently pretty.

"Mom, where were you going?"

First Linda tried her daughter's left forefinger with the diamond ring. Then she tried the right. That bus left three days a week. She had an envelope flap for Rainey with Ask's name and address on it. She said, "To visit a friend named Ask."

"If my name was Ask, I'd kill myself."

Linda worked the ring over her daughter's knuckle, finally. "Don't let your father sell this," she said. "It's worth four thousand dollars."

"If I even *knew* some guy named Ask, I'd kill myself," said Rainey.

In the breath that followed, Linda looked into her own clasped hands and understood that a normal mother would race into the burning building and save her daughter's life. Your words reverberate in the cracked vase of my heart, she would say. I will stay.

But when Linda looked up, she saw her daughter's eyes blacked by the closing of the gates of the city. What did she expect? Benediction? She had let her own heart get blacked in this house till it lay panting beneath the boiler, a thing to be poked at from time to time.

In the bathroom that day, only Gordy had thought to ask about Linda's wish. I wish her beauty, said Linda, and in a voice harder than she knew she had: I want her *armed*.

You can't mother a daughter, Ask had written, *till you can mother yourself.* Could she be drawn, carnally, to a fifty-one-year-old man? If he was kind, and slow, maybe she could be shy, and new.

The ring was a glint on her daughter's finger. It had traveled from mother to mother to daughter; it was traveling still.

FEAR KNOT

1972

They are talking about sluts. Who is, who isn't. Angeline is an expert on it, has scratched the word into their lab bench with the knife she keeps in her sock, and Rainey believes the word is the blade itself.

"You're obsessed," she tells Angeline. "Who cares?"

It's lunch period at Washington Irving High School, a wet October Thursday under an ash-can sky. The four girls shiver outside the school without coats because the lockers are out of the way. Hugging themselves, smoking Rainey's Kools and Leah's Virginia Slims, pressing their backs to the wall. They are sophomores.

Rainey Royal and Tina Dial and Leah Levinson and the one who doesn't quite belong but is harping on it, Angeline Yost. Angeline is the only one who dyes her hair, white-blond with roots, and she is the only one who starts fights, scratches girls' faces if they challenge her. Rainey tolerates her because she brings news from another, more violent world. An idea persists that Angeline herself might be a slut, and Rainey can't look away.

"I heard something about a girl who goes here," says Angeline. Rainey sees the shutters close over her face as she blows a stream of smoke at the sky, which has started to squeeze out droplets here and there like a sponge.

"Who?" says Leah, quivering with the chill. She is a willow branch, the one who scuffs her feet and watches herself do it, the one who secretly wishes, Rainey knows, she were at a school without boys. Whereas Tina just ignores the distractions. Rainey meets boys everywhere. She doesn't need school to set her up.

Angeline shrugs. "I heard she got in a car with a guy she didn't know, which is asking for it, and he took her to a biker bar. Locked her bag in the trunk."

"Urban legend." Rainey thinks Angeline must be taunting her. She twists her mother's diamond ring and watches the traffic stream by on Irving Place: bike messengers with their heads tucked down, people in office clothes with umbrellas and sack lunches. The wind lifts the flag of her long dark hair, and she flings it back.

"I love urban legends." Tina props up one foot behind her. She wears a short tartan kilt with black tights and a black turtleneck. Most of Tina's pretty clothes come from thrift shops. Rainey goes with her to places like Unique Boutique, rooting through bins and racks for seventy-five-cent vintage beaded cardigans. "I want to hear it. Remember the Doberman with the fingers in his mouth? How did that go?"

"He tells her," says Angeline, her gravelly voice nailing them in place, "he can leave her there alone and she can take her chances getting raped, *or* . . ."

"What about her bag?" Leah, tremulous, tugs at her red hair.

"This is a really dumb story, Angeline," says Rainey.

"If it's just a dumb story, why do you care?" says Tina, challenging. When Tina comes over to the townhouse on West Tenth Street, she lingers by the double parlor and listens to the live jazz, Rainey's father on piano and his acolytes on every other damn thing, and Rainey has to drag her upstairs to her pink bedroom. Howard calls Tina Miss Temptation and smiles at her with eyes of intent. He has offered her clarinet lessons. Don't you dare, Rainey said. He's not *your* father. But Tina has somehow ended up with a clarinet.

They are virgins, supposedly.

"I just care, Tina, that's all." Rainey opens her fist; the diamond has dented her palm.

"*Or* she can give him a blow job in the car and get her bag back and a ride home." Angeline looks triumphant.

"What did she *do*," says Leah, wide-eyed, as if she herself might get the answer wrong.

"She totally whored herself out." Angeline pushes off from the wall and faces the three girls. She wears silver eyeshadow, a bit of moonlight on her face on a shadowy day. Drizzle glints in her hair. "The guy told my brother. They were laughing about it. What would *you* do?"

"Oh, that's easy," says Tina, and Rainey eyes the crucifix gleaming on her honeyed skin. "You walk. Pray and walk. You don't let some jerk make a slut out of you. What a pig."

"Which one is the pig?" Leah murmurs to Rainey.

"You people," says Rainey. "This whole story is a lie. And you shouldn't say *slut*. Or *whore*. That's so judgmental." In her own home, the sexual revolution has been in full swing forever. The fifth-floor bedrooms of the West Tenth Street townhouse are a revolving home to the young musicians, mainly female musicians, who revere her father. Rainey's always known, big deal, that they do this revering in bed, and that her mother took part in lots of group revering back when she lived at home. In fact when Rainey was young, it was like having big sisters, teaching her to smoke and how to roll emergency Tampax from toilet paper, because with all those chicks in the house it often came down to that.

Angeline looks at her sharply. Rainey holds her gaze. Then she takes a last drag on her Kool and brutalizes the butt under the toe of her sneaker. "Let's go in."

The girls don't move, though, because fifth period bell hasn't rung yet and there seems to be more to unwind. And Rainey's lying—she's never heard the biker bar story and it's not an urban legend. Something just like this happened to her Monday night. She hasn't told anyone, not even Tina, maybe especially not Tina the weird way she's reacting.

"Where was this?" Rainey demands, and Angeline shrugs.

"Around," she says. "Maybe Long Island." She says it *Lawn Guyland*.

WHEN RAINEY MET the boy she was sitting midway up on the steps of the Metropolitan Museum, smoking one of the Kools she'd snicked from the pocket of her father's leather jacket, which she also had borrowed without asking. It was two o'clock and the thin October sun was shifting over the museum. She was cutting school after lunch, by herself, because Tina, who wanted to be a doctor, wouldn't skip chemistry. Rainey looked like trouble. She felt like a model for *Seventeen*. She wore Love's Soft Camel eyeshadow and Mary Quant Black Cherry lip gloss, and she smelled of tea rose oil, which strangers accosted her to sniff. The boy stood below on the street, eating a pretzel and looking up thoughtfully at the people on the steps. He had blond curls to his shoulders like Roger Daltrey, wide-set eyes with a Roman nose. His T-shirt was a rainbow tie-dye. See me, she thought. Pay attention to me.

His gaze slid over to her. A bridge formed between them, gold and silver strands shining in the watery sun. He looked older than her by at least several years. He would be skipping class, too—she guessed he was an NYU brat. He did not take his eyes off her. She tipped her head and smiled down at him.

After a moment, he held the pretzel at his side and ambled up the steps slowly till he reached her. The silvery bridge collapsed into thin air. They did not need it anymore.

"Maybe you're my guardian angel," he said. "I have to write a paper on Renaissance art. It's not really my area."

"It will be," she said, and tugged him down by the hand not holding the pretzel. "What's your area?"

He sat and toyed with her fingers, and ate. He didn't offer any but she wasn't hungry. His pits smelled of eucalyptus. "Hockey," he said. "You know where to go, inside?"

She thought about hockey players breaking out into fights, and found herself getting excited. She wanted to see this beautiful boy bleeding and breathing hard. "I come here all the time," she said. "You definitely want to see some Hieronymus Bosch. They just have a couple of engravings made after he died, but he was *weird*. He painted nightmares. Da Vinci, Titian, El Greco. No one did fabric and sky like El Greco. We'll have a blast."

"You think?" He leaned toward her, and the furrow between his brows deepened.

"C'mon, you already know some Renaissance art. Michelangelo painted the Sistine Chapel. You heard of that?"

"Yeah."

"And Da Vinci painted *The Last Supper*. You've seen pictures of that?"

"I guess." He popped an arc of pretzel into his mouth and turned his blue eyes on hers. She wanted to nestle a finger under the ledges of his cheekbones. "Can you show me that stuff?"

"Well, they're in Italy. But we can see other things. Where's your notebook?"

"I'm just looking. Today's for background."

This didn't seem like much of a studying system to Rainey, but she wasn't the one with a paper due. He really should go to the library. She could take him to the Rose Reading Room. Or she could write the thing for him. Maybe he would pay her twenty bucks to do it. He had rich-boy's hair, those springy coils. She wanted to sink her hands into them.

They paid the dragon ladies their admission. Rainey laid down a quarter. She said, "That's all I have." She was a high school student, for Chrissake, she didn't have $1.75 to throw around. She led him up the Grand Staircase and to the galleries with the Renaissance artists. "Look at the turn in her body, the way she's moving with the infant." She had stopped before a Botticelli Madonna. "The Renaissance artists really studied anatomy. That was what made it an artistic rebirth. Da Vinci dissected dead people to look at muscle and bone, how the human body was articulated."

"Yes, the anatomy is perfect," he said, taking her arm, pressing it through the leather jacket as if he could feel the flesh.

OUTSIDE THE HIGH school, Rainey moves toward the double doors but no one follows, so she stops. "You all," she says, turning back, "are so harsh. A girl could get killed." She sees Angeline's smile of dismissal. "Never mind raped," she goes on. "Plus, what if she had heels on? You can't walk home in heels."

They all look down as if to check their footwear, mostly sneakers. Angeline is in Candies, what's with that? Her feet must be freezing, never mind wet. "I'd rather get blisters than be a slut," says Tina righteously, and Rainey sees Leah blanch.

"You could use some compassion," Rainey says softly. "You

don't know what you would do." She feels Tina and Angeline watching her closely. She feels her best friend slipping away. She knows Leah would open her mouth wide in a minute to stay in a safe car.

Angeline presses the glowing ash of her Virginia Slim gingerly to the wall, touches it, and tucks the butt in her back pocket. Sometimes she doesn't have money for lunch, either, and Rainey has seen her eat the crusts of their sandwiches on the sly.

"So what would you do, Rain?"

IN THE MUSEUM, she passed by the dark canvases and the flower pictures and led him to the El Grecos. "Look at that sky," she said, "so lurid, as if he'd dreamed it, and those fabrics, all rumpled and alive."

"And lustrous," said the boy. His hand moved to her hair and lifted a hank of it, sampling.

Was he getting it, or was he only half listening? She resolved to try harder. She stopped him again in front of her favorite painting, a Bronzino portrait of an arrogant young man with his hand on a book. His body, too, had a subtle twist and the hands were exquisite, long-fingered, one over the book and the other clasping a hip. She showed these details to the boy, explained how the face was fully human, fully realized, in a way that also symbolized the Renaissance. He nodded, examining. "Don't you want to write it down?" she asked him.

"I remember shit," he said.

There is no paper, she thought. He isn't taking art history at all. He just wants to be with me. She showed him one more, a da Vinci painting on wood of a young woman with disheveled ringlets, the loveliest girl she'd seen. "See how natural she looks?" she said. "That was another aspect of Renaissance art." She hadn't yet said how religious everyone was back then. "Do you want to see more?" She knew what he wanted was not in the museum.

"I want you to let me drive you somewhere," he said. "A friend of mine keeps a boat on City Island. I'll take you out. We can see the sunset from the water."

She had never been on a boat except for that loud tour around Manhattan. City Island was a mystery. She did not even know how it attached to New York—somewhere off the Bronx? And *attached* was the wrong word. Islands floated, didn't they? "You have a car?" she said, marveling. A car was a kind of island, too.

"Old Mercedes 300 SL," he said. "It used to be my father's."

A father *and* a car. It fleshed him out. Her own father would be too busy at the piano to wonder where she was. They walked down the Grand Staircase, toward the main doors. "I don't know who you are," she said. "I'm Rainey Royal."

"Let's not do the biographical thing," he said. "It's more exciting without it."

Was it? A person's name is what you grip, Rainey thought, a radiant little handle attached to their inner being. It got screwed on at birth for a reason. "I need to know who you are," she said.

He laughed. "What's the hurry? You can get to know me in the car. We can exchange names on the boat, will that work? I'll get a bottle of wine and tell you my name and my social and the circumference of my head." He was funny, and his smile was the real thing. They walked to his garage on Seventy-Ninth Street holding hands. I've got a boyfriend in college with a *car*, Rainey thought. Tina is going to be so impressed. Tina was her *best friend*. Unless something was happening in those hateful clarinet lessons, she was still a virgin. Gordy had nearly overpowered Rainey once, but Tina had told her virginity was a state of mind, so Rainey had concentrated till she sealed herself up. She was saving this new feeling of purity for something special. Maybe for this boy, if his name was as exotic as his hair. Maybe the boat was a yacht with billowing flags and steps leading down to a circular bed.

The doors of his little silver car flew up like wings, and for a moment she was too astonished to fold herself inside. Then they sped through the Central Park Transverse. Stone walls raced alongside, and trees glittered overhead. The boy had Frank Zappa on cassette, and she chanted with Frank as they shot out of the park, maneuvered west on Seventy-Ninth, then drove north along the Hudson River. Zappa was just crazy. Who named their daughter Moon Unit? Maybe that was a pretty radiant handle, though. She watched his hand, long and sculptural, leave the stick shift and clamp halfway up her thigh, and she rested her head against the seat back as the sign for the Cross Bronx Expressway whipped by.

She pretended that without his name she knew who he was deep inside. She asked him what he liked to read, the question sounded so adult, and he said he read mechanical engineering and chemistry for school, which didn't sound like a rock star at all, though Mick Jagger had gone to the London School of Economics, so maybe. "Do you play guitar?" she asked.

He squeezed her leg. "How did you guess?"

She felt a tiny swell of pride in her rib cage. "Acoustic or electric?"

He glanced at her as if checking for the answer and said: "Electric." So he could be Roger after all. He asked what she liked in school and she said art most of all, because she was going to be an artist, and English second. "We just read that short story 'The Lottery.' Do you know it?"

"I slept through English," he said. "Tell it to me." The Dead were playing now. He turned the music down, and she told him about the townspeople drawing lots to see who would be stoned to death that year. He looked at her briefly. "Shirley Jackson's mind must look like that Hieronymus guy's brain," he said. He'd been paying attention! It pleased her; she felt useful. "You told that really well," he said. "Now I want to read the story." And Rainey thought, This is how our love begins, when we get inside each other's heads.

He took the exit for Orchard Beach and drove straight and straight till they were in a village of little brick and wooden buildings with lots of restaurants, and that was it: City Island.

THE FIRST BELL rings for fifth period. The girls look at Rainey, and she wants to tell them there are so many things the boy left out, but she burns for the maligned girl standing in for her in the story, a nonexistent girl who cannot defend herself.

"I'd do anything to stay alive," she says, raising her chin, and Tina lifts her eyebrows, skeptical. Her brows are plucked into fine swoops. She does Rainey's arches, too, but Rainey has a more natural beauty, and Tina leaves them lush. "I'd have no intention of dying to prove a point," Rainey says, but Angeline just shakes her head.

"Gross," she says.

THE BOY PARKED near a marina with two long walkways. He unslotted the cassette player from the dashboard and took it out of the car with him. It was late afternoon, with long shadows, but not yet dusk. The boats were all white and different sizes, bobbing on the water, and she made out a few of the names: *Best of Boat Worlds, Pura Vida, Lady of the Lake.* Farther out were the sailboats, anchored offshore. The breeze off the Sound was whippy and cool. A Fritos bag blew against her ankle and rested there. She was glad she had her father's leather jacket on.

He opened the trunk and tucked the cassette player inside. "You wanna put your purse in here?" he said. "Nothing's safe anymore. Besides, it might get wet."

Rainey held her bag tight, considering this. The bag was woven and might soak through. She had an image of her ring coming off as she trailed her hand in the water, flashing its way to the bottom of the sea. The ring was her mother's, a succulent diamond. Before that it had been her maternal grandmother's, and there was no replacing it, ever. She had to suck her finger and tongue the ring till she could fight it over her knuckle, by which time she realized it would never have slid off, but rather than cram it back on she slipped it into her bag, then tucked her bag inside the trunk.

After that they walked till they found a package store. He bought a corkscrew, too, and carried the bottle-shaped paper bag by the neck, his other arm draped around her. She leaned into him, rubbing her naked finger and imagining that a famous rock star had fallen for her, a half-virgin groupie. The marina had boats tethered to each side of its walkways, some with people sitting on them, mostly dressed in white and drinking in groups or tending to mysterious chores. He knew exactly where to go; he must have borrowed it before. If it was a big enough boat, maybe they could take trips on it, and bring Tina. Leah would be too scared.

But the one he finally stopped at was one of the smallest. It was like a big rowboat with a motor in back, and a few benches with blue vinyl cushions, one of them torn with white stuffing. The name on the back was *Fear Knot*.

Rainey remembered suddenly that she didn't like wine. She remembered that she didn't swim. The Sound stretched endlessly on all sides, and she couldn't drive a boat. At least with a moving car you could fling yourself out onto the street.

"I changed my mind," she said, edging away.

"Aw, Rainey." He lifted his arm from her shoulders. "I thought you'd love it. It was my way of saying thanks."

He stood with his hands in his front pockets and no apparent urgency. She could decide either way for all he cared, that's how it felt. The wind lifted the hairs on his arms but in his T-shirt he didn't seem to register the chill.

"My name is Andrew Nicely, if that helps," he said.

It didn't sound like a mass murderer's name. It didn't sound like anyone's name, but she guessed it was his. She watched his golden skin prickle under the risen hairs. "Are you at NYU?"

"How did you guess?" he said again. The paper bag crinkled under his arm. It was close enough to a yes if she wanted it to be. "You're a very intuitive girl," he said. "Has anyone ever told you that?"

She figured it was all right. Tina knew she had cut school and gone to the Met. A man was on the boat next to theirs, cleaning something with a giant sponge. And every time she narrowed her eyes, he looked exactly like Roger Daltrey, except taller. She felt like he had climbed off the stage at Leeds and extended his hand to her, only to her, and when she finally nodded, that was exactly what he did—held out his hand to steady her so she could step into the boat. It rocked, lurching her brain, till he released her onto the middle of the bench. He handed her the bottle and got in behind her. She turned and saw him untie the rope from the dock thingy and coil it up on the deck. Then he removed something from under a seat cushion and started the motor. I'm having an adventure, she thought. I'm brave. I collect adventures. I'm out here with the sexiest member of the Who. The boat putt-putted slowly out of the marina and then roared out to sea, slamming onto the water and rearing up. It must be like riding a horse, she thought.

When they were really far out, she saw that the shoreline had thinned, like the edge of a plate. Her hair went crazy in the wind. The water was a midnight blue, with tips glittering like dabs of silver nail polish where the aching rays of late sun struck. She moved carefully to the edge and trailed her fingers down, feeling a cold so profound it spoke of another side of the world.

Then they were out past the sailboats that had seemed so distant from the marina, and it seemed he would keep plowing the water forever. "Hey, Andrew Nicely," she shouted, "I need to stop." He looked startled, but he slowed the boat and cut the motor, then crept forward to sit beside her.

With the motor finally silent, she heard water slapping the sides of the boat. They drifted peaceably. Light was starting to die out of the sky. He took the bag from her, opened the bottle with the corkscrew, and handed it back. She waved it away. She felt like a ladybug trapped in a bright mayonnaise jar with a hulking emerald mantis.

"It's romantic out here. Why don't you drink?" He slipped the bag off the bottle and dropped it over the side.

"Andrew, seriously?" She had never seen someone injure the ocean. The bag floated on his side; if she lunged for it, climbing over his knees, the boat would get tippy. "You have to pick that up."

"It's a big bay," he said soothingly, "and a very small bag." He held out the bottle again. She shook her head and watched the bag drift, darkening with the wet. He squeezed her with the arm that curtained her shoulders. "Nobody's going to notice it."

"It's like scribbling on a painting. Please. If you don't get it, we can't be together."

Andrew Nicely took a swallow of wine, then another. His lips were stained an innocent red. He offered the wine for the third time. "We're already together, Rainey Royal," he said. "But you're not being sweet anymore."

It felt hateful that he was staring at her, a little smile on his lips. Her throat constricted. She was relieved to find that she could still swallow. "I was never sweet," she said fiercely.

"I'm not sweet, either," he told her.

She stood and tried to reach across him for the bag in the water. But it was too far gone, and everything began to rock wildly. He grabbed her around the waist and thrust her back onto her seat. She felt chastened and afraid. Why wouldn't he start the boat and take her back? She clearly despised him now.

"You should be nicer to me," he said, draping his arm around her again.

"I want to go home." She heaved off the arm. Daylight was bruising and the sun had dropped. She hadn't been paying attention.

He shook his head as if she were making a huge mistake, and began to drink alone, saying nothing. She looked out over the water, afraid to meet his eyes. She wondered if he would try something out here, but if she struggled they could both end up in the Sound. He would know that, right? When much of the bottle was gone, he corked it, went behind her with a slight lurch, started the motor, and piloted them back across the Sound to the marina. It was nearly dark and the chill was sinking through her father's leather jacket. He had to be freezing, but he didn't show it. The lights on the dock and the streets had been turned on, and gleamed through the fallen dusk. She struggled to get out without his steadying hand and fell against the wooden dock, banging her shin. She limped quickly after him. At the car, he opened his own door, got inside, and reached over to unlock hers. But she stood beside his door and thumped hard on his window. He had her mother's ring locked in his trunk and she wanted it now. He looked straight at the windshield, so she opened his door.

"I want my bag," she said.

"Just get in," he said. "I'll open the trunk when you get out."

"Press the lever." She touched her stinging shin, felt the nub of a splinter, and wondered if they had a tweezer at home.

"What lever?" he said. "There is no lever. Get in the car."

He closed his door again and left her standing outside. He could drive off with the bag and leave her there at the marina, taking her mother's diamond. She didn't have a dime for a phone call. The bag held her tokens and her school ID and her subway pass, which would be hard to replace, and her keys. And the ring. She didn't have much of her mom's. Her father had thrown nearly all of it out.

She walked around the front of the car and got inside.

"Good girl," he said. She told him where she lived. After that, they drove in a silence that wrapped around her like a shroud and she didn't know how to peel it off. At first they backtracked.

Then they took an exit she didn't recognize. She noticed they were in a neighborhood they had not passed before. It looked poor, with some houses boarded up or sagging and yards paved with cracked concrete. Here and there a plaster Virgin reigned over the shrubbery. Finally they approached a corner with a lonely bodega, its window gated but lit, three young men clustered outside, lounging. The boy pulled over about twenty yards ahead and cut the lights.

"Why are we getting out here?"

He smiled at her. The shroud tightened.

"I don't get it," she said. "Where are we?"

He palmed the back of her neck and tightened his fingers. "So," he said, "you can get out and take your chances here, or you can be nice to me and get a ride back."

The whole speech sounded fake. She tried to jerk her head away. "I have to pee," she said. "Take me to a restaurant. Give me my bag. Then I'll decide."

"Go in the bushes. If you can find any." He slid his seat back and settled in. Maybe he'd done this with other girls and gotten his way. She held the door handle. He didn't look like Roger Daltrey anymore. He was acting like a mass murderer now. "Give me my bag and I'll take my chances."

"Soon," he said.

"You're just like your name," she said. "Nicely. I'm going to scream." She rolled her window down.

"It's not my name," he said calmly. "I got it off a tombstone. Go ahead and scream."

Her spine rippled like the Sound. They were seated so close. It was a small car. His biceps bulged. The little gearshift stuck up bravely between them and she wondered if it would poke her ribs if she leaned over him. Her sinuses swelled with tears. The young men on the corner might rescue her if she screamed. Unless they were all in cahoots.

"If I have to blow you, I'll bite it off," she said.

"Oh, you don't want to hurt me," he said, smiling.

NOW SHE IS standing outside the school with Angeline and Tina and Leah, where a light drizzle, almost a mist, envelopes them. "It's not a binary ending like you have it," says Rainey loudly, as they edge along the wall toward the double doors. "She could call a car service. She could knock on people's doors till she found a woman at home. She could gouge his eyes out with her keys. Listen, Angeline. She doesn't have to do what he wants. The guy who told you the story is full of it."

"Yeah, well, I know him and you don't," says Angeline, turning. They are going to be late for class, pushing open the door and squeezing in with a crowd of other students as the second bell rings, then lingering a moment, still shivering. Rainey gets another eyeful of the grand fireplace with the plaster bas-relief panel above it. It's a historic building, their school. The panel is called THE LEGEND OF SLEEPY HOLLOW, but instead of showing a headless horseman, which would have been extremely cool, it shows three ladies in flowing garments reading the legend from a book. Like the three of them, listening to Angeline's lurid lies.

The words slip out before she can bite them back.

"I think I know him," she says, furious at Angeline's story, and by then it's too late. Her friends look at her, amazed. "Is his name Andrew Nicely? Blond curls, blue eyes, drives a vintage black Mercedes?"

Angeline looks puzzled. "His name's not Andrew Nicely, but yeah, all the rest. How do *you* know what he drives?" Leah and Tina lean in; they want to hear this.

"Goes to NYU, right?"

Angeline laughs. "Seriously? He hangs around. Gets high. Tries to get girls in his car. They're idiots if they go. I don't feel sorry for them."

"Ciao," says Tina, and moves off with Leah, turning down a corridor with a swirl of kids.

The sound of sneakers on marble eddies in Rainey's ears. "Tell him to change the end of his stupid story," she tells Angeline. "It's a lie. I know the girl. In fact if you know where to find him, I'll get her purse back for her." If she has his address, maybe she can take revenge, mail him something repellent.

"Why do you care about her stupid purse?" Angeline peers into Rainey's face. Her nose flares wide like a baby's and her silver eyeshadow is starting to crack in the crease. "Don't tell me." Her eyes go wide. The irises are the same midnight blue as the Sound. "It was *you*."

"I'm not kidding," says Rainey. "He's ruining her reputation, and you're helping him."

A teacher pokes his head out of a classroom and vehemently

waves them on; they are late. "Look," says Angeline, her voice abrasive, "so maybe you're the one who got into his car. It's not my problem. You got home, right?" She starts to walk away, but Rainey wrenches her back by a slender arm, feeling the bone within so lanky and fragile that she realizes that even Angeline has been in Andrew's Mercedes, and Angeline stumbles.

"I'm making it your problem," Rainey says.

THIS WAS THE ending, the nonbinary one, the one she would tell Angeline, even Tina, the one she would own till the end of her life.

She yanked the keys out of the ignition, finally. Wrenched herself out of his grip and out of the car, and leaning over the pristine hood gouged two parallel long lines into the paint. She expected blood to seep through the inky black lacquer and wet her hand. He shouted and got out, but by then the boys on the corner had drifted over. "Pop the trunk," she demanded, as they mobilized around her little scene. "Pop the trunk and I'll quit." She carved an angry *X* into the hood as the boys laughed and egged her on, and Andrew Nicely cursed and lunged at her uselessly. She got no particular joy out of it, just a mute flow of power that streamed through her back and arms. Swearing, he reached into the car, the trunk wafted open, and she walked over and extracted her purse. He came around and stopped her there. "*Bitch*," he said, trying to block her as she played keep-away with his keys. The corner boys hooted.

"He tried to steal my bag," she told them, keeping her eyes on Roger Daltrey. She feinted left, right, then tossed the keys to the three young men. And as he pled his case with them, she strolled into the lit bodega.

STRING TENSION

1977

It's March, eleven degrees below freezing. West Tenth Street is fucking *desolate*.

Rainey parts the velvet drapes of the townhouse parlor and ices her forehead on a windowpane. When she releases the red curtains and turns back toward the double parlor, she sees Radmila, who may or may not still be her father's girlfriend, waiting by the Louis Quinze sofa with expectant eyes.

"Just fling yourself down," suggests Rainey. She has promised Radmila a portrait. "Be your most sensual self." She takes her sketchbook from the Biedermeier secretary desk and sits cross-legged on a bergère.

Radmila arranges herself on the sofa. She is a sniffling odalisque in an old sweatshirt belonging to Rainey's father, who's at the piano. The sweatshirt has a splotch of bleach over the heart.

Radmila's hair, extravagant with distress, climbs the cushions and crawls down her clothes. On the wall above her hangs an oversexed interpretation of Rebecca at the Well, in which Rebecca's low-cut frock seems about to creep below her left nipple. In this painting—so tall and heavy in its frame that it was bolted to the studs when Howard's mother, Lala, first married and moved in—Abraham's servant Eliezer, who seeks a bride for Abraham's son, Isaac, stands so very close that the virginal Rebecca has to lean away from him to avoid, like, frottage.

Rainey uncaps her Rapidograph with a delectable click. "You know, if you took your top off, it would look kind of classical."

Radmila strips off the sweatshirt. Howard keeps pounding on the piano. Radmila thrusts her breasts at the ceiling cherubs. They ignore her, too.

"Howard," says Radmila. The piano gets louder. She raises her voice. "At least say we give her your name." Radmila has gotten preggers, seemingly all by herself, gauging from Howard's interest.

The drawing is to be a birthday present. It's a blind contour. That means Rainey can't look away from the model, nor lift her pen from the page. In other words, the artist must trust her eyes.

Her father makes up a little song, variations on his name, drizzling his fingers up in the high notes. "Howardina, Howardette," he sings.

In the other bergère, Tina's studying. Her gaze bores into a blue textbook. *Next to Tina, you're a centerfold*, Howard told his daughter once. They were twelve then. He must have thrilled to that viola back of Tina's, because he even named a composition for her, later: *The Tina Temptation*.

Now they are nineteen and Tina lives on the top floor. Here she is in black sheep pajamas, ignoring them all with the single-minded focus of a scholarship premed at midterms. From the dark heart of the oven come top notes of chocolate, sweetening the cigarette smoke that hangs over the parlor. This is Rainey's other present to Radmila: the cake.

She begins to draw. Radmila stretches like a woman awaiting her demon lover. "I mean give her your *last* name, dahling." Radmila is Romanian, Hungarian, something exotic—Howard calls her a Gypsy; there might be no correlation. She had a full scholarship for classical flute at the Manhattan School of Music. Then Howard found her playing in the park on Sundays for change and introduced her to jazz, and then she dropped out and moved in. Now she's due in five months and infected with Barbie Brain. Let that be a lesson, Rainey thinks to herself.

Howard releases a flock of frenzied notes; they lift off the piano, swarming. "Maybe," he says, "you'd like to fuck me up the ass with a hot poker next."

Rainey tells her father, "Hey, you agreed to this kid." She leads her Rapidograph into the blind alley of a knee crease and shoots an eyeball message into Radmila's brain. *Run*, it says.

The doorbell rings. Radmila doesn't flicker. Tina stirs as if from a dream.

"I *agreed* we'd make beautiful babies. That's an abstract truth."

Howard pumps the syllables on the downbeats. "I also *agreed* to get rid of it. That's concrete. Howardsdottir—get the damn door."

"It's your dealer, you get it."

The doorbell chimes again. Howard stops playing. The hiss of radiators rushes in to fill the quiet. Tina shakes off her afghan, twisting up her long caramel hair as she walks to the foyer. Radmila lunges for the afghan, which Tina salvaged from the Spanish Harlem walk-up where her dead Catholic grandmother raised her, and sarongs her half-naked self.

As for the man lying face up on the floor at Rainey's feet, he hasn't stirred. Who knows if the door chime penetrates his traveling mind? His name is Gordy Vine, and his white-blond hair streams across the Aubusson. Only the cigarette between his fingers looks alive.

THE DEALER IS a new dude. A stripling. Boyish, his face a meadow, the dealer stands with Tina in the arched doorway as if posing for a marriage portrait: a tall, fair man with a new haircut and a watchful, pretty wife, her only adornment the crucifix at her neck.

Rainey likes him. She likes the pink of his high freckled cheekbones and the fine supple wool of his trousers. She likes the gleam of his shoe leather. When has anyone worn dress shoes in this house? He'll be coming from his real job, Howard has told them. He is an analyst at Merrill Lynch. What is that? Rainey asked, and Howard said helpfully, An analyst is a grunt.

Tina goes to the sofa this time, freeing up a chair, and snugs in next to Radmila, who deals out a bit of the afghan. The dealer looks at Rainey, finally. She falls through blue wariness in his eyes, through cold, clear water, then deeper toward a sunless bottom. She thinks he might nurture a secret hurt there, like dark rabbity moss.

Howard steps forward and folds into a Shakespearean bow. "Ah, King Jupiter."

"Jesus H. Christ," says Rainey.

"Don't call me that." Her father looks aggrieved. "It's his *name*."

She can't stop herself—she laughs. "What's his wife's name?"

Howard says, "You're the most welcome man to enter this house in a fool's age. Let's have a taste, shall we? A taste and a toast."

Rainey heads to the kitchen, but she can't resist. "Hey," she says. "If you marry me, can I be Queen Jupiter?" But King Jupiter is watching her father, who's trying to splice himself between Tina and Radmila on the sofa. It's like trying to part the waters.

"Radmila, *git*," he says, as Radmila cocoons herself more tightly against Tina.

In the kitchen, a timer ticks on white Formica, tightly wound. Rainey gets the chilled champagne. She lays the bottle on a tray, adds five of Lala's Waterford coupes and carries it all, clinking, back to the parlor.

King Jupiter remains in the parlor doorway, one ear cocked toward the staircase. From the top floor comes the distant sound of acolytes practicing—a swanky clarinet, a maniacal violin. He sniffs hard: chocolate air.

"Double Dutch Intrigue Cake," Rainey says, and sets the tray on the coffee table.

Then she pulls her hair back, lifting her chest to high heaven.

But it's the light glancing off her mother's diamond ring that seems to catch his eye. "You can have cake," she teases, "if the guy you stole that name off doesn't get you first."

King Jupiter studies Rainey as if considering whether to buy her. Then he utters a gorgeous word. "It's Ashkenazi. Jupiter." He looks down at Gordy Vine, who is stoned and has left his body behind like a dropped coat. "You sold tickets, Howard?" he says. "Went through Ticketron?"

Tina glances at him, then lapses into her book as if Radmila were not ardently pressed to her side.

This room is full of such tenuous blessings. Every day, Lala gazes at her granddaughter with clueless love from a portrait over the hearth, diamonds distending her earlobes. She left Rainey the house, and left her also Howard, who is to run the house in trust till Rainey turns twenty-five. *Trust.* It seems a lousy word for anything involving Howard. Or money. Or, what the hell, trust.

"I don't play to a crowd," King Jupiter says, though he steps closer to the coffee table, and Rainey wants to drape herself across him like a scarf.

Howard peruses him with wizened eyes. "Crowd? This here is a well of loneliness, baby. Show me a room that violates the fire code and I'll show you a crowd." He grips a bottle by the neck.

"Sit yourself down. Have some Champs." He gives Radmila an instructive prod. Radmila bites her lip and sits tight. On her lap now are pieces of a flute she's assembling, four bright knuckled tubes.

In six years, Rainey will own the house. She will make them all leave. Gordy, the acolytes, Howard. She goes over to King Jupiter and stands an inch too close. He smells like morning, like when you cut school and take the ferry just to see water from a boat.

"We all *live* here," she says patiently. With the toe of her Ked she nudges Gordy Vine. "He's trumpet," she says. "And this is Tina. She's my best friend. She's premed." Rainey can hardly remember a time when she did not know and love Tina Marie Dial. She leans into the dealer. Since they are going to marry and all. "And that's Radmila, my dad's girlfriend. Electric flute."

King Jupiter speaks low into the spot on Rainey's neck where every morning she dabs tea rose oil, the scent her mother left behind.

"You got 'em reversed," he says.

Outside on the street, or maybe deep in her brain, a car alarm begins to wail.

"Reversed how?" If she shakes him, maybe something ugly will fall out, like a cockroach from a curtain fold. Her voice turns harsh. "You think the one with the flute is premed?"

The car alarm is muffled by the drapes, but urgent, relentless. Sometimes this happens during rehearsal, and eventually Howard sends an acolyte out to write *dickwad* across the windshield in lipstick, which comes off only with rubbing alcohol, paper towels, and grief.

Tina says, "I can't study here." She tries to rise, but Howard grips her book.

"Your mind is a laser. You're fine." What an asshole. He says, "Radmila. Scoot the fuck over. Jealousy won't get you tenure."

In the painting, Eliezer, who really should step back, dangles near Rebecca's loins a string of beads. But that's wrong. In the Bible, he gives her bracelets and earrings, which she runs home to show her mother: Rainey looked it up. Eliezer has ten camels packed with this shit—gold, jewels, and *raiment*, which means *designer clothes*.

"Reversed *how*?" Rainey demands, pressing into King Jupiter now with a breast. It's a high-burner breast—it can melt anyone.

She has missed something, but what? Is it the timer? Maybe the cake is on its own now. How do you confuse *best friend* and *girlfriend*? Howard leaves Radmila frantic for love.

"Seven years," says Radmila, "*I have fucking tenure.*" That accent! He relished it once. He keeps trying to knee his way in, and Tina wears the heavy-lidded look of a mother dog harassed by puppies.

King Jupiter unsuctions himself, astonishingly, from the breast. He walks to the piano and brings his fist down on the keys. The piano is furious. From the piano innards comes an angry clanging as from a union of radiators.

"Jesus God, man." Howard turns toward the sound so fast he

pitches into the coffee table. Radmila cringes. "That Steinway is *signed*," says Howard. "*Putain de merde.*"

"My time is money," says King Jupiter. "*Putain*," he adds, tasting the word.

Radmila scoots over and tugs at Howard, crooning *baby, baby*, so he can drop between the two women and be soothed, a bearded minotaur sunk into down-filled cushions.

Revived, Howard spreads his knees wide and clamps a hand onto Tina's thigh. "Peace, King. Let an old man have a taste and get you paid."

King Jupiter looks down at the coffee table and withdraws from his shirt pocket a test tube.

As for Tina's thigh, it sparks like a welder's torch. Rainey can feel it. "Tina hates that," she informs her father. "Tina is not a piece of meat."

"Doctor Dial a piece of meat? Mercy no." Howard pulls his hand off the hotplate that is Tina's leg, blows on his burning fingers to cool them, and untwists the champagne's wire hood.

King Jupiter says, "I want a clean surface, Howard." He squats at the table, his wing tips emanating light, and holds the test tube as if the white powder inside might detonate.

Tina and Rainey have been talking without talking since the sixth grade. They do this now. Tina leans in and lifts the tray with the glasses, and Rainey, kneeling by King Jupiter in her holey red Keds, reaches out with an arm and sweeps the table clean of everything else like a windshield wiper. Jazz magazines, a hash pipe, rolling papers, a box of reeds, and the full Cinzano ashtray fall softly around Gordy's legs and onto Lala's Aubusson.

King Jupiter whips his hand up as if to slap Rainey's face, then freezes it inches from her skin. But Rainey doesn't blink. She picks her father's pack of Kools from the mess on the rug and lights one. Two things make her proud in this world: what she achieves, which is her *art*, and what she denies to others, which is *satisfaction*. She's not giving him a damn thing.

"Disobedient daughter," he observes.

"If only you knew," says Howard proudly.

One radiator bangs, another hisses. Tina sets the tray back down and stands the glasses up. Howard pours champagne in sibilant streams. Does he hear it, too, this accidental jazz?

King Jupiter now pulls from his shirt pocket a Popsicle stick.

"What did you mean," says Rainey, "*I got 'em reversed?*"

In the kitchen, the timer buzzes. Rainey starts, but feels King Jupiter's hand on her arm. His touch is light, yet, strangely, the hand is a clamp. His skin speaks to her skin. *Don't move*, it says, and, in a whisper, *If one prevail against him, two shall withstand him; and a threefold cord is not quickly broken*. Bewildered, she stays. Chocolate molecules swirl, distressed.

"Nirvana has corners," says Gordy. The cigarette is dead in his fingers, the ash long.

King Jupiter releases her.

"I didn't reverse *shit*," says Rainey. She decides the cake can wait another minute. Champagne seethes in the glasses as Howard slides them across.

"Sound waves bounce around in there, man," says Gordy.

With the Popsicle stick, King Jupiter quarries out a tiny mound of coke onto the table in front of Howard. "Well, if that's your truth, daughter," King Jupiter says, "you hang on tight."

But he is so wrong! Tina is just *studying*. Whereas Radmila is ignoring Howard's hand, the one now back on Tina's thigh, at a hundred miles an hour. Any faster and she will crash and burn. Her ovaries will explode like tiny wrecked Ferraris. Six years ago, when Rainey's mother split, Radmila was the one who taught Rainey how to filch cigarettes and ones and sometimes even fives from the purses and packs of the acolytes, because Howard had so many chicks around the place playing excellent jazz and giving excellent blow jobs it was all just sitting around on the fifth floor asking to be boosted.

Radmila was cool then. Everyone was cool then.

"Timer went off," says Tina.

"Could you maybe *extricate* yourself?" says Rainey. "Check the cake?"

Tina tries, but her leg is collared by Howard's hand. She wavers, glances at Rainey, sits back. Radmila laughs, a dark utterance in her nose.

Howard pulls Tina's book over. "*Extremes of Life.*" He looks pleased. "My memoirs."

King Jupiter plugs the vial and sets it down.

"Seven hundred buckaroos, huh?" says Howard, as if he's just spotted it. King Jupiter takes a straightedge from his pocket and unwraps it. Rainey finds her footing and starts to rise, but he touches her wrist and funnels liquid paralysis through her veins.

"*Extremes of Life*," says Tina patiently, "refers to the beginning, and the end."

Radmila bounces around to face her. "You *study* that?"

Tina nods. It seems to decide something for Radmila. "Toast, *to the beginning*," she tells Howard.

Last night Howard and Gordy played till four and came home with one chick for the both of them. Radmila sat on the floor outside Howardland, the blue bedroom, and cried. But why? There've always been girls. Sober, stoned, sliding needles into pretty veins, playing sorrowful clarinets and straitlaced cellos. On school nights, when Rainey was young, they veered into her pink room and told her how darling she was. They gathered needles and corks to pierce her ears. They crashed on her floor and shared their cigarettes. She grew up on the jazz of girls: electric violin, vomiting, singing, sobbing, and fucking whoever happened to be sprawled in Howardland—her mother, Gordy, Howard—under those gilded foil stars. What got to Radmila last night? She could have just gone in.

"Don't be so predictable." Howard wraps Tina's fingers, then his own, around a champagne coupe, a shape molded on Marie Antoinette's left breast—that would be, Lala once confided, the larger one. Lala ordered Taittinger by the case, but Rainey's pouring Freixenet.

Tina, eyes narrowed, starts squirming in Howard's grip like a cat held too tight.

Rainey feels twilight purpling behind the curtains; she feels one cake darkening in the kitchen, another charring behind her ribs. "Daddy. Tina wants you to let go."

King Jupiter, dicing up the coke, slides her a thin, metallic glance.

Radmila lifts her glass. "To our baby, a musical genius." Christ, she ticks louder than the kitchen timer; Rainey knows her father hears it, too, and is goading Radmila toward some jangly and shrill detonation, some state of misery he can pick apart like a coroner. "To me," she persists, "because I refuse abortion."

King Jupiter stares right through Howard, razoring the coke crossways now like a chef decimating a toe of garlic. He has what Rainey's mother used to call *knife skills*.

"Good for you," says Tina softly to Radmila.

Rainey brightens. What a great little broadcast from the core of Tina Dial, who believes in Our Lord Jesus Christ, yet because man is fallen, she sins with a vengeance, and judges no one, and these are things Rainey loves about her. The first day of junior high, she fell in love with Tina, a bully in tight bell-bottoms who concurred that shifting into the Pearl Drops tongue move when men teachers looked their way was a stellar use of seventh grade. Tina lied with precision about the one thing she wanted to hide, which was living with her one-legged Puerto Rican grandmother, and Rainey lied with conviction about the one thing *she* wanted to hide, which was Gordy Vine and the night visits, and words were not required.

But now Tina seems to have no love for anything but becoming a doctor.

King Jupiter deftly arranges two lines on the glass tabletop before Howard.

Howard takes from King Jupiter a tightly rolled bill. He relinquishes the glass to Tina as if it were his beating heart; and Rainey sees Radmila sail through the walls of the house and down the street, across the Hudson, over the chemical plants of New Jersey, never to return.

When Rebecca, who proved her kindness by watering all ten camels, left her mother's home to marry, her people blessed her. Specifically, they said: *Let thy seed possess the gate of those which hate them.* What precisely would that look like? When Rainey possesses her enemies' gates, she will line those suckers up in her basement like so many brass headboards.

Her father snarfs up a long white scar. He switches nostrils and vacuums up the second. He is beautiful, biblically so, his face just ragged enough to intimate the kind of suffering bound up with jazz, lust, and a direct line to God. Soon his fingers will drum on the table, reporting back from the interior of some complex tune, twisted as DNA. That's some shit, he will say, gazing with rapture at the ceiling cherubs.

But he doesn't say it. Instead, Rainey watches him bind a hank of Tina's hair around one fist and ease her head close so that her ear is fastened to his heart. Then he turns to Radmila, the rolled bill jutting from his nose. He is the Minotaur.

"I'll toast you, girl," he says, "if I can suck champagne off Tina's long sweet toes."

"*Howard.*" Tina's voice is a warning shot.

He releases her instantly. "What, baby? Did I hurt you?"

"Pay up, Howard," says King Jupiter. Tina, rubbing her scalp, shoots Rainey a high-speed telegraph. *I don't like this*, the telegraph says. *I swear on the grave of my grandmother.* Rainey gets it—Tina doesn't want Howard. She manages him. Everyone manages him.

Rainey nudges King Jupiter with her whole self. The nudge is slow, sensual, generous. Why doesn't it register? "I didn't reverse anything," she says.

When King Jupiter stands, he leaves Rainey on her knees in the pale, wilting garden of the Aubusson. He snaps his fingers, hard as castanets. "*Dinero,*" he says.

"Oh, yeah." Her father starts bopping to music that only he can hear. "Howardsdottir," he says kindly. "White envelope. Nightstand drawer. Do me a favor."

Radmila crooning: "A family, Howard—toast to that." Rainey ascends to one knee. She will get the envelope. She will rescue the cake. She will toast Radmila and this fetus to whom she is so intimately related they could share makeup tips, and even makeup.

"I *got* a family. You don't listen," says Howard, and that is true. "Don't you have limits, baby? Try this—I'll toast you if I can suck champagne off Tina's fat pink nipples."

Rainey, half risen, stops moving.

King Jupiter bends low and speaks into her hair. "*They seeing see not,*" he murmurs. "*And hearing they hear not.*"

Whatever that means. But Tina's nipples. They are, in fact, fat. Howard knows this how, exactly? Tina is private about her *lady places*—that's the dead grandmother. Tina gets into her nightie with her back turned. Best friends for years, though, you spied on sleepovers. You marveled at nipple differences.

You seeing, saw.

I swear on the lives of the saints. This telegraphed from Tina: long pajama'd legs crossed on the Louis Quinze, *Extremes of Life* open across her lap, plowing furrows of text.

Rainey picks up the vial.

Hands swim toward her slowly, but Rainey is in dream time now. She plucks the stopper, tips the vial over Tina and Howard's barely touched glass, and raps it sharply on the rim.

And the vial is emptied, and the wine made bitter. *No man may buy or sell now, save that he has the mark, or the name of the beast, or the number of his name.*

Her father leans out of his seat, braces himself on the coffee table, and smacks her.

Never has he done this. She feels like she is three, and she feels like a woman. The vial flies from her hand and cracks on the marble hearth. Salt is on her tongue, and the ruins of her cake scent the air. It is thrilling, not to have cried out.

King Jupiter says, "I'll be wanting that cash immediately."

The razor gleams between his fingertips. Rainey looks up at him from the floor. He drapes raiment upon his flesh and strides among beings who shuttle, blind as salamanders, along the streets of the city.

Her father spits syllables at her. "My bitch daughter will get your money."

Rainey scrambles to her feet. Her cheek flames. She faces Howard, unashamed. Tina's face flames, too; her finger is stabbed to some kind of list, a list with bullets. Ways of being born, reborn, dying, who the fuck knows. Radmila begins her incantation: "I'm sorry. I'm sorry. Baby, I'm sorry." But it is too late for that. Her glass, too, is full of abominations.

"Don't think you won't regret this," Howard tells Rainey. But he is here on borrowed time.

As Rainey climbs the stairs, she hears him. "Dude," he says, placating, "what'd you cut this shit with? Procaine? *Chalk?*" Her father's body is not and never has been a temple. "Lemme jew you down a little."

He sleeps in his dead mother's room, the big blue one on the second floor facing the leafy sunlight of West Tenth. The four posts of the bed prick the air, dangerous as thorns. A storm has whirled briefs and T-shirts everywhere but left neat stacks of sheet music intact.

Rainey opens the nightstand drawer. It's scattered with gold foil stars the size of Christmas cards. Years ago Radmila found them in a craft store and puttied them to the ceiling, where some still glint. A shooting star foretells luck, Rainey knows, but a star that falls straight down—what does that signify?

Signs and symbols float up at her from the drawer. Kool, Bayer, Trojan, Vandoren—those are reeds; and in the detritus of the life her father lives in the dark, a white envelope glows.

From below comes Radmila's shriek. "I *live* here, you son of a bitch."

Rainey extracts the envelope, shedding golden stars. Seven hundred buckaroos, belonging to whom, exactly? She hears Gordy's slow, reluctant tread on the stairs, and on the floor she sees Radmila's big suede purse, a time capsule from early Beatles. Rainey picks it up. Under the flap are coin slots, and a white comb strapped in by elastic. Behind a plastic window, a little boy smiles.

Wherever he is, he isn't here.

From the stairs, Gordy calls: "Raineleh? Everyone's waiting."

Hidden behind the broad canvas pocket that lines the purse is another, just as wide but with a gusset for depth and a zipper for security. Here Radmila stashes her dowry—the tens and gold earrings she filches from Howard's take-home girls. Rainey sewed that pocket in. She was what, thirteen? She can set zippers and sleeves with her eyes shut. She puts the envelope in the pocket. Zips it closed. Drops the purse back onto the floor.

On the stairs, she shoves past Gordy, then skirts Radmila, who sits on the bottom step, weeping, wearing the sweatshirt now and rocking herself like a child.

In the parlor doorway, she stops. Her father gapes at her from the sofa. King Jupiter has found Gordy's mute and studies Rainey and her empty hands through its rubber eye.

Then he throws the mute.

Hard, not at her, but at the painting above the sofa. The mute hits Rebecca in the face, denting the canvas, then drops and lolls on the Aubusson, circling itself, going nowhere. On the sofa, Howard and Tina look out at him from under raised, protective arms.

"You're fucking with me," he tells Howard.

Howard slowly stands, leaning on Tina's shoulder. He looks like he could use a daughter about now. "Daddy—" says Rainey, but he walks right past her and heavily climbs the stairs.

Tina gathers up her book. King Jupiter turns on her. "Sit you there, girlfriend." A theater of sound plays overhead. What might be a nightstand drawer smashes into what might be a wall. Coins clatter and roll.

"What if it's gone?" Rainey saunters through the parlor like a woman in red stilettos, though one Ked is untied. She stands near King Jupiter at the piano.

"Gone?" He touches her arm. Feeling chosen, she lets him lace his fingers through hers. "Money is never gone." He turns her hand and sets her ring glittering. "It is only transformed."

Upstairs her father shouts: "Where'd you hide it, Gypsy?" She hears the thud of sailing clothes hitting the stairs. "Whore of Babylon," her father shouts. "Third-rate flutist." A spray of coins and Maybelline clatters in the foyer: a hurled purse.

They watch Howard reenter the parlor, stretching his fingers. "King, I'm at your mercy. I'm good for a check. Or I can hit the bank Monday. *Hey*—don't lean on the instrument."

"He won't take a *check*, Daddy." She touches King Jupiter's white cuff. They can be partners. She'll be the saucy one who talks too much. He'll pack that Popsicle stick and the tube.

"I accept alternate forms of payment." He twists her hand into the air. The diamond of Rainey's mother shoots light through them all.

Tina speaks as if from Rainey's mind. "She's not giving you that."

"Her cooperation is not required." And to Rainey: "Take it off."

"I did not reverse them," she whispers. His vice on her hand tightens.

Howard says, "That's worth four thousand bucks, King. I owe you seven hundred. Give us till Monday."

Tina says, "Plus it's stuck," and that is true.

"The finger ain't." He whomps Rainey's hand on the piano lid, hard.

It's the most interesting thing to happen in this house in a fool's age, even if it hurts.

"*I was eyes to the blind*," he tells her, his face close to her face. Then electricity lifts the roots of her hair, by which time it's over: switchblade, flick, slash. The finger remains attached, but slightly less so.

"She'll give you the ring," her father shouts. "Rainey, please."

"I know," says King Jupiter. "She'll beg me to take it."

The pain is the pain is the pain. Who said that? The pain is the biggest thing in the room, it is a rose with razor-petals. It shrills in her brain at the exact pitch of high B-flat from her own eighth-grade flute. That pathetic instrument! When she was twelve and cutting school with Tina, she would brag to the boys in Central Park that she played jazz flute, when all she played was scales. Tina looked fifteen and Rainey sixteen, and the boys were old enough to drink.

That pain. Instinctively she tries to tourniquet her bleeding forefinger with her other fist, but he's pinned her hand to the piano.

"Skin-deep," says King Jupiter warmly. It is the same tone her father used when she would bring him a skinned knee and he would say, mysteriously, *'Tis not so deep as a well, nor so wide as a church door.* King Jupiter says, "Twist the ring off while the blood's wet."

Howard is shrieking like the person in *The Scream* painting. When he gets control of his face, he says, "I'll pay you *eight hundred* Monday morning."

King Jupiter ignores him. "Twist," he says. "Next one goes through the bone."

She twists. The knuckle is slippery but it's still a manhole cover.

Man, her blood is gorgeous on the lacquered piano lid. And from up here on the ceiling she's riveted by the sight of Tina, who ambles up on their little group like a disinterested cat while King Jupiter watches with eyes in the back of his head.

Upstairs, a file drawer glides and slams. From the ceiling, Rainey sees herself lean into King Jupiter. "Tell Gordy to look under *J*," she says dreamily. "For *jagoff*."

Her father says sadly, "Howardsdottir, don't make it worse."

"Don't call me that." She has knife skills, too. She has awesome fucking knife skills.

"You might get us some Crisco, Howard," King Jupiter says. "Before we try surgery."

Her father bolts from the room. Rainey, on the ceiling, listens as the townhouse keeps playing its particular improvisational jazz—Radmila crawling after the disgorgements of her purse, knees bumping the floorboards; the cake, in the oven, skulking and smoking; the kitchen crashing and shattering as Howard pillages the cupboards.

"That needs Mercurochrome," says Tina calmly.

"I said: Sit you down, girlfriend," says King Jupiter.

Tina goes on, as if this were an actual conversation, "Did you sterilize that knife?"

It turns out that a person on the ceiling can say anything. "Maybe your daddy was a *putain de merde*, too," says Rainey. Her father was a kid in Paris; he can say the most egregious things in French. "Maybe you were the great disappointment of his life."

"Who are you trying to hurt?" says King Jupiter.

"From the time you could walk, right?" says Rainey. His grip makes her fingers go numb. "Oh, I bet it sucked, being you."

The knife flashes, growls. A long blond ellipse appears in the piano lid.

The piano lid is a virgin, a pristine surface upon which elbows do not lean, beer bottles do not rest, magazines do not collect. Amazed, Rainey stares at the gouge. It is the crescent moon, which, waxing, portends intention and, waning, surrender.

King Jupiter calls into the kitchen, "I think you spared the rod with this one, Howard."

Her father emerges. When he spots the damage, he looks at first like a man who has decided never to speak again. But then he wails. He is a raging prophet, his thurible a can of Crisco.

Radmila, holding her things in the parlor doorway, sputters at the carnage—whether the piano's or her own, Rainey is not sure.

"Jesus H.," says Rainey. The pain still sings soprano and her blood has browned on King Jupiter's white shirt cuff. "You'd think the piano bleeds worse than me."

"Actually. It doesn't." Tina slithers partway between King Jupiter and the piano. She has to grind her hips to do it and she looks right up at him through those long flamenco eyelashes of hers. Tina can be hot. She tells him, "That piano is stronger than you are." Rainey is struck by the sweetness of Tina's breath, as if her mouth might taste delicious. Tina is putting her life in the way of Rainey's mother's diamond. Or is it Rainey's father's piano?

"You can't hurt it," says Tina. "There's twenty tons of string tension in there."

"Wake up," snaps King Jupiter, and Rainey's father, as if awakened by thunder, thrusts out the oily blue can from across the grand piano. King Jupiter says, "Slide it over," and Howard, holding the can in midair, trembles.

"Not on the piano." He jerks the Crisco back.

King Jupiter lets Rainey wrest her hand free. Her blood tastes like pennies.

"Howwwward," says King Jupiter slowly, across many notes, as if calling to a child he is about to whip.

Her father plants the Crisco on the piano. Rainey dips her bleeding fist into the open tin. The lard feels creamy and cool. She lets her hand bathe in it.

"When did my father tell you about *string* tension?" she asks Tina.

Radmila steps into the parlor, rustling and cursing. In one hand she has her flute case and purse, in the other a knotted Hefty bag. She is radiant with snot and tears. "You. Mister drug dealer," she says. "You should get him where he lives with that knife." The power and the glory, if not the kingdom, shine in her face. She looks at King Jupiter with such intent that Rainey wonders, not for the first time, what she has missed. And then she sees it. The knife has moved. It is an inch from Tina's eye.

"Check her flute case," says Howard quietly. "Lift the lining."

"I did," says Rainey quickly. "It was the second place I looked. After her purse."

Radmila flicks Rainey the finger. But why? She's seen every one of Howard's women leave this house, one way or another.

Rainey taps Tina on the arm, though Tina is not looking, not with a knife to her eye. "What else did my father teach you?" She does not ask: How many minutes alone in a room, a room with a bed like a beating heart, does it take to impart the physics of string tension?

No part of Tina moves.

"Hey, King," says Howard. How do you distract a cobra? He tries. He walks to Radmila where she holds her belongings and kisses her, hard, on the mouth. It is the *bacio della morte*. "Take *her*, why don't you," says Howard. "Chain her to the radiator. Make her earn her keep."

Radmila scrapes out a sound like a gate barking closed. Tina says, "Howard, shut up."

King Jupiter lowers the knife. The light in his eyes changes. He walks to Radmila and looks her over, touching the tip of his knife to the fine meter that is the tip of his tongue.

"The ring came off," says Rainey. "Pay attention." She holds out an emerald-cut diamond ring. It was an engagement gift from her maternal grandfather, Marty, to his betrothed, Sophie; thence to Rainey's mother, Linda, when Linda decided to escape Howard, and thence (in a fit of maternal remorse) to Rainey. Marty has declined to meet Rainey, ever. He is Jewish, extremely, and she is not remotely Jewish enough, because of Howard. She is nothing, really.

"It's yours," she sings, and holds it up, but the light has died in the facets, smothered in both lard and blood, and besides, he isn't looking. He is deep into an appraisal of the disbelieving Radmila.

"Deal," he says. "Wrap it up and I'll take it."

He is not talking about the ring.

Rainey has one piece of advice for Radmila. It remains the best advice she's ever given. "Run," she says clearly. But Radmila is stalled, riveted by the last act of a bad play.

"Take a joke, man," says Howard. "Rainey, give him the goddamn ring."

Rainey comes up behind King Jupiter and takes his hand—as if they were lovers, as if his fingers belonged on her lips—and presses the ring to his palm. He lets it drop to the floor so that she lunges after it. "Jokes elude me," he says. He takes Radmila's arm, denting her flesh, and shunts her toward the foyer. Tina drifts their way like a translucent sea creature, but Rainey gets ahead and flattens herself against the front door.

Gordy shouting from upstairs: "I got seventeen dollars from pockets and shit."

Tina touches the dealer's arm. She opens her palm. Something glints there. She talks even lower than he does, but he won't look. "My grandmother's crucifix," she murmurs. Rainey keeps her eye roll to herself. "It has great meaning," says Tina.

And here we stand with our jewels out, Rainey wants to say. You, Eliezer, and me. And whose seed, Rebecca's or Radmila's, will possess the gate of their enemy?

Meanwhile, eighteen feet from the painting, Radmila has become an insect. She grapples with one sticky, spidery strand, then another, entangling herself until she, too, feels that strange liquid paralysis. "Kill him, Howard," she says. "What are you cowards staring at?"

"He's got a knife, sweetie," Tina says, and Rainey thinks she has never heard such tenderness in Tina's voice.

The cake is fighting for its life, too, that much is true. This cake has turned hard without adult supervision. Rainey can smell it, the dark crust, all the sweetness burned off. Inside, though, there might still be soft, delicious bits.

The knife is small and sharp and quick. It is a stiletto, illegal to carry, illegal to own. It merely glints through Radmila's hair, but there it is, chewing on light from the foyer sconces, which were gaslights in 1888 when the townhouse was built. Rainey steps aside. Tina does the same. King Jupiter opens the front door to a dark street, admitting an icy blast. He steers Radmila and her thumping baggage down the steps to a car that idles, shadowy, at the hydrant. The night sky releases a soft mist with no irony whatsoever.

"Don't," says Howard, though no one does anything but shiver in the shock of cold.

"Don't what?" says Rainey. "We could rush him." Tina looks at her, waiting. Rainey thinks, *Knife*, and Tina nods, barely.

The rear car door opens from inside and Radmila's body locks in refusal.

"He's a twerp. He won't hurt her," says Howard. He drapes an arm around Rainey's shoulders and she feels him shaking from cold before she jerks it off. Radmila looks back up at their little group. Her face is pale as a pearl in the dark. "For all we know, she planned it," says Howard. Radmila looks straight at Howard, spits on the sidewalk, then folds herself into the backseat with her flute case and purse. "Making off with him. Christ, my poor piano."

King Jupiter opens the trunk and places the Hefty bag inside. He gets into the backseat after Radmila. Noiselessly, the car pulls away. Up and down the block, bluestone sidewalks peak crazily over frozen tree roots.

In the warm foyer, Tina says quietly, "That finger needs Mercurochrome and stitches."

Rainey takes Howard's bomber jacket off a hook in the foyer. Her father is now tearing his hair over the piano damage. In his jacket pockets are Kools and a yellow BIC lighter, keys, and a bunch of bills. Jammed in a sleeve is a thrift-shop ruby cashmere scarf, a gift from Rainey's mother. This jacket could nurture her for days.

Tina watches her, then takes her own white down jacket off the hook.

And this is one more thing Rainey loves about Tina, how she doesn't talk if she has nothing to say. Like right now, how Tina simply follows her out the front door, no *Where we going* or *Bye, Howard* or *I have to just . . .* No words, just some sticky blood.

On the stoop, Tina sighs, her breath swirling white and vanishing into the dark. Rainey taps two Kools out of the pack. She feels Tina's hand in the pocket of Howard's jacket, fishing for the lighter. Then Tina offers up a flame in the chalice of her cupped hands.

Rainey hands her a lit cigarette. They walk west. The night is still, and midnight dark, and cold enough to snap in half. Every townhouse they look up into has a parlor. In every parlor hangs a chandelier. And beneath those crystals, who knows, a King might even now be chopping up little cicatrices of coke.

On her right hand, Linda's diamond has changed. It is heavy, a glass doorknob, still mired in Crisco. She tried to give it up and it flew back. Maybe, if she wears it hard enough, other things will fly back. Radmila, her mother, Tina—maybe Tina will tell Howard to drop dead.

· STRING TENSION ·

Those stars! Rainey remembers walking into Howardland balancing a tray for Mother's Day. She was a kid, maybe twelve, the tray heavy, coffee lapping the two cups, and Radmila and Linda Royal sat up in bed with their tops off under those gold foil stars, talking and smoking, magazines across their laps. They looked happy. It was strangely not confusing. To apply the stars, Radmila had dragged the bed aside and hauled the ladder up from the basement. Howard laughed and wouldn't help. Rainey handed up one star at a time, first dabbing on putty with an ice-cream paddle, and when the putty ran out Radmila said, Go get the toothpaste, and that held fine, too, for a while.

MR. APOLOGY

1980

In the chilled air of the Metropolitan Museum, Rainey Royal studies the dark orchid mouth of Bashi-Bazouk.

His name means *headless*, the label says. That's just weird. The dude has an exquisite head.

Bashi-Bazouk glances sidelong at Rainey from the painting. His eyes are onyx. His ear is a complicated bronze shell.

She wants to kiss this painted warrior before she sketches him, but the painter has captured him turning away. Rainey thinks: *Would you fucking* look *at me?* A woman donated him, a Mrs. Someone. Maybe it was unrequited love.

I saw you, says Bashi-Bazouk. *You're hot. But I am a warrior, pure of body and heart.*

She drops her army pack noisily. *I could fix that.*

Rainey figures if she sketches every portrait in every museum in New York, or at least the ones she likes, it will be a graduate art education. She is twenty-two years old; she has dozens of sketchbooks filled from her trips to museums. Cooper Union rejected her twice after Washington Irving. Since then, she's gone part time to the College of Rainey Royal in the University of New York Museums, so Cooper Union can just go fuck itself.

She turns from the painting, drawn by nothing: a prickling on her scalp.

Across the gallery, a man, too, turns from a picture to look back at Rainey, and when he shifts his weight, the herringbone wood floor grunts. Tiny antennae prickle on the scalp of the woman who is with him. *Lie flat*, the woman commands her antennae.

Bashi-Bazouk tells Rainey: *Quit it. Those two got married a year ago.*

So? says Rainey. She knows some things, too. She knows that he, the guy, has a voice like bourbon and cigarettes. She knows he can handle himself with a knife, which is the sexiest thing ever. His hair is thick and black and curls over his sweater.

She pulls the sketchbook out of her pack, fishes around noisily for whatever pencil comes to hand, and considers the wife.

The chick wears a beret. As in, she *wears* it. It does not wear her. She does the damn thing justice. Her head tilts right and her hip juts left, and the hip is a bowl of fruit. The wife has cheeks like lady apples, and obviously that is *his* leather jacket she has on. It is zippery, hard-worn. He may have slept in it, somewhere down the line. Rainey wants to get this man alone in that leather jacket. She wants to lick it.

Quit sparking, says Bashi-Bazouk.

The man looks over. His eyes are doorways, left ajar for her. He wears a wedding band, but it does not wear him. Rainey and the man gaze at each other with intent.

Stop making trouble, says Bashi-Bazouk.

To perceive someone, that is a powerful thing. It is beyond sexual. You could be with a person forever and never see them. Besides, she wants to make trouble. Just the tiniest bit of trouble. Then he can go home with the sexy cow and Rainey will never look for him in the Met again.

She smiles at the man. Then, to show her power, she turns her smile to Bashi-Bazouk. He looks disdainful now. With that attitude, maybe that's why he got donated.

As for the dark-haired man, he's drawn to the way she rustles paper. It makes him hot. She feels it. She flips the sketchbook to a new page, then back to study her previous efforts, then forward. She feels her bones radiant, like those nuclear rods they encase in concrete and stash away in caves.

The man and the woman cannot stare at one picture forever. They ease forward two squares. "Kevin," says the woman softly.

This seems a good moment to stretch.

Rainey leans the sketchbook against her leg, laces her hands behind her neck, presses her shoulder blades together behind her back and makes a muscular purr.

The man and his wife both turn. Rainey's chest is in the sticking-out phase of the stretch. What the hell, right? She beams right at him.

Of course, the woman sees.

She shoots Rainey a terrific smile of her own. *Sister!* the smile says. *I am alive all over,* the smile says. *I have so much lovely money,* the smile says. *I have a Princeton education. I know so much about art. I have this husband-lover who never read a page of Shakespeare but holy moly, the shit he does in bed. Isn't it great? Life?*

IN THE STALL of the ladies' room of the Met, the yellow paper peeks out mockingly from her pack. She crammed in the whole flyer at Union Square. You were supposed to tear off just the phone number, a single eyelash, from the bottom.

YOU HAVE WRONGED PEOPLE.

It actually says that, in paranoid-looking black text on a neon-yellow page. "Fuckin' A I have *wronged* people," Rainey says combatively.

"You need some paper, honey?" This from the next-door stall, a disembodied woman's voice. "Or you okay?"

"*You* ever wronged anybody?" Rainey demands. She smooths the wrinkles out while she does her business.

APOLOGY WILL AUTOMATICALLY TAPE-RECORD YOUR ANONYMOUS PHONE CALL, the flyer says.

How has she wronged, exactly? Let her count the ways. She slapped Leah in the girls' room till Leah said uncle, but that was seventh grade. Tina dumped Leah's purse in the toilet, too. She and Tina were an absolute bitch to that poor girl. Is that what Mr. Apology means?

And what about things done unto you, do those count? Like last weekend, when her father took her and Tina shopping to celebrate his selling a record in France, and Tina got a three-hundred-dollar hand-painted, silk and velvet scarf from Bergdorf Goodman, while Rainey got fake patent leather boots from Macy's that are too tight and can't be returned?

She listens to water running. Toilets flush, sinks flow.

How Rainey got the bad present was, Howard got visibly restless in the Macy's shoe department, so she said yes to the first boots she put on her feet because they only hurt a little. And how Tina got the good present was, they stepped out of Macy's, and Howard swooped open a taxi door and said smoothly, "Tina's turn. On to Bergdorf's."

No, Rainey wanted to say, you've got us mixed up. I'm the daughter. I get the fancy store. But Howard could be so snappish about money, even though the money is technically hers. Hers in trust. Hers in three years when she turns twenty-five. Anyway, Tina got Bergdorf's—why? The question needles her. Tina has lived in the townhouse with them since her grandmother died, on the top floor, rent-free, in one of the narrow, chilly attic rooms where Rainey's grandmother used to stash the servants. Tina chose that room. Rainey figures it's because Tina lives like a nun.

Every line of the Apology flyer is alluring to her. DESCRIBE IN DETAIL WHAT YOU HAVE DONE AND HOW YOU FEEL ABOUT IT. Tina would go crazy. Tina would say, Don't tell them about the gun. She would say, It's a trap.

But it's not. It's an art installation. Rainey can tell. WHEN YOU CALL, YOU WILL BE ALONE WITH A TAPE RECORDER.

Can she spell *felony*?

But the gun was years ago. The gun was high school. The fire, that was eons ago, too.

She folds the phone-number eyelashes carefully into the flyer, then folds the flyer into quarters.

Maybe she feels apologetic now.

She zips her jeans and leaves without washing her hands. Outside the Met it's a brilliant May day, bright and blue. She waits for a bus that will whisk her down Fifth Avenue to almost the Marble Arch. Near the stop, a Sabrett guy's radio scratches out Jermaine Jackson. You have to feel sorry for Jermaine. He was the lead, originally. Then Michael opened that pretty mouth.

In Bergdorf's the saleswoman wore pumps and black tights and kept her gaze fixed above the garish red Macy's bag. How may I be of help? she asked Howard, who had a celebratory arm around Tina, and Rainey said, Oh, I think we're way the fuck beyond help.

HELLO?

You want to know if I *wronged* someone. If I tell you, what, you forgive me? You're a *machine*. This is conceptual art. So really I should forgive myself. Come on, that's fucking ridiculous. I'm hanging up.

Wait. Wait. Okay. I'm lighting a cigarette.

Man, you don't say a thing. What are you, a Freudian analyst?

Okay, I smoke Kools. My father smokes Kools. Ha. Go interpret that.

This has to be a gas for you. Listening.

I found a gun. Are you happy? No? Tina and I showed it to some people. That is to say, we shoved it in their face and they almost died. Wait, not because we shot them—because they almost had a *canary*. Tina with a gun? Scary. That's how I got this cape. And these beautiful old handwritten letters I used in my tapestries. She said they were her mother's. The woman. The letters. We were, like, kids—does that count? If you're fifteen?

What if I tell you all this and don't apologize?

Is there a time limit on this thing? Three minutes and then you hang up on me?

Fuck, I used Tina's name. She's going to kill me.

Hang on.

Do you like the music? It's my contribution. *Soundtrack by Patti Smith.*

Okay, so. We put the gun in my purse and we changed our identities and we followed this man and this woman down a bunch of streets in the Village to where they lived. Whoa. I'm not saying which village. We could be in *Connecticut*. The woman was wearing the cape I told you about. And these Frye boots that didn't fit. Well, they fit *her*. We wore Gordy's T-shirts over our real clothes. That's my father's best friend who lives in our house, if you need to know. I wore Chick Corea and Tina wore Larry Coryell. Do you believe I remember? Eight years and I remember Larry Coryell? I had to iron the shirts and sneak them back into

Gordy's room. They're signed. He says they're his retirement. Ya *think*? In three years that townhouse is legally mine and I am throwing his ass on the street.

Maybe that's harsh. Ummmm, no. This is harsh. You have a daughter and you let a grown man live down the hall from her her whole life while you sleep on another floor.

I don't know why I even called. Maybe *you* should apologize. Fucking with people's heads.

AT THE CLINIC, Tina's sister, Carmen, reclines in her orange plastic chair as if she got spilled there, and Tina snaps, "*Carmen.*"

Carmen is fourteen and has a boyfriend, sixteen. Rainey's opinion is that Tina missed the boat on this one. And Carmen lives with their mother, who is worse than useless.

Tina yawns till her eyes water. She is always tired. She studies like a typical premed. She volunteers in the ER now.

Rainey wants to tap Carmen on the shoulder and say, Let's split. They are crowded into this little room where you meet before the clinic people send you home.

"It's okay," says the nurse. Her tone says, How about you let me do my job? Lazily, Carmen fiddles with a pink plastic pelvis. Tina plucks it from her hands and sets it back on the desk. Rainey wants to take Carmen to the townhouse on West Tenth Street and get her out of those tight clothes and say, This is how you dress. This is how you say no to boys. This is how you look at art and this is how you make art, too.

They are having the talk. The nurse holds up a luminous bone-white dome the size of a demitasse cup.

"I'm not putting that thing inside me," says Carmen.

"Why not?" says Tina. "You put everything else in there." With the nurse, she lowers her voice and talks right across the patient. "My sister wants an IUD. If it's in her, she'll use it. And the failure rate is oh-point-eight percent."

Tina is missing the boat again. Rainey watches her lean across the desk and narrow her eyes at the nurse like she wants that IUD coughed up one, two, three. The nurse, too, leans across the other side of the desk facing Tina. Rainey likes how she swings herself lightly under that white dress and saves her sweetness for Carmen, who needs it. She decides not to say anything about the boat.

Instead, she gathers up Carmen's hair and begins braiding it.

The nurse looks hard at Tina's hands on her desk till Tina steps back. Then the nurse opens a drawer and pulls out a bit of metal scrap. "This is an IUD," she says.

Carmen rolls her head into Rainey's hands. "I want the Pill."

"She's a tobacco user," says Tina in her doctor voice. "And she'll be noncompliant. She wants an IUD."

"Are you a doctor?" says the nurse, and Rainey can tell she knows the answer.

Tina cocks her head. "Premed."

"Huh," the nurse says. "Maybe you'd be more comfortable outside."

Rainey lifts the tip of the braid, looking around for a rubber band; if she stops holding tight, the ends will fray. "The Pill works great," she says lyrically.

Tina looks at Rainey and says, very slowly, "When you are thirteen, and your father gives you the Pill every morning with a glass of milk, it works. You think our mother's going to do that?"

The nurse looks hard at Rainey. Carmen's eyes go wide.

"Fourteen," says Rainey.

And Tina is right about the mother. Tina grew up with her grandmother, who had four rooms and one leg and three words of English, including *beautiful,* and who taught her to cook and study and pray, and who straightened her the *fuck out*. The grandmother is a saint, literally, because she's dead. So now Tina has Barnard on a full scholarship and also a rent-free room in the townhouse and a silk and velvet scarf from Howard, and also she has Jesus Christ, whereas Carmen has one abortion down.

"Why don't you sit outside and study?" the nurse tells Tina.

"Jesus," says Carmen. "Your dad did that for you?"

"Don't take the name of the Lord in vain," says Tina, on her way out.

"Not *for* me," Rainey says. "More like *to* me. But yeah."

THE NEXT WEEK at the Met, Rainey wears a buccaneer shirt she sewed herself. She unbuttons it low. She wears jeans she's tailored with seams down the front. She wears boots with heels.

Heels make her taller than the dragon ladies.

You have to stare them down, these ladies who sit in Admissions under the big SUGGESTED sign and look at your single dollar like you fished it out of the toilet. What is SUGGESTED on the sign is four dollars. Her father always says, Just walk the fuck in, Rain, it's tax-supported. Suggests. He SUGGESTS that.

She finds the lady with the parrot way over on the second floor. In the painting, the lady is naked on a green velvet chaise. They just about crucified Courbet over this pic, not because of a naked chick, that was cool in France in 1866, but because her hair was unkempt, her clothes strewn about, all that *abandon*. But they put it in the Salon because it was *good*.

Rainey spends a lot of time in the Rose Reading Room at the NYPL. Right now she is working her way through the gossipy second volume of Vasari's *The Lives of the Most Excellent Painters, Sculptors, and Architects*.

Two men peer at the painting. Their arms touch all the way. "It showed in the X-ray," the first man says. He draws an emphatic curlicue in the air. "Right *there*. He painted himself in, nude. Then he painted himself out."

"No kidding," says Rainey. She moves closer. One of the men smells of almonds.

"No kidding," he tells her.

"Well, that bird stand is pretty phallic," says the second man. He is baby-plump and wears a baby-blue sweater.

Two boys burst into the gallery and chase each other around a bench. One, pale as a bone, abruptly stops and stares at the nude. The second boy collides with him and stares, too. The painting has news that they need and Rainey watches them consume it.

She tells them, "You know museums are full of pictures like this."

"He was pulchritudinous," the first man says, tasting the word. "He often painted himself into things."

A woman walks into the gallery with a red-eyed robot tucked under one arm and shakes her head. The boys get tugged away. One flashes a plum-colored stain on his face. He has been marked, but for what?

Rainey sketches the lady with the parrot, wondering about the artist who lurked between layers of pigment and light, deeply concealed. It was like sketching Madame X with her strap up, knowing she'd let the real strap slip. You could almost see the ghost of the thing.

Tina likes birds—maybe she'll give Tina the sketch, in a thrift store frame. And maybe, while she is up in Tina's room on the fifth floor, extending this gift, she will caress the hand-painted scarf till Tina offers to let her borrow it. It is only fair. 'Cause if Howard had thought of Bergdorf's *first*, he might have given his daughter the genuine gift and Tina the plastic boots.

Not that it matters. They are best friends.

YOU DON'T GET bored, hearing all this confessing? Last time all I did was whine. I'm sorry I bored you. Ha! I apologized.

I was telling about the gun, but I think we covered that. We robbed those people. I'm not sorry. Does that fuck up your art? I'm not sorry I have the cape. You think Tina's sorry she has the dude's leather jacket that she still wears? God, don't get me going on leather jackets. And I am not sorry about the guy at the museum. Ask me if I care that he's married.

Ask me.

I'm waiting.

Okay. There was this fire? You are scouring me out, I swear to God. I never meant to scorch half her apartment. It's just, you don't insult my family. At least not after fucking my boyfriend. So what if I was raised by wolves? Who was she to say it?

I could tell you about Mrs. Teagan. I'm not sorry about her *at all*. Mrs. Teagan was second grade and she taught me everything I know about art in one day. She was teaching us the story of Icarus. His father made those wings out of feathers and wax. He said, You can fly, Ic, but if you go near the sun the wax will melt and you'll fall and *die* even though you're only, like, twelve. You know what that story means, right. It means *aim low*. It means rein yourself in.

They should never tell that story to children.

So Mrs. Teagan tells us to take out our crayons and draw Icarus. Every kid in the class draws Icarus flying. But not me. *I* draw him plummeting, with his wings dripping, and feathers everywhere. She walks up and down the rows of desks, praising us in alphabetical order, and she gets to me and goes, Rainey Royal, that is morbid. Draw it again, please.

Shit. If you're listening, splice that out. My name. Not the *shit*.

Anyway, I said no. So they called my father to come get me. He *loved* my picture of Icarus falling, and he was so proud that I refused to draw it again. Because what I drew the first time was true. But Mrs. Teagan said, Art is not about truth, Mr. Royal. Art is about beauty.

My father said, This woman is a danger to children. I don't want her near my daughter.

This is wild. I keep calling Mr. Apology and refusing to apologize. I'm sorry I keep not saying I'm sorry. I'll leave you alone now. Bye.

THE NEXT DAY, she goes straight to Bashi-Bazouk, in case the guy in the leather jacket is telepathic. *You should not*, says Bashi-Bazouk, *do this*.

It doesn't matter. He isn't there.

She stalks off to Drawings and Prints, looking for a Mary with some steel to her, or a Mary who secretly wants to be an artist, and wanders the rooms till she's arrested by a Leonardo Mary, specifically the *Head of the Virgin in Three-Quarter View Facing Right*. A dreamy, sweet-faced chick who probably made candles and tie-dye T-shirts.

Rainey kneels to dig out her supplies. Then, for a time, all she feels is her pencil on the page. So she doesn't feel him. And then she feels him. She *knows* him. She knows his thumbnail is half blackened. She knows his laughing wife made the bed that morning with peach sheets. She knows. She knows. And she turns.

He has that unruly Jim Morrison hair going on. His eyes are a well with old hurt at the bottom. He aims a low beam at her. He lets her *see*.

Rainey, still kneeling, takes in that beam and lets the light traverse her. Then she resumes sketching Mary's face. Through her back, she feels the guard in the tall doorway, watching without watching. Some kind of golden mean plays out between Mary's eyes and lips, and a wisp of kinked hair escapes her cap. Rainey draws the wisp. She smudges it. She bites her lower lip and begins the flirtation of her pencil with the Virgin's philtrum.

"All that beauty and all that pain," the man says. "You feel it, don't you."

His voice: tobacco, gravel. The pressure of his knees against her back.

"I bet you've wronged someone," she says, and gets to her feet.

"I'm thinking about it," he says.

She senses his wife nearby—the water fountain, the ladies' room. A timer whirs in Rainey's mind as the wife, nearing the stall, gives her reflection a quick appraisal.

The man tips his head toward the corridor. *One minute*, he is telling her, *maybe two*. Good. You can ink a future in that time. Later today she will go see Louise Nevelson at Pace, where the gallery girl will fix her green Bryn Mawr gaze on Rainey's sneakers and jeans. Sometimes you have to see work by a woman for a change. A woman who wanted to sculpt things from the age of ten, for Chrissake, who would give up her marriage for art.

The man says, "I want to buy you a cup of coffee."

He doesn't mean coffee. And he doesn't mean now. She traces her front teeth with the tip of her pretty tongue. Let the wife find them like this. Let a nagging little fear shadow her, like a half-seen stray cat, around the corners of the marriage.

"Milk," says Rainey. She makes it two syllables. "I drink milk."

He growls. He cups her face hard. In the doorway, the guard's radar pings. In the ladies' room, the wife pulls a black Chanel lipstick case from her bag.

Rainey loops a finger through the leather cord around the man's neck.

He kisses her.

His tongue is respectful. Rainey tastes toothpaste, pot, salami, and the fresh basil he filches from the windowsill, not in that order. She presses her most private part against him. She ankles up to the bad-behavior line and feels it spread beneath her. It is a wider place than she imagined, not linear like Broadway but leafy like Central Park, as tangled as the Ramble and as dangerous, too. She could linger there. It is a place where she might live.

The wife paints her mouth carmine. A woman down the line of sinks says, At your age, honey, a red lip is all you need.

In the gallery, the guard tells them to *step back*. He means from each other. Far off, heels tick in the corridor. Rainey pulls a BIC pen from her pack and opens her left palm wide.

He prints the marks upon her flesh.

And he's barely handed back the pen when his wife clicks into the gallery. She does the calculus. Rainey sees it. Then she shakes it off, walks over to her man, and claims him. She calls him *honey*. He calls her *hey*. Her voice is a lynx coat. His hands go to his pockets. She murmurs into his hair. Rainey watches like she knows them. The wife glances at Rainey and Rainey smiles at her, a slowball smile that says, *There is no house I can't break into.*

She can't wait to tell Tina: My God, it was like the first kiss ever. It was like we had *the same mouth.*

SICK OF ME yet?

Ha, you're a machine. You have to listen to me. It's your *job.*

So I do want to apologize. But I don't know if it's for a crime.

I was in school and I found this little cat, pure black, a kitten. She was outside our townhouse lifting her paws out of snow like she didn't know if it was freezing or hot. When I hold out my hand, she rubs against it, and when she purrs she lifts her tail. So I know it's a girl. She's got a tiny white target, right there. I pick her up and take her inside and start carrying her up to my room, and of course I get stopped.

My dad goes, Whatcha got? He's in the parlor with Gordy, who's doodling around with a clarinet, and an acolyte on violin and one on flute. And Gordy starts sneezing. But majorly sneezing.

Big deal, right? Some kid gets abandoned every five seconds and I'm whining about a cat. You're a tape recorder, you deal with it. My dad won't let the acolytes touch the cat. He says, "Gordy can't play if he's sick." And Gordy keeps sneezing. He sounds like he's choking. From one little hair that floats across the foyer. He's not just an asshole trumpeter. He's an asthmatic asshole trumpeter. Then my mother comes down and baby talks to the cat and says, I'm so sorry, sweet pea, she's got to go. But we'll put milk out every day.

How stupid am I? I figure this little cat can live in a box with sweaters behind the trash bins. I didn't know cats can't drink cow milk. So I hold her while my mother heats the milk, and then I set down the cat. She sniffs the bowl, tucks her tail between her legs, wobbles down the steps, and folds herself under a parked car. I try to get under there. My knees are freezing on the snow but I want to take her to the ASPCA. I stick my arm under the car and I guess it scares her because she shoots across the street, just as a car backs out of a space. I don't look but I hear it, all squeak and yowl, and then I do look. The driver is freaked. She pukes a little. My mother's sympathetic but I tell her, I hate you. The next summer she was gone.

Oh. No. I'm not sorry for saying that.

I think about that little cat. I apologize to her.

THE ANGEL OF the Waters wears a bronze dress, because she's a statue. Rainey wears a top she made from part of a tight, white man-tailored blouse and a lot of lace yardage.

At Bethesda Fountain, in the park, under the Angel, waiting for Kevin, Rainey wears also a full-gored black skirt and brown suede boots that her mother abandoned. With majesty and excellence she has decked herself. Black patent boots would cinch it, but they hurt that first day out. Howard wasn't interested, so she tried to return them herself. The salesman just glanced at the soles. *You're kidding me, right?*

On a broken bench at Bethesda Terrace, a man in an olive suit nurses a paper bag. Before him, two girls twirl ropes while a third jumps. They chant, *Not last night but the night before, fourteen robbers came to my door.* Rainey sits straight-backed on the fountain lip, looking dreamily up at Terrace Bridge. *Stole my watch and stole my ring. Then they all began to sing.* Thoughtfully she unbuttons the lace one more button. *Policeman, policeman, do your duty.* She wishes she had something to sketch with.

He stands before her.

He stands before her lean as a branch, his mouth a chalice, hands jammed in the pockets of his jeans. His eyes map her. That leather cord around his neck—she wants to snag it with a finger again, wants to pull him down to her.

The rhyme shifts, and Rainey senses it is taking on a moral stance. *Wiggle, wobble, do the split*, the girls chant. *Can't wear her dress above her hips.*

Oh, but she can. Arrayed with art and abandon and glory and rage, she can do anything. Under the bridge, she can hike her skirt past her hips if she wants. He ditched the wife; he did that for *her*. For what should she apologize; for whom should she go into the clefts of the ragged rocks?

"Isn't she beautiful?" Rainey tips her head. She means the angel, but he doesn't look up.

They are waiting for the thing to begin.

LIFE IS LIKE THAT

1981

Rainey woke in her pink room to a ringing phone. Kira was furious. "I can't wait for you another minute," she said. "I'm late for work."

"Oh, Kira." Rainey meant *I am fucking up both of our lives*; she meant *please don't yell at me*. Rainey was supposed to be painting Kira's little apartment to resemble a loggia, glazing three walls like terra-cotta, with high arches on the fourth wall revealing pastoral Italian views. She painted while Kira was at work, which meant getting there by eight fifteen in the morning so Kira could leave. At eight fifteen, Rainey was still cycling in REM sleep.

"If you made me keys, it wouldn't matter," she said. It was 8:38 A.M.

"I told you, I can't," said Kira. "They're Do Not Duplicate."

Kira Kendricks was built like a praying mantis. She worked at a Condé Nast magazine where half the editors and editorial assistants went to the ladies' after lunch and stuck their fingers down their throats. Kira had told her this with pride. Yeah, but your *teeth*, Rainey said. She personally liked having boobs you could rest on a scale and they weighed something. Kira's mother was paying Rainey $1,500 to decorate the studio, but that included brushes and paint. If Rainey wanted Kira to have creditable antiques, she had to do faux bird's-eye maple on the bureau and dining table. More brushes, more paint.

"Be sweet to the locksmith." Rainey stretched audibly. "He'll cut you keys."

"Life isn't like that," said Kira.

Rainey got her decorative painting jobs from a sympathetic dude in the employment office at Cooper Union, the art college that had turned her down. "My life is like that," she said.

Kira hung up on her.

The dark studio on Horatio Street was a fifteen-minute walk in the October chill from the townhouse on West Tenth. At least it might have been fifteen minutes. Time wasn't Rainey's strong point. Kira was waiting at the door, sighing heavily. It was 9:25 A.M. "I'm really, really late for work," she said. She wore a swing coat, and her scarf was tied the French way. Lately Rainey had been copying that, and she was thinking of shoplifting a pair of ballet flats like the ones Kira wore to the office. Her friends were a year or two out of college but Rainey had been working straight from high school, making and selling memory tapestries that memorialized the dead. She didn't get many commissions but a single one paid five hundred dollars, so that was huge.

"My boss is freaking," Kira said, stalking toward the elevator. "What happened yesterday? I waited till nine thirty."

"Yesterday I blew it." Rainey entered the apartment, her cape, a heavy sluice of black lapping at her boots, whirling even more than Kira's swing coat. She had taken it years earlier in that robbery she'd committed with Tina Dial. She eyed Kira's sink full of unwashed dishes, set her army pack on the unmade bed, and poked her head back into the hall where Kira was jabbing the elevator button. "I'll set the bottom lock if I leave early."

"I need both locks," said Kira severely. "It's not a secure building. Can't you wait till I get home with the keys, for Chrissake?"

"Could you please please please not worry? I will personally vouch for your apartment and everything in it." She ducked back inside just as she heard the elevator door glide shut. Yes! God was good. She went straight to the stereo. Please don't, Kira had said, it's very delicate. But Rainey grew up with delicate. Howard had the best components. He was a professional jazz pianist; he had a fucking signed Steinway, of course he had the best stereo. He had a Pioneer SX-1980 receiver with 270 watts per channel; it weighed as much as the refrigerator. He had a new Micro Seiki SX-8000 turntable. Rainey could recite stereo equipment the way their friend Leah Levinson knew horoscope signs. Kira had an Onkyo deck, which was good, but it was not the Second Coming of Christ.

She opened the window, leaned out into the courtyard, and smoked a Kool. The truth was she felt for Kira. This chick had a mother who criticized her weight in ounces and her boyfriends and her hair and her clothes. That was one thing about Linda. She didn't judge. Well, hell, Linda wasn't *there*. She hadn't been there for years.

She flicked her lit cigarette toward the razor wire, pulled off her black cowboy boots to save them from drips, and spread her drop cloth. Her church key lay on the can of McCloskey glazing liquid, and she used it to pry off the lid. She poured some glaze into a bucket. It looked as white as milk. You had to mix four parts glaze with one part colored paint to make something interesting.

But the real trick with glazing liquid was after you dabbed it on the wall, you had to work the wet edge fast and smear it with conviction. You couldn't hesitate and step back and think, Is that a persuasive smear? You had to have looked at terra-cotta in the Met. You had to have looked at photographs of villa interiors in the library. So you could swipe and swirl and cloud and not ask questions. Rainey used a sheepskin mitt meant for washing cars, and she felt herself on intimate terms with terra-cotta.

She opened the ladder and climbed it, holding the bucket of colored glaze.

Stevie Nicks was singing "Stop Draggin' My Heart Around," and Rainey danced and swiped and made of the glaze an umbery smoke on the walls and thought, But that is what people *do*, Stevie. She herself was half in love with a guy whose heart got regularly dragged home by his wife, and she had a mother who had loved her but packed her heart into a suitcase and split, and a father who loved only himself and kicked other people's hearts down the front stoop. The whole point was to hold on as tight as you could.

The glaze was the color of tobacco. She could almost taste it. She had painted the walls a lighter base coat first, graham cracker, and she could almost taste that, too. Journey did "Who's Crying Now," and she danced to that up on the ladder and thought, Not me, baby, I haven't cried since I was thirteen, dabbing color on the wall and swirling it with the mitt.

Howard had almost ruined rock for her. Never mind that he was white, he called it *white boys whining*. Getting chased by the sheriff my ass, he liked to say, they probably grew up in the suburbs. He couldn't make Rainey love jazz but jazz was like— jazz was abstract art. Jazz was Mark Rothko, Joan Mitchell. Stuff that made other art seem dull, even guys like Courbet, whom she adored. Modern art wasn't beautiful but it made you *feel*. It made you think. If you stood there long enough, it made you see. The way jazz taught you to hear.

Outer voice. Sideslipping. Inner voice. Crush. Broken time. Howard was all about broken time. He had taught her how to listen, even if he spent way the fuck too much time with her best friend.

She took another cigarette break, hanging out the window into a fine drizzle. She climbed back up and worked awhile. She was on the ladder, singing with Michael Jackson and doing a modified Cabbage Patch, a dumb dance, and the third wall was half done and looked fantastic but it still wasn't enough. The two arches and the Italian landscape on the fourth wall needed a week and the faux tortoise inlay on the kitchen cabinets needed another. She couldn't believe she'd signed a contract where the mother got to dock her pay.

And then "Fame" came on and she lost it.

Rainey could sing every word of "Fame." She climbed down and turned the stereo up. Then she poured her body into Irene Cara.

She *was* gonna live forever. *Kick.* She *was* gonna learn how to fly, *pivot*, only it would be through art. She decided to make a tapestry of things stolen from Howardland, the big blue bedroom on the second floor. Her father would live between layers of fabric and *objets* just as Courbet hid between pigment and light. Howard would be the truth, the good and evil, that she would stitch instead of speak. She spun again. *Click.* She tipped her head back. *Click.*

Two locks unclicked. "Jesus, Rainey?"

Kira, soaked, with streaked mascara, stood in the doorway holding a sodden cardboard carton. A picture frame stuck out of it. Rainey stopped dancing. Irene Cara kept singing. "You got me fired," said Kira thickly. "For fucking lateness." Her thin, pretty face looked carved, and strands of hair stuck wetly to her neck. "What are you *doing*?"

Rainey pointed to the third wall, on which she had made significant progress.

"This is *your fault.*" Kira set the box on the foyer table, strode to the tuner, her coat swinging admirably, and turned off the radio. The silence was silver around the edges. "You should go," said Kira.

Were those raindrops or tears? "I'll make you some tea," said Rainey gently. "Then I'll finish. You won't even know I'm here."

"I hate tea," said Kira. "Just go. You can come back Monday. Monday I'll be temping." Today was Thursday.

"Your mother will dock me if I don't finish." Rainey tugged the ladder a few feet over and climbed back up, slipping the mitt on. She dabbed some glazing liquid on the wall and rubbed it artfully.

Kira was not impressed. "If you don't get out," she said, "I'll call the super." She waited. "I'll call the *police.*"

Rainey applied more glaze. "You've had a trauma," she said. "And I'm really sorry. But only your mother can fire me."

"I'll get a can of white paint. I'll undo everything you did. I swear."

That did it. "Okay," said Rainey. "Okay, okay, okay, okay, okay."

FRIDAY MORNING. KIRA had relented, but Rainey was frozen at her own front door, listening, late again, because Tina Dial was clumping down the stairs from high up in the house, and something was off. Four flights down, normally, but the clumping stopped on the second floor.

Howardland, the blue bedroom.

"Ya think?" said Rainey. She was talking to herself.

Her father would sleep till noon. The acolytes, his girl musicians who lived on the fifth floor with Tina, pretty much kept his schedule. Tina was in medical school; she had loans up the wazoo.

Rainey smoked an entire cigarette while she waited for Tina. She stubbed it out in Howard's overflowing ashtray in the double parlor, where a depleted pot baggie and a coke mirror sat with empty glasses on the coffee table, a trumpet lay on a bergère, and the grand piano lorded it over the whole mess.

Finally Tina came downstairs looking edible with her cat-green eyes and that blunt-cut caramel hair. Miss Temptation, that was what Howard called her. In junior high, Tina had a cute sash of fat around her waist, and Rainey had loved that sash because it was necessary that only one of them be perfect. Admit it, Howard had said, you hang with Tina because next to her you look like a centerfold. But he was wrong. Rainey hung with Tina because she adored her. Now here she was, all slim, carrying the leather jacket that she and Rainey took off a guy named Paul back when they had stolen Howard's loaded gun for a day, and Rainey had gotten her cape from Paul's girl. It was a long story. It was intense. It was, okay, felonious. They never talked about it, but it bonded them as if they'd cut themselves and rubbed their blood together.

Tina was wearing Howard's Fair Isle sweater.

Rainey could smell it as well as see it. She might as well have buried her nose in that sweater, picking up notes of Old Spice and

LIFE IS LIKE THAT

patchouli. "Hey," she said, and Tina stopped. She had no right to barge in and paw through Howard's clothing—Howardland was a vault. It was Rainey's vault.

"That fits well," Rainey said coolly. What was she supposed to say? *Leave my father's shit alone?* She looked hungrily at the sweater, oatmeal and cobalt. Tina's collarbones came hauntingly through the worn wool, and when after a moment she slipped on her jacket, the sleeves slunk past the chapped leather cuffs.

"He was sleeping. I just borrowed it."

"It took twenty minutes to borrow?"

"We talked a little. Aren't you late?" and Tina gave her a sweet smile and sailed out of the townhouse in Howard's sweater.

FIFTEEN MINUTES LATER, Kira opened the door and looked at Rainey and said, "Fuck." She wore gold hoop earrings and a red suit. "You know anything about music people?" she demanded.

On the stereo, public radio was droning away. That wasn't going to teach her anything. Rainey laughed. "Yeah," she said. "A lot." She didn't ask Kira why. Sometimes it was more delicious to let the answers snake their way to you.

She set her pack and her cape on the disheveled bed. The gift-shop artwork she had taken off the walls in order to paint leaned against the bureau, and soon would come painful negotiations over images like *Water Lilies* or a framed poster captioned I CANNOT LIVE WITHOUT BOOKS. Kira owned two books. One was a collection of *The Far Side* cartoons.

"I'm screwed," said Kira. "I have an interview at Electric Lady Studios and my clothes say Condé Nast. *Rainey.* Fucking help me." White blouse, chain belt, red skirt, black pumps—she looked like the assistant to the assistant VP of something stupefying. Kira said, "Pretend you're Iron Maiden. They're recording as we speak."

"Iron Maiden isn't awake at ten in the morning." Rainey turned the radio dial and found the Talking Heads. It was nice, being needed. "Your makeup says *secretary*," she said. "We can start there. And you might as well take everything off. Including that stinky perfume."

Kira disappeared down the hall. Her heels were a metronome. She came back with her face bare and shining, but still dressed. "This is a power suit," she said. "It's Anne Klein. The chain belt is faux Chanel. The shoes are perfectly neutral."

"I know," said Rainey. "It sucks."

"Yeah, but." Kira put her hands on her hips, defiant. "They said I can become a PA in a year. So I wouldn't be just some receptionist. It's called dressing for the job you want."

"Okay." Rainey shrugged. She picked up her church key and worked the lid off the glaze. Her powers were growing by the minute. She was absorbing light like a black hole.

Kira let her arms flop in the aspect of supreme disappointment. "So tell me what to do."

Rainey set down the sticky lid, went to Kira's closet, and began pulling out everything black. She held up one piece at a time, examined it, then dropped it on the floor. "Is that necessary?"

said Kira. Rainey found a black satin corset that Kira probably wore to clubs, and draped it over the love seat. "No fucking way," said Kira, but Rainey kept sliding hangers till she found a black cotton blouse and a skinny black skirt.

"This," she said. "And black tights."

"If I don't get this job, you're supporting me." But Kira stripped down to a white bra and panties and painstakingly hooked the corset on. Rainey tied the black shirt in a knot over the corset, leaving it partly open to flash some satin.

Kira slipped on the black tights and skirt and examined herself in the mirror. "What about that rose oil you wear?"

But it was back at the townhouse. Rainey said, "Those low black boots you wore last week. Find those."

Kira posed in the mirror and flung out a hip, which was like waving a box cutter around, she was so angular. "My mother would *die*," she said. It sounded like a compliment. It sounded like *thank you*.

"This is not about your mother," said Rainey, which meant *you look terrific*. "Hang on." She got her cape from the bed and draped it around Kira, who twirled it in the mirror and swooned, holding her face with both hands.

Rainey seized her advantage. "Hey, those tortoiseshell cabinets." She couldn't afford to spend a week on them. "They're really overkill. They'd rock just black enamel."

Kira smiled at her reflection. "No, I really love the idea of tortoiseshell," she said distractedly. "Oh!" She found her purse, dug into it, and pressed something into Rainey's palm: two keys.

"It took three locksmiths, but you were right," she said. "Life is like that. Wish me luck."

"Ciao, bella," Rainey said.

LATE AFTERNOON. SHE sat on the drop cloth–draped love seat and dialed Kevin on Kira's phone. The phone was pink. It clashed with the terra-cotta. It would have to be replaced.

"Art studio," said Kevin, and she smelled leather, Zest, and sweaty, slept-in sheets.

"Hey," she said.

"Thank you, Jesus." She heard a match strike. "God, this makes me happy," he said. Then the long expulsion of cigarette smoke. Kira's phone wouldn't stretch to the window. Fuck it. She lit a Kool right in the studio. A man was singing distantly at the other end of the line, slow, soulful, strange.

"Who's that?" she asked him.

"You like it?" The singer had a voice of streaming crimson. "It's Boris Godunov," he said.

"I don't know him," she said cautiously.

He laughed. The laugh had gravel in it. Budweiser in the fridge, she thought. And bourbon in bars, straight up, water back. "He's crying for a ray of joy," said Kevin. "He won't get one. Murderers never do." He paused. "Not really fair, is it? Come over and listen."

Howard would say, What are you, kidding? Daughter, *go*. Soak up some opera. But Kevin was a married man. She should quit fooling around.

· LIFE IS LIKE THAT ·

No ashtray. She nudged the ash of her Kool onto her jeans and rubbed it in. "How's your day going?"

"Sublime," he said. "I drew a lady in a girdle. Bonwit Teller sent a messenger for it. Help me celebrate, Rainey Royal. I'm a free man." He wasn't actually.

"Yeah, well, I'm not a free woman." But if Tina could fuck her father, Rainey sure as hell could keep seeing Kevin. Well, probably she was being unfair. Tina would never in a million years do that to her. She gave Kevin a millisecond to persuade her, and he said urgently, "*Wait.*" She waited. She tucked her feet up under her and basked in the terra-cotta. It looked almost powdery to the touch, sunbaked.

"Look, come to the studio for an hour," he said. "Before my wife gets home. Let me draw you."

An hour was nothing. An hour was a garden with a high wall around it. "Can I keep the drawing?"

She would not fuck him. Of course she would fuck him. Again she heard the cigarette suck, the deep exhale. "Babe," he said, "anything you want."

Kira had her cape, but she had the swing coat. She slipped it on and swirled out the door.

"AM I *WHAT*?" said Howard the next morning.

Tina had just left for Mount Sinai, and Howard sat up in bed when Rainey burst in, the covers pulled up just barely enough to hide his groin, as if he couldn't be bothered to notice such things. Next to him, the girl he'd picked up in a jazz club the night before lay clutching the sheet to her chest as if Rainey had not seen such things all her life.

"You heard me." Rainey leaned on the doorpost. She demanded satisfaction.

"Lord, you are a paranoid thing. Tina and I talk. This is your business why?"

Howard smiled at her, reached for the Kools on his cluttered nightstand and crumpled the empty pack. "Give me a cigarette, Daughter."

Rainey ignored him. "She woke you up to talk?"

"Why not? You woke me to interrogate me. Have you met Dandelion?"

The girl with the heart-shaped face shot him a glittering look. "It's Daisy."

"Ha," said Rainey. "Dandelion's better." Howard betrayed people so casually it was hard to tell what was criminal with him and what was everyday misbehavior.

Rainey left him in Howardland bitching about cigarettes and climbed the creaking stairs to the fifth floor, the last flight narrow and dimly lit because it was only meant for servants back in the day. Tina always closed her door when she left, as if this afforded some kind of privacy. The hell, thought Rainey. She'd rarely been up here. Tina always came down. She turned the knob and found herself standing in Tina's nun's cell of a room. It held a battered bureau, a student desk, and a crucifix on the wall that had belonged to the dead grandmother. Tina could commit all kinds of bad shit yet dedicate her mind to

Christ. She could have chosen a real bedroom, yet here she was, in the attic.

It felt almost punitive. What was she doing wrong?

Rainey searched methodically. Bureau, closet, desk. Clothes, notebooks, textbooks, a cardboard carton of novels. The grandmother's Bible and rosary. A little gold jewelry, a *Vogue* on the nightstand, two packs of Marlboro Lights and Howard's yellow Cinzano ashtray, which looked just like the one on his nightstand—Rainey made a note of that.

She saw nowhere else to look. And then she regarded the bed—a twin, narrow as something for a cloister, and tightly made up, its corner folded into a triangular flap. That grandmother had sure taught her how to make a bed. Rainey couldn't remember a single lesson from Linda about how to make a bed. As far as Rainey was concerned, you woke up and got dressed and the bed took care of itself.

She lifted the pillow. Nothing. She stood back and looked at the bed and it looked back at her, neat as a pin.

Intrigued, she lifted the rear corner of the mattress and stuck her hand beneath, groping. Indeed, Tina had hidden something: a sheaf of papers. She pulled it out.

Sheet music.

The Tina Temptation was written across the top. She knew about this piece of jazz. Howard had composed it years ago, when the girls were sixteen, when he had started with the fucking clarinet lessons. Eventually Rainey had enough of those closeted lessons and made Tina throw the clarinet in a dumpster. Just like Tina had rescued this sheet music, she thought, but that was not the real issue. Anyone might want a copy of the music composed in their honor. It was what Howard had written in the top right corner. *For Tina, my love*, it said in his spidery blue handwriting.

Tina my love? Tina my *love*? Tina my fucking *love*?

Of course he probably meant it sardonically. Howard meant almost everything sardonically. Especially if he wrote it for a mere sixteen-year-old girl. But he *had* written it, at some point, and Tina had saved it, and she had kept it a secret from Rainey.

Tina my *love*?

Rainey shoved the music back under the mattress and tried to fold the sheet and quilt back into a flap. Impossible. Tina would come home and know she had looked, and they would have a conversation or they would not, and either way Rainey would never love anyone the way she loved Tina Dial.

Even if Tina had betrayed her. Which Tina would never do. They were *best friends*.

RAINEY WAS TORTOISESHELLING the kitchen cabinets on Tuesday when Kira draped herself in the doorway, suspiciously not saying something. She wore the narrow black skirt Rainey had chosen for her last Friday, a new low-cut black top, black tights, the short black boots. She had pierced her ears again, so double holes now, and she had a new choppy haircut. Plus her hair was now dyed raven black: Rainey's idea. This Kira had attitude. The mother hated it, but Kira was now the daytime receptionist at Electric Lady and was dressing for the job she wanted.

"I think it's gorgeous," Kira said. "I love the walls and I fucking *love* the cabinets. And I love the look you put together for me," she added graciously.

"But?" She heard something in Kira's voice. Rainey had sectioned the cabinet doors into squares with painter's tape and was on a ladder with a narrow brush, dabbing slanted black marks over the raw umber glaze.

"It's my mother," said Kira. Rainey kept working. "I'm really sorry but she's sticking to her guns about having it done in a week."

"Kira, no one alive could do this job in a week." Each square would have its black marks on a different diagonal. Not that you ever saw faux inlaid tortoiseshell on a large scale like this, but it would be stunning.

"I'm really, really sorry, Rainey. I didn't think she'd do it but she's docking your pay."

Rainey climbed down off the ladder and walked over to face Kira. She was rocking the new look. Her lips were scarlet and her eyes were darkly lined, the way Rainey had showed her. "Then you have to make it up to me," Rainey said flatly. "I still have to do the fourth wall and that's a whole other week."

Kira dabbed at the corners of her mouth with a pinkie as if checking for errant lipstick. "I can't afford it. I took a pay cut."

Rainey took one step closer. Maybe it would make her seem bigger, maybe not. "Your mother's being a bitch. It's only fair. And it wouldn't cost you much."

Kira stiffened and stepped back. "You knew the terms when you took the job," she said, reddening. "Look, I really am sorry, but I have to go to work."

Rainey walked to Blaustein on Bleecker and bought two gallons of paint and a roller with a tray. Back at the studio she poured paint into the tray and fed the roller into the liquid. She stopped twice to smoke and once to raid Kira's fridge. She went into the kitchen and rolled paint across the cabinets she had tortoised. Then she painted over the studio's terra-cotta walls.

By five o'clock the studio had become a thundercloud, dark and oppressive. It felt shocking to destroy her own work but she was damned if she would give it away.

She dipped a brush into the battleship-gray paint and wrote a huge letter to Kira on the fourth wall, where two high arches, already sketched in pencil, were to have overlooked a sunlit Tuscan countryside.

LIFE IS LIKE THAT, the letter said.

THE WATER OR THE FISH

1982

Carmen Morales carried a two-inch penknife, street legal in NYC, and this morning after Danny hit her, she'd etched her initials onto a green-painted pillar in the 103rd Street station. The letters ran thin and small, like the knife, and she wished she'd had the wherewithal to do them fat. An old white lady scolded her, but Carmen said, Stay away from me, you withered old cunt. She got the nerve from her mother, who drank and cursed the whole time Carmen was growing up on East 137th. Thank God Danny took her away from that mess.

Danny worked at Midtown Lumber; he cut boards for people's shelves. That May afternoon, Tina Dial, Carmen's older half sister, sat catlike on a dining chair in Danny's basement air shaft apartment on Amsterdam and 104th. She was drinking one of his beers under the dreary ceiling light and problem-solving for Carmen when there wasn't a thing wrong. Tina tucked her sock feet beneath her and wore her long hair in a high ponytail, but it was the suspicion in her eyes that made her look most like a cat. Carmen, her own hair loose and bedroom-y the way Danny liked it, lolled in the recliner with a beer, too. The T-shirt under her sweater said *KNOCKED UP*, which she was glad Tina couldn't see. Above her was a movie poster that demanded in blunt letters, WHO WILL SURVIVE AND WHAT WILL BE LEFT OF THEM? Danny had picked it up from the street in Chelsea, where he worked, and the image of a man wielding a chainsaw, a woman strung up behind him, made Carmen half sick.

Likewise, Danny had found the recliner when he was out on a walk. He was not too proud to scavenge. Danny was thirty-six and Carmen was sixteen, and she could tell she was starting to grate on his last nerve, just a few months in. She had a vague sense it was her shrill voice when she didn't get what she wanted. She'd have to work on that, her temper. When he hit her, first and only time, it left a red mark on her cheekbone, because he'd used the back of his hand and he always wore his high school ring.

But when he said he was sorry, he'd gotten down on his knees and kissed her Keds, so she knew it would be okay between them.

Better than okay. *Beautiful.*

Tina was in medical school, she was going to be an obstetrician, and she was a nonbeliever when it came to Danny. "They all get down on their knees at some point," she told Carmen, swiping the air with her beer bottle for emphasis. "But I've had it with Danny beating up on my little sister."

"It was one slap." Carmen liked being called *little sister*. "I deserved it. Mom dished out a lot worse."

She watched Tina look around the living room, from the Formica table, another castoff, to the mostly bare walls to the windows with their bristling blinds. "You need a grow light and some ivy here," Tina said, with a degree of feeling that surprised Carmen. "That air shaft, I don't know how you take it."

"I just take it," said Carmen defiantly. She tried never to look, was how she took it. The air shaft was a dark gray upright tunnel into which no birds ever flew and no sun penetrated, and there was no climbing out from the bottom.

"Carmen. When's the last time you went to school?" Tina leaned toward her, the deep *V* of her olive green sweater falling forward. The color looked rich on her. Both sisters had caramel hair and green eyes, but only Carmen appeared Puerto Rican. Tina had to announce it, and maybe she did and maybe she didn't.

"I go to school," said Carmen. "My homework's on the table."

Inside her the fetus clung to the uterine wall, calling, *Keep me.* It had a spine like the tiniest of shrimp, no need yet for fingers or eyes. But to Carmen it felt like the size of a baby doll, with eyelids and eyelashes like the real thing. The fetus did not correct her.

She saw Tina study the dining table, slick with *Cosmo*s and *Seventeen*s. Carmen took magazines from the laundry room, where there was a shelf for reading materials. She should have set the dinner plates out by now. "Show me a textbook," said Tina, challenging her. Carmen looked down at her jeans. Danny liked her better in skirts. "Just one notebook," demanded Tina. Now Carmen tried staring her down. "Tell me you didn't drop out."

"Don't get too comfy." Carmen checked the pearlescent wristwatch she'd stolen from her mother when she left. "Danny gets home in half an hour. I have to fix his dinner." And change her clothes. But Tina looked like she might curl into that dining chair and cry.

"Yeah? Or?" said Tina.

"Or he goes hungry," retorted Carmen, struggling out of the recliner. "And school's not really part of my *agenda*, Sis." Might as well get it done, since Tina was going to kill her. "I'm pregnant." She rubbed her still-flat stomach tenderly through her thrift-shop cashmere sweater, which was pilling. She picked off a couple of tiny woolen nubs.

"Not again," said Tina. "Your third? Put that beer down right now." She rose and reached for it, but Carmen held it away, teasing. "What happened to the Pill we got you on?" Carmen knew where Tina stood on abortion, Tina being a committed Catholic who would never end her own pregnancy but who nonetheless had dragged Carmen twice to get scraped out. That's how badly Tina wanted her to get an education, and look how great that was going. School was a doomed enterprise from the beginning, Carmen thought morosely. Tina grew up with her own grandmother, because Tina's father, who was not Carmen's father, had plucked her out of the girls' mother's home early on, and the grandmother changed everything, made Tina believe in God and college and medical school. Whereas Carmen grew up with a violent drunk who made her see that Danny was as good as she was going to get—Danny, who kissed her feet! She'd like to see Tina find a man who did that. She'd like to see Tina find a man, period. Carmen would take Danny over a high school diploma any day, a man who loved her enough to keep her in line.

"I can't remember to take pills," Carmen said.

"Where's your super?" demanded Tina. "We have to rekey the lock. We have to keep Danny out if he hits you when you're pregnant."

Carmen took another swallow of beer and yanked the bottle away when Tina lunged for it. "Omar lives next door. But I'm not locking Danny out of *his apartment*." She stretched and went to the Pullman kitchen laid out along one wall, ignoring a fallen *TV Guide* as she walked. "You're the only person who's upset here, Teen."

"You were crying when you called me."

"Now I'm happy. See?"

Carmen hung in the doorway and watched Tina pad through the hallway's undersea fluorescence to ring at Omar's. Carmen had never heard a name so beautiful; *Omar Alas* made her think of Arabian horses, or stars in the domed night sky, or getting her feet kissed. She wondered if Danny would ever do that again, maybe without hitting her first.

Next time he's going to hit us both, the fetus said, spinning inside her.

That was a one-off, said Carmen. Relax.

Omar was not visible from where she stood; she wanted to see his face, faintly amused at Tina's pomp. "I'm a doctor," she heard Tina saying, which wasn't quite true. "He left a mark on her face. So we need to rekey her locks before we file a police report."

Oh, really? The only thing Carmen was going to file was her nails.

"I think you mean Mr. Pelletier's locks." Omar sounded friendly, unsuspicious. "You can't do that without his consent." Carmen retreated to neaten the magazines. She knew how this was going to go. Tina wouldn't leave till she'd told Danny off, and Danny wouldn't be happy to find her there.

But she was wrong. Danny greeted Tina warmly when he came home. "Heyyy," he said. "Big sister." He had an open face, creases at the eyes proving that he smiled often, an expressive mustache, dark eyes carrying light. "Stay for dinner. Carmen's got something *good* in the oven." He sniffed. "What is that, babe?" Carmen could hardly believe this man had backhanded her this morning. She must have been a real bitch.

"Lamb burgers. I thought it would make a nice change from beef." Danny was not big on her Puerto Rican food—*fricasé de pollo, bistec encebollado*—he liked to eat his American food one ingredient at a time. She wondered if he could pick up radar from her stomach yet, three months on, and how he would feel about it when he did.

"Expensive change," said Danny, the mustache shifting downward, and Carmen saw Tina's antennae quiver.

"Carmen was trying to please you." Tina bit off each word.

"Lamb was on sale," Carmen lied. She would skip some lunches, or economize someplace else. Maybe they'd eat hot dogs tomorrow night. Maybe Tina would lend her five dollars if she could get her out of Danny's earshot.

"That's my girl," said Danny. "Careful shopper." He stooped to pick up the *TV Guide* without comment and settled into his recliner. Both he and the chair sighed. "So how's the doc?"

But Tina wasn't going to make this easy for her. "I saw what you did to my sister's face."

"You my sister-in-law already?" Danny's eyelid twitched. He crossed his arms in an anti-Tina shield. "That was one mistake," he said. "I've been forgiven."

"Not by me," said Tina, as Carmen noisily set out two places for dinner, making conversation difficult. "Don't do it again. I'll call the cops. Sixteen is automatic statutory rape."

"Don't threaten me," said Danny. "Carmen, am I raping you?"

Carmen understood this as her cue to move to the recliner and let herself be hugged, which felt sweet and also like a loss in advance, and slithering out of Danny's arms she watched her sister unhook her purse and sweater from the shoulder of a dining chair and slip out the scarred front door before Carmen could ask about the five dollars. She envied Tina her little room high up in her friend Rainey's townhouse, even with that massive crucifix above the dresser and the walls peeling paint. Tina had a *home*.

The air between Carmen and Danny was thick and irritable now that the injury to her cheekbone, a mark no larger than a dime but as red as a lipstick kiss, had been raised again. Danny tipped his head back and noisily exhaled. Finally he said, "So what did you do all day, babe?"

She stopped where she was, knives and forks in one hand and two glasses pinched in the other. "I crocheted," she said. "On that throw for the sofa. And I went marketing." The truth was she hadn't worked on the throw for weeks, and she'd marketed yesterday. Today she went to the park and fell into a romance novel from the laundry room. It had a man, a woman, and a horse on the cover, and enough sex to fasten her to the page.

"You didn't look for work?" Danny chewed his lip.

"I did that first," said Carmen. "I tried the Chinese place, the Jewish deli, and the stationary place." But going door-to-door was mortifying, and it was so easy to lie and say she'd hit some kind of quota. She set the silverware and glasses on the table and fetched two bottles of beer. "No one needs anyone." She didn't say, I'm pregnant and I'd just have to quit. She didn't say, I like being bored and hanging out in the park. She had no idea what to do with herself since she'd quit going to school. She wanted to be Danny's princess, but he acted like there was no money for princesses. He might or might not be a prince himself.

"You're doing it too random, sweetheart," said Danny. "You got to knock on one door after the next. Did you apply at Gristedes like I said?"

"Tomorrow. Come sit. I'll get your dinner." She sounded like a perfect housewife, everything her mother wasn't. Who cared if she bullshitted about her day? *I roller-skated in Central Park and bummed cigarettes from boys.* Maybe it was time to tell Danny about the baby. Maybe he'd tell her to put her feet up and just watch daytime television.

She cracked the oven door as Danny pushed himself out of the recliner's embrace, and the fragrance of cooked lamb sent her reeling with nausea. She bolted for the bathroom. Danny had left the seat up from when he'd gotten home, a black hair coiled on the porcelain. Carmen knelt and let her stomach evacuate. When she was done throwing up, her hair shone sticky at the ends.

I want you to do a thing or two, the fetus said, punching her ineffectually. *I want you to stay in school. I want you to read the encyclopedia A to Z and get yourself a library card.*

I want you to shut up, Carmen said, thumping herself on the stomach.

A dab of toothpaste took care of the smell. She tongued it over her teeth and licked it off a fingertip. Danny lumbered over and rubbed her back. His hands felt big, and fatherly. "Are you sick, babe?" When she met his eyes in the mirror, he said, "Whoa, you're not preggers?" She shook her head and leaned briefly against him, then went back to slide the burgers onto the plates.

Danny sat when she did, the furrow between his brows deep with worry. "What's going on, Carm?"

She could have another abortion. It was only a few months along. She'd survived the first two just fine, though the second time, when she saw the circular plastic bin full of blood and gunk, she almost got sick. Sick, but fascinated. Her baby was in that mess. Tina would take her to Planned Parenthood in a New York minute, would pay for it somehow.

"Stomach flu," she said. "It'll pass, hon." That was when she knew she was going to do it, leave herself unencumbered in case there was a place she could escape to. Though where that might be she had no idea. The problem was that nothing, no *thing*, called to her. She didn't love quilting, or car engines, or even clothing design, which might steer her toward FIT. She didn't love nature, which might lead to forestry, and she didn't love books or history shows on TV, which might make her want to finish high school. If you loved one thing hard enough, you were unlikely to starve, that was Tina's theory. At least you might not get smacked in your pregnant face.

"Danny," said Carmen, pushing the salt toward him, "do something for me and I'll tell you a secret."

Maybe, down here in the basement, all she could love was the very notion of sun pouring into a window, the way passion might gush into a person's heart, or grace pour into a pew. And that kind of thing you couldn't hustle for, could you? You had to wait for it to slip around a corner, kind of nestle into your life.

"Sure, sweetheart," he said. "Do what?"

It was a test. If he did it, she'd stay and have his baby. "Kiss my feet again. That was the sweetest thing ever."

He raised his head and put his fork down. It clattered onto the plate. His dark eyes turned hard as statue eyes. "You want your man on his *knees*?"

Something started up and rumbled deep in her brain. "No," she said quickly. "Of course not."

"That's not a thing you ask a man for," said Danny. "What's the big secret?"

If she told him she was pregnant, he'd keep her here in this sunless apartment, tied to a screaming baby like her own mother at sixteen, making a liar out of her at every dinner. She'd go to the park with a baby carriage instead of skates, and the boys would stay away. Danny was a strong man, and she had nowhere else to live, unless Rainey would put her up in that Village townhouse. But Rainey barely knew her. Carmen was never going back to her mother's shouting, that was for sure.

"The secret's just that I love you," she said weakly.

Danny picked up his fork and held it in his fist. "That's no secret, baby." He looked back at his plate. "I love you, too." He ignored the canned green beans and asked for more lamb, and Carmen, still nauseated, gave him hers.

After dinner Danny watched TV and Carmen flopped onto the bed alone to read her novel. Her only light came from the overhead bulb; shades blocked out the air shaft, though it wasn't yet dark. Abruptly she saw something drop onto the blue acrylic blanket.

Like an earring, but not. She sat up to investigate.

Their ceiling was the floor of the Espina family's apartment. She saw them in the elevator sometimes with a little girl swathed in lace and a froth of small dogs. The mother always said *buenos días*. There was a faint spot on the bed now, and when Carmen triangulated up to the source on the ceiling, she perceived a slightly grayed area and—if she wasn't imagining it—a bulge near the light fixture. Running across the bulge was a thin crack. It could have been drawn with a needle dipped in ink. The thing was as fine as a hair.

Another earring dropped onto the blanket. She squinted up again. *I dare you.* A glimmering drop of water squeezed out from the crack, which seemed, somehow, as improbable as birth. As she watched, it grew into a pearl. The pearl hung there, shimmering, thinking. Then it released.

She couldn't see it fall. But she imagined she heard it, a soft *thup.*

Spaghetti pot, she thought. Kitchen. Get Omar. Yet she sat mesmerized, watching another pearl form. The ceiling was pregnant. She scrutinized the faint bulge. Slight as it was, minnows could be swimming in there. Other buildings had hidden roaches—Danny's had silvery fish flashing and darting in the water between apartments.

Danny walked in to use the bathroom and saw her staring, followed her gaze to the ceiling, peered at the crack. His attention snapped into focus. "Oh, shit," he said. "Is that what I think it is?" They watched another drop fall. "We need Omar before that ceiling comes down."

He was in his undershirt, so Carmen put her book down. "I'm already gone."

The hall wavered in that murky underwater light; seaweed swam around her as she walked. Omar Alas opened his door. His apartment sounded like football and smelled like omelets. He looked at Carmen with eyes full of *alas*: alas you are next to married, alas you are about to kill that baby, alas your heart remains unstruck. "Omar," she said, "it's raining in our apartment."

"Again?" He had a long face with a wide, thin mouth, and he focused on a spot about two inches deeper than her eyes, as if speaking without words to some secret place in her brain about something entirely different. "Where is this rain?"

"Above the bed. Where else?" She saw a slight movement at the edges of his lips. His scalp shone under the hallway fluorescent.

"Let's go see," he said. "Do you need a bucket?"

"I need a million dollars," she said. "How is Mrs. Alas?"

About Mrs. Alas he said nothing. He followed her into Danny's apartment carrying a bucket, and from the back of her head Carmen felt him scanning her body. She wore snug jeans and one of Danny's black T's knotted tight at the belly. She was a package.

She led Omar into the bedroom where Danny had arranged Carmen's green towel on the blanket and set down a pot. What was it they said about water in science? It seeks its own level. The Espinas' water wanted to drown them. Maybe they should let it.

"Thank God you're here," said Danny. "It's got to be their damn tub again."

In the liquid in Carmen's womb, dark as the air shaft with as little view, the fetus twirled and flipped. Dripping water excited it. Stay still, she told it. You aren't helping your case.

"Oh, it's the tub. I'm going up," said Omar.

"I'll move the bed," said Danny.

"The bureau, too," said Omar.

"You guys move things," said Carmen. "I'll go up and tell them."

She took the fire stairs and rang at 1A, enjoying the Spanish TV that carried faintly into the hall. Those small tenacious dogs began yapping, then the door opened slowly, revealing an apparition of lace and curls. A small child stared up at her with enormous dark eyes, a dachshund and a ratty-looking terrier boiling around her legs.

Carmen squatted on the doormat. "Well, hello," she said as the dogs licked her hands. "I'm Carmen. Who are you?"

"Nina." The child gripped the doorknob and hung from it, swaying.

"Well, Nina," said Carmen, stroking the dachshund, "I like your dress. Is your *mami* running your bath?"

"*Sí*," said Nina. With her free hand she lifted her fancy dress and thoughtfully scratched the crotch of her white tights. The seam was crooked, her fingernails tinier than Victorian buttons.

Carmen reached out and tucked back a strand of Nina's hair. The dachshund had ears like heavy silk. Everything in Carmen's life had slowed down all of a sudden in the presence of this small child. She saw water lapping the sides of the Espinas' tub, spilling onto the tiled floor, and slipping into the basement through imperceptible cracks. She felt it moving in currents above Danny's apartment, weighing heavily on his ceiling—a ceiling that needed to come bursting down, drowning everything in Carmen's life so she would be forced to move on in some spectacular fashion without having made a single decision. Because she'd only ever made one, so far, which was moving in with Danny, and look how brilliantly that turned out.

And where was this mother who ran the tub and then dematerialized?

"How old are you, honey?" she asked the child.

"*Tres*," said Nina. "I have to make *pipí*."

"Wait one second, honey." Carmen could talk to Nina in Spanish all day. Indeed, she could scarcely remember why she'd come. "Will you tell your *mami* your bath is running over, sweetheart?"

"*Sí*," said Nina.

But the girl did not move. She seemed less than reliable. "Wait," said Carmen, "I have a better idea—will you tell your *mami* I'm here and it's very important? *Ahora*, now?"

"*Sí*," Nina said, and firmly shut the door.

Kids enslave you, her mother had said once when they were having a bitter facts-of-life talk, and Carmen had thought then, *Free me*. Now, thinking of Nina, she thought, *Enslave me*. But maybe just for a little while.

She waited a full minute—she counted it. She heard Omar climbing the stairs, and rang again.

Nina opened the front door once more, this time holding a troll doll with pink hair. From far inside a man's voice yelled, "*Quién es?*" Everything was happening in Spanish up here on the first floor, where they at least had a view of the street. She missed the sound of Spanish in her life with Danny Pelletier; she listened for it in the park.

"Honey, tell your *mami* and *papi* it's the lady downstairs." She tried to sound urgent so Omar, appearing at the top of the stairs now, would know she took the situation seriously. But Omar shook his head.

"Hello, Nina," he said, and stepped right past Carmen and Nina into the Espinas' darkened front hall. He moved toward the sound of the TV, turned, and looked back at Carmen.

"You don't have this kind of time," he said.

She watched him turn a corner into the living room and disappear, and out in the hall she put a hand on her quivering stomach and breathed into her baby.

WHEN DANNY CAME to bed that night, he studied her in dismay. The bed was pushed into a corner and Omar's bucket stood in the middle of the room, collecting pearls, which fell more slowly now. The ceiling was visibly damp and swollen. It couldn't be painted till it dried, she knew that from the last overflow. What was it with the dreamy Mrs. Espina, who turned on the faucet and then drifted away? Carmen still wore Danny's T-shirt, and he grimaced and said, "Try wearing a dress tomorrow. Stop hiding your beautiful self under a bushel, wouldja?"

But now Carmen was thinking about seeking her own level, like the Espinas' water. She might be the water or she might be the fish. She imagined clearing off all those magazines and studying for her GED; she saw herself flowing between apartments, finding one with windows that framed the sun. She gazed back at Danny, wanting to know everything now, *A* to *Z*, and said, "What's a bushel?"

He shook his head at her and climbed under the sheet. His large hands and his mouth moved as if Carmen had a series of erotic switches that must be flicked on in a rigorous order: mouth, left breast, right breast, lower down. Was this statutory rape? Why had he stopped looking like an older John Travolta, so that their lovemaking no longer felt like a movie scene and she no longer played a disco girl writhing under his muscular chest? Now everything was real, and dull.

Pay attention, the fetus demanded, and Carmen loosely tuned in, the current in the ceiling sweeping her along, while Danny worked his way through the stations of the cross. *I can't grow in a basement.*

I'd be a better mother than you think, she retorted, even with an air shaft. Anyway, you're out of here.

You wouldn't dare, the fetus said. *I have plans for us.*

But Carmen dared. She had plans, too. In the morning she'd call Tina, after Danny left for work. She'd leave a message with Howard Royal, Rainey's flirty father, because that's where Tina lived now. Well, hello, pretty lady, he'd say, Tina's not here, but you're welcome to come hang out—because Tina would be in class studying bone or nerve or bits of tissue, and Carmen would leave her message, and read her novel, and watch the fish swim in the ceiling, and wait.

That night, when Danny finally slept, Carmen gazed up at the darkened ceiling where the fish flittered between layers of wet plaster. She wandered into the unlit living room and raised the blinds, wondering what a grow light was and hoping that this time the air shaft might show her something new—a skyline twinkling with stars, perhaps, or maybe a cistern of rainwater, rippling and pure, that would let her swim free to the top.

But she found herself again at the base of a twelve-story vertical tunnel pierced only by occasional rectangles of veiled incandescence and seasick fluorescence, a shadowed place where it seemed like no baby could thrive. *Help me*, said the fetus, *light my way in the world*, and Carmen said, Help me, light my way out of this one.

BERNARD LANDRY, SAVE ME

1983

The padlock hangs open on the Sweetwater County dump and the gate is partly ajar. A weeping willow rains over the chain-link. Ask pulls the scarred white F-150 onto the weedy grass. Peace hoists herself down, and Linda Royal follows her out under a sweet blue bowl of Colorado sky. She can't look at Peace's pregnant stomach so she looks west at the green majesty of the Flatirons, the drapes of their snowy capes.

She opens the gate, both sides, and Ask drives them between hills of trash on the left and a vast flat carpet of garbage on the right. Linda feels the ugly, exciting weight of all this refuse against the rumpled folds of the implacable mountains. Two boys, maybe ten or eleven, tread the carpet's edge, kicking bits of trash, stirring things up. One of them carries a slingshot.

When they pull up to the appliance graveyard, Ask parks and they all get out. Linda watches Ask circle the truck, the way he moves like an athlete, muscular in his mid-sixties, but also ginger in the way he holds his head, his neck fused after a climbing fall. He pulls the litter stick from the flatbed and hands it to Peace, who cradles her belly with one arm. Linda reaches in for her gardening gloves.

She loves the dump. It reminds her of how she once felt in her sister Laurette's apartment, a mixture of disgust and excitement, as if beneath Laurette's hoard of clutter might lie a nugget of treasure, and she might find it if she dug around. Once she did, in fact, find in the dump a piece of jewelry, a sterling ring with an amethyst cabochon. Linda wears it every day; it's her treasure since she gave up her mother's diamond ring to Rainey, her daughter, all those years ago. *I can't take this where I'm going.*

Ask's idea of treasure is more stringent: a credit card application in a stranger's name. The women change the address to the farmhouse, and when it works, a new credit card arrives. It's only good till the calls start and the card gets closed. They quickly charge what they need—a whole bunch of gas and groceries, maybe some nice clothes or truck repairs, and quit using the card while they're ahead. Then they wait for the next one.

"I'm freezing but this sun feels glorious," says Peace.

May that baby of yours freeze inside you, Linda thinks. She shivers, grateful for her layers of fleece, salvaged and secondhand.

A van pulls up behind the truck. Two men get out and slam their doors. Ask touches his cap in greeting. Peace can stab away with that damn stick all she wants but she is having that baby without a husband. Ask belongs to Linda. The baby was an Accident, a onetime slip.

"Good luck, babe," Ask tells Linda, or maybe Peace. "We need it."

The last two trips turned up nothing.

Linda hesitates, because Peace is standing by Ask as if they are a team.

But he heads off alone toward the part of the dump they long ago nicknamed the Attic. He's found armchairs there, a sofa for which Linda stitched slipcovers in white cotton. Peace strolls off using the litter stick as a cane. Linda watches the two men unload a washing machine from the van, struggle with it toward the other appliances—dryers and lawn mowers and big broken things. She feels a breeze in her hair; it wisps away the scent of rot almost before it registers.

Linda walks onto a hill of trash. Her sneakers crunch and wobble and sink as she strains for balance, watching for sharp things, metallic edges, or wet areas that might give way, the debris so varied she barely takes it in. As she treads, her eye picks out a blue hospital gown, a spiral notebook, a child's mitten, a clutch of empty bottles with bright yellow labels, and she steps on all of it, indiscriminate. I am a divining rod, she thinks, and she stops at a brown grocery bag. It looks clean but reeks of kitty litter up close. She moves on to a knotted white plastic bag and tears a hole in the side. Slick broken eggshells and a coffee filter redolent with grinds; jumbo orange juice cans that made terrific hair curlers when she was a girl. If there is mail at the bottom, it can stay there.

The boys stop and observe her. The two men drop the washer with a thud.

Ask whistles. He holds up to Linda what appears to be a bread box. She gives him a thumbs-up. Maybe Peace's baby can sleep in that.

She opens more bags. One perfumes the air with rubbing alcohol and spilled blossoms of cotton balls.

"Hey, lady."

The boys wear shit-kicker boots, which she admires. The one who spoke is tanned and skinny, with inky slits for eyes. The other is rugged and bleached and doesn't blink.

"What are you looking for?" says the dark-eyed boy.

"Useful things." She watches Peace sidle up to Ask, twirling the stick.

"You ever find money?"

She laughs. "You know anyone rich enough to toss their money?" She needs them to leave. At her feet is a half-spilled shopping bag full of paper.

"We're looking for rats," says the bleached boy, holding up the slingshot. "We're going to stone them."

"Well," says Linda, "good luck to you." And more luck to the rats. She smiles till they back off. Then she squats by the bag and upends it.

Finally. But first she is going to torture herself—first she is going to look.

And in fact Peace has fastened Ask's palm to her belly. *There, feel that? Feel it kick? We made that.* You *made that.*

Pained, Linda looks down. The bag is spilling old issues of the *Daily Camera*, crumpled sheets from a yellow legal pad, and many envelopes, both opened and sealed.

She stands in a sea of garbage. A syringe cracks under her left Ked. She takes off her gardening gloves, and begins sifting.

Yes. It's only for a department store card, but it is something: a Sears application sent to Bernard R. Landry on Old Town Road, Saint Mary's. They can get a lot from Sears. Clothes and boots and new curtains for the living room. As of this afternoon Mr. Landry will have officially moved to Baseline Road, Bitter Creek. Bernard Landry is a find.

Ask will be pleased.

She's about to stand, to call out, but Jesus H. Christ. Ask's two hands are cupping Peace's face and he is talking to her intently.

Bernard Landry, save me from this.

Linda uncrumples one of the yellow pages. What do people write in their private time, besides letters to their abandoned daughters?

"Island Rueful View," Mr. Landry has printed neatly, and below it are words both crossed out and written over:

> *My father stood straight but his spirit was*
> *Bent when he said with a laugh:*
> *My get-up-and-go has got up and went.*
> *And now, his age, I lament with no laugh:*

That old get-up-and-go has got up and
Went. Still everyday wonders fly
Drunkenly by
Gulls through low clouds
Feather the sky
Azure below, tangerine wind
Oh sweet ongoing now, God's gift to rescind.

Linda reads it twice. How long has it been since she's seen a poem—high school? Does Mr. Landry really sense wonders in his everyday life, and could she see them, too? His poem moves her far more than anything Ask says, such as *Be born every moment*. But is that possible, really? Sometimes she's wondered, over the years, if lies and love haven't all been snarled up for her like so much pretty yarn. She should do something better and wiser before her own get-up-and-go departs, that's what Bernard Landry's telling her—and he's got nothing to gain by it.

"What've you got?" Ask calls to her from the Attic. Peace stands close by him. They look like a couple. When, exactly, did this happen? And what has Linda got, if she doesn't have Ask?

Sweet ongoing now. She's got that.

She's got a daughter she hasn't seen in years, and whose fault is that? She's got an actual poem that now belongs to her. And Bernard Landry's got a credit application that should still belong to him.

Waving at Ask, she calls back, "Still looking," and sweeps her gaze across the cloudless sky.

She folds up the rumpled yellow page and tucks it in the pocket of her jeans. Then she tears up the Sears application, scatters the pieces, and covers them with a copy of the *Daily Camera*.

LINDA LIES ON their bed by the window in the Bitter Creek farmhouse, studying Ask's face while he floats his palm above her throat: fifth chakra.

His close-cropped beard says *serious*, it says *intimate*, it says *spiritually inclined*. His sweatshirt says *Shakedown Street*.

She struggles to relax but she has to pee. This seems the wrong time to announce such a need. "It's probably not very blue," she says apologetically of her Vishuddhi. "It's probably pale pale pale—"

"Don't talk, love." He moves his palm as if rolling a ball against her neck, and Linda believes the ball is energy.

Meanwhile, her mind is a movie screen. Only one film plays, and it is a twenty-four-hour theater up there. Sometimes, in her mind-movie, Peace touches Ask on the waist, and he locks into her brown irises and passionately pulls her toward him. Or Ask backs Peace onto the long kitchen table till her dark curls spill across the wood. Or else Peace, naked, tugs Ask, fully dressed, into a warm shower. Linda needs to know how the Accident happened, and Ask will not discuss it. She needs Ask to know that the name *Peace* is some made-up bullshit, and he will not discuss that, either.

A big mistake, Ask says. It just happened once. But Peace, tall and beatific, is thirty-three weeks pregnant.

Howard would laugh himself to death if he hadn't died five months ago. *You? Jealous?* And it is true, on West Tenth Street Linda was never jealous because she knew where she stood: Howard would fuck a folding chair. She lived in a kind of three-way marriage with Howard and Gordy Vine, plus whatever girls drifted in and out of that blue bedroom. But here on their pastureland—which they lease to a neighboring farmer, whose black-and-white Holstein cows graze placidly on the tall fescue—Ask is all about fidelity, and now her jealousy has a beating heart. She struggles to see the pure and risen thing in him that keeps her here. And instead her cortex plays *Ask and Peace Locked in Love* on the rag rug that they ordered with the Reeves credit card, when that still worked.

Ask touches her wrist and says, "Raise your arm."

Linda raises her arm. Or begins to. Or sends the signal from her brain, but nothing works.

"Your Vishuddhi is blocked," says Ask. "You had things to tell Howard before he died."

Her throat is concrete. Whatever she had to say, Howard never wanted to hear. What was his line? *Fuck 'em if they can't take a joke.* And those people he couldn't stand. *Eggshell people.* Linda refuses to be an eggshell person.

Her bladder is a melon about to burst.

Out the window, she sees a black pickup truck pull up. Sometimes the farmhouse feels like witness protection. Ask's friend Lisa works with a women's shelter in New Mexico and once in a while she sends a woman his way. *How can I say no?* Ask says. But

Peace has stayed *three years*. Linda *asked* her to stay. They were best friends until the Accident. Wanda seems to be staying, too, but she lives out back, in a yurt thing, raising vegetables and keeping chickens and grinding her own ink, or corn, something. Wanda smiles at Ask as if he were a five-year-old child. Wanda is *safe*. Linda remembers the day Wanda first stepped out of Ask's truck in her denim overalls, twirling as she looked around at all of it—sky, barn, house, fields, Flatirons—while Ask held her pack and smiled. And then she ran straight toward Linda, shouting, Linda Royal, I am so filled with spirit. I have so much love for you. I feel so blessed to be in your presence. And Linda murmured, Already?

Linda exhales, and poison gas flows out of her.

"You can speak your truth," Ask says.

"I can speak my truth," she repeats carefully.

"You honor the truth that you speak," he says.

"I honor the truth that I speak. Ask, my truth is that I have to pee."

"Breathe into it," he says. "We come into this world on an in-breath. We leave on an out-breath. It's all one big pose."

It seems to Linda that *pose* can be taken both ways, but Ask keeps moving his palm from her throat to her heart to her groin, never touching. "I want us to go outside and have you make a new connection with the earth." His voice is a warm bath. "But I have a question for you first."

Outside, the pickup door slams. Linda raises herself up on her elbows and sees Cathy Crowell climbing out of the driver's seat, her medical bag swinging, her spiky black hair and black boots making her a jagged form against the green-and-violet mountains. Some local folks say Cathy once sang backup for Joan Jett, but Cathy only offers a mysterious smile if she's asked. She drives over from Niwot every two weeks to check on Peace. Linda considers with disgust the view up her speculum, that little pucker of a kiss that is Peace's cervix.

"I have to talk to Cathy," says Ask, heading for the bedroom door. "Don't move."

"Stay," says Linda. The need she wants him to fill is bottomless. She's lucky it doesn't scare him off. When Howard saw the hint of need, he would send her off to sleep with his friends. She remembers a party at their home when he put an arm around Gordy in front of all their friends and said loudly, We share everything. Except for the Steinway, my friends, *everything*. And Linda had felt their stares, their nervous and excited glances at her body, right before they laughed.

Whereas Ask has been faithful and respectful in all ways—that is, until the Accident.

Out the window, she watches him stride up to Cathy at the truck. Peace ambles out holding her stomach. Fern, her eight-year-old girl, is with her, clinging to her dress. Peace looks swaybacked and contented. Ask touches his spread fingertips to a spot between her shoulder blades. Peace and Ask, the mother and the father. The real family.

Linda wants to run outside and say, Ask, this baby is an *artifact*. Let it go. Instead, she watches the four of them walk toward the farmhouse, Fern hanging on tight.

Once Linda thought that Peace was the bravest woman she knew. Peace was pregnant at fifteen, married at sixteen to a sexy, charming drinker. JT beat her when she began studying for her GED, and when she tried to move back home, her parents said, No, you'll bring shame on both our families. Carrabelle, Florida, poor. She started hitchhiking with her little girl and just the money she stole from JT's wallet. Now Fern is a long bean of a child who bites her fingernails till the rosebuds show beneath them. If she can't sleep with her mother, she cries. She is nothing like Rainey, who didn't cry at Fern's age, who didn't cry at thirteen when Linda walked out of her bedroom for the last time ever.

Linda runs to the toilet, finally, and sits there wondering if Rainey has ever cried for her since. Grieved, she thinks, probably not. She returns to find Ask back in the bedroom, pacing.

"Peace is fine," says Ask.

Because Linda has left the channel open, her heart speaks up now, when she least wants to hear from it. Not fine, it says. Not fine at all.

"You had a question for me, before."

His fingers, when he touches her, are cold from outside. "I know Rainey's been asking you to come home since her father died," he says softly. "Are you tempted to go?"

Out of loyalty, she starts to tell him no when the urge to pack a bag and see her daughter squeezes something internally, like a fist around her organs. "Maybe," she says cautiously.

Ask stops her from continuing with a raised hand. "There are many ways to honor the dead," he says. "You can stay here and plant a garden. You can talk things through on the phone with your daughter. But if you fly home, my love . . ." He strokes the back of her neck and she leans into it. "You won't come back."

She swallows.

"Love is a stream of water," says Ask. "It can erode a mountain into grains of sand. But a stream of water is also easily broken. Don't take love for granted."

Linda tries to perceive the wisdom of this. But *love* can be taken in so many ways, too, and she is thinking not of the passion of a woman for her man but of the bond between a mother and her daughter left behind.

"That's my humble request," says Ask lightly, releasing her neck. "Surrender it."

Outside, the sun has speared itself on a mountain peak. It could crack like a yolk and bleed. He looks where she's looking and finally says: "Two cards got canceled."

So he's worried about money. That leaves one credit card. They found nothing yesterday in the dump, and it's too easy to get caught raiding mailboxes.

Linda runs the numbers. "Sennecot had a five-hundred-dollar limit," she says. "We can survive without that."

"Yes, but Ryder had fifteen hundred. It's okay. I'll get a stint in retail. If I can find it." He palms her cheek. "Nothing changes for us except you make more room in your heart."

In the townhouse on West Tenth Street, Howard always made space for one more acolyte. But Linda's heart is not a townhouse. She hasn't had a best friend since after high school because Howard demanded all her light. But she had come to love Peace. And then came the day she noticed that the flaps of Peace's waistband were poking through her T-shirt, unbuttoned, like tiny fins.

Linda had rested her hand on Peace's belly and said, When? meaning *when did you do it*, and Peace said, Oh God, and turned to embrace her. Linda struggled out of her arms like a feral cat.

In the movie that never ends, Ask brushes past Peace on the stairs and grabs her arm, and she murmurs, I thought you'd never. Her hips were can openers before the pregnancy. A man could get sliced on those things. Whereas Linda is a bowl of ripe fruit.

When she first arrived at the Denver bus terminal twelve years ago, she'd been on Trailways for two days. She remembers sniffing her pits before she climbed down. She wore a short denim skirt with embroidered pot leaves and a fringed suede jacket, and she'd chipped off her nail polish while the bus rumbled across the prairie.

She looked self-consciously around the waiting area for a guy who resembled aging Jesus. He stepped toward her, hands in his pockets, smiling. His T-shirt said *Earth Day* and a strand of puka shells hung around his neck.

She had fifty dollars and Ask's letters tucked into a shirred satin pocket of her suitcase. They'd met through the Personals in the back of the *Voice. Farmhouse. Family. Peace. New life.*

What new life? she had written him. *There's no peace in my life—what do you mean?*

He'd written back: *You've had it with people who use you up.*

Exsanguinātus, *drained of blood. I am talking about family as life raft.* Sustineō, *to sustain.*

He wrote, *You will be a better mother if you first find your own truth.* He wrote: *Sometimes you have to leave home before you can go home.*

At the bus terminal, he had raised her chin with his fingers. He was exactly her height. I've been waiting for you my whole life, he said, and gazed into her eyes as if watching fish flash in their depths.

He drove them past Boulder, past Gunbarrel, past Niwot, to a place so rural it lay off a long dirt road the color of milky coffee. Twenty minutes, said Ask, from the nearest stores. So no one will hear me scream, she thought, and tightened her grip on her purse. A pretty two-story farmhouse came into view. I call it *el Alma*, he said, for *soul*. The hydrangeas by the porch were flushed with violet, and the side garden blazed, flowers blooming in crazy colors as if begging for their lives. Mountains rose in the distance, deep gray folds mantled with patches of green.

Do you have books here? She felt shy saying it, and a little scared that this stranger to whom she'd committed herself might take it as an insult.

But he did not; he smiled, and when she saw that smile go straight to his eyes, her shoulders finally let go. There's a library in the valley. I'll take you. And I'll teach you what can't be found in books. We'll study the Vedas together. I'll even teach you how to breathe, Ask said, and Linda thought, Yes, you will.

Now, in the bedroom, he turns to leave, then says over his shoulder, "Just think about it, Linda. You're my world. I hope you'll stay."

GIRL, GORDY VINE'S letter begins. It is three days after the dump visit, early morning, and Linda has scrounged a bunch of Gordy's and Rainey's letters out of a bureau drawer. This one's on music manuscript paper, full of misspellings and news. Since Rainey threw Gordy out of the townhouse, he's been living with his mother in a rented room up in Washington Heights. It's full of her Kleenex, he says, and smells like rotting flowers.

Talk to Rainey, he begs Linda. It's an older letter, written just a few weeks after Howard's death. *She's lost her mind*, he writes. *She locked her own father out of the house, and me, I was like an uncle to her. She won't talk to me. Linda I miss you so much. I want to be with you girl. Only with you. Come back.*

Well, Gordy is a dog still scratching at the townhouse door. Rainey won't let him back in unless Linda's there to smooth the way. But he also loves Linda, she knows that for sure. Just as she also believes it's way too late to fix the shit show of damage she's done to Rainey. Or is it? Since Howard died Rainey's begged her to come home. *Mommy, why aren't you here?* All grown up and she still says *mommy*. It makes Linda shiver.

She shoves the letters back in her drawer, slips into her robe, and puts on her Barbarella wig. At least Ask responded reverently when she revealed to him that her own hair fell out in clumps years ago. Howard was a torment in this department.

She remembers him winding his finger slowly in her hair as if he found it lovely, then drawing her head in so close she became his prisoner.

She goes downstairs to find Peace smiling into her hibiscus tea as if secrets are scrawled in the steam. Fern claps at the air in a complicated way and chants in a whisper. *Miss Mary Mack, Mack, Mack.* Linda finishes the rhyme in her head, pours herself a black coffee, and sits across the table.

She says softly, "Your time is up, Peace."

"Oh, I know," says Peace. "Three more weeks." She has cheekbones like aqueducts and the bridge of her nose is strangely lovely and wide. She is young, still in her twenties. Linda has a good fifteen years on her, speaking charitably. Indeed, Linda feels at this very moment as if her skin were sagging right off her face.

"I mean," Linda tells her, "it's time for you to leave."

Peace's eyes fly open. When she speaks, her voice is as hard as the little quartz heart she wears around her throat. "Boy, do you have it backwards," she says. "He promised me—"

But Ask is clomping down the staircase now. Linda, Peace, and Fern look watchful until he appears. "Good morning, all," he says. When he scratches the back of his neck, his T-shirt rides up and one cochlear hip bone shows above the drawstring of his PJ bottoms. Promised Peace *what?* Touch me, thinks Linda as he approaches, but it is the coffeepot he wants.

Peace says, her voice now a lilt, "We had a good night." Linda understands this means the baby is sending out pulses from some interior solar system where only Peace and Ask can travel. She probably looks at Linda every day and thinks, In your bed, honey. On the kitchen table. In Wanda's yurt.

The back door opens and Wanda clops in. On her head is what she calls *the fur factory*, a copious and lovely fountain of braids, waves, and coils that Linda would murder for, and on her feet are the Dr. Scholl's she scuffs and clacks as if wearing percussive instruments. Give that girl a tambourine, thinks Linda, and she'd be the whole band.

"Glory, you guys," says Wanda. "Hope you slept a blessed sleep."

"Always," agrees Ask. "We have someone new arriving today."

Peace looks astonished. Linda feels proud that Ask has told only her about the stranger's arrival, a woman fleeing an abusive husband in Los Angeles, a man who'd tracked her to a shelter and later to a safe house. Colorado is supposed to be *unfindable*.

Sally, tell my mother I will never come back, chants Fern in a whisper, clapping the air.

Once upon a time Linda had a beautiful daughter and she taught the daughter how to sew. At twelve Rainey could copy a dress out of a magazine, just like Linda; zippers were nothing to her. She sewed lace to her school blouses and darts in her T-shirts and long seams up the front of her jeans. Linda and Rainey made matching wrap dresses in a red diamond print, even better than Diane von Furstenberg's.

Now Linda is teaching Fern, who stiffens with anxiety at the sewing machine, jams the needle, snarls the thread.

Linda remembers suddenly that when Rainey was eight, like

Fern, she drew an elaborate diagrammatic picture of the townhouse that showed Linda in Gordy's bedroom. It showed Gordy in Rainey's bedroom, with Rainey. But that's all wrong, Linda had said. You have the bedrooms mixed up.

Rainey just looked at her.

In the kitchen, Peace says, "Tell me about the new woman."

Ask plants his chin on his palm and looks at her. His eyes are blades of light. Only Linda knows his secret, she is sure. One night, years ago, he sat back on the porch and told her how his daddy had walked into the garage one Christmas Eve, slid into the front seat of his Ford Super Deluxe, and shot himself through the mouth. Ask found the body. He was sixteen, the eldest son of strict older parents in Duluth, Minnesota. Linda has been extra tender with Ask since that story. She tries to do this so it won't look like pity. Men hate pity.

"I think she'll keep to herself a bit more than you might expect," says Ask, "and she's got a daughter."

"How old?" says Peace. "Fern, stop poking." Fern sinks a cloying finger into her mother's hair. I couldn't take it, thinks Linda.

"All shall be revealed," says Ask. "I'm leaving for the bus station"—he looks up at the kitchen clock—"now."

MAGDA, THE NEW woman, alights from Ask's truck starting with one Lucite platform shoe. Linda marvels at that shoe. Magda is clearly not like any other woman who has been drawn to the steady flame of Ask. For one thing, she is Black. Not so common in the Colorado countryside. For another, she's dressed for the city. Her earrings are big ram's head hoops and her pants are a dressy, clingy white under a swirly halter top.

While Magda stands by the truck and looks around warily, shouldering her large leather purse, out climbs a tall, elegant teenager with a Chanel-looking bag, gold chains and all, dangling low from one hand. "Oh my," Linda whispers to herself.

And then there is her name. Where would someone get an awkward name like that? Of course: *Magdalene.* The first to see Christ when he rose from the dead. Ask looks like Christ; maybe Magda will elicit something extraordinary from him that she, Linda, has failed to perceive. Why would you lop off a radiant name like Magdalene?

No suitcases appear. Not even shopping bags. In the kitchen, Linda tries not to stare, because Magda's elegant face is marred by a scar that slices from eye to earlobe. One of the daughter's palms, she then sees, is shiny in the way of burned skin, as if someone had held it to a stove.

"Oh my God, welcome, welcome. You are both absolutely gorgeous. I'm Linda." She hugs Magda, who endures it with her arms at her sides. Startled, Linda pulls back. She smells something expensive clinging to Magda, maybe JOY. She turns to the daughter. "What's your name, sweetheart?"

The girl walks to the window. She's almost six feet tall; how can she be fourteen, as Ask had told her?

"My daughter is Rosamund," Magda says.

"Hi, Rosamund," Linda says softly, as if trying to coax over a cat. It doesn't work.

Ask says, "How about fixing them something to eat, sweetheart?"

Linda would like to have offered this herself but says, "You must be starving—I can make chicken salad, scrambled eggs and bacon, beans and rice—the fridge is stuffed with food, I can get you—"

"I'd like to see where we sleep," says Magda. "Before anything."

"Why don't you show her, Linda?" says Ask, and she realizes he is just being the good host, saying everything first.

"Come see the upstairs," she says. "It's very pretty."

She leads them up the kitchen stairs, down a hall, and to a bright room with two twin beds. At the foot of each bed stands a simple chair, and facing the chairs is a tall bureau. On the bureau is a green ceramic lamp that Linda found at the dump and cleaned up. Other than that, the room is a blank slate. Linda thinks it is serenely beautiful.

From the windows she watches Magda, who stands in the doorway with her hand on a hip, gazing in without entering. Rosamund collapses onto one of the beds, looking bored.

"It's *pure*," says Linda. "The paint is fresh. The sheets are new. You'll love it."

Magda gives her a slanted glance. "I'll reserve judgment on that," she says, as Rosamund bounces up and wanders into the hall. "You mind if I ask who you are?"

Linda is startled. How hard is it to figure out? "I'm Linda. I live here. We're a family. We're blessed with abundance." Didn't she talk to Ask before she got on the bus? "You'll love Ask," she says. "He's a good man."

"He certainly rescued *us*." Magda steps inside, opens an empty bureau drawer, then closes it. God knows what she'll put inside, besides those sleek clothes she arrived in. Someone will have to take them shopping at the Goodwill. Indeed, she urgently wants to be the one. She hears Rosamund's fingers knocking restlessly on the wall.

"That sounds like Ask, rescuing," says Linda. Magda's scar gleams. "Our room is across the hall if you want to talk, anything," she says. "What can I fix you to eat?"

At lunch Fern stares at Rosamund, gaping, chewing with her mouth open. Wanda watches her but doesn't correct, and Rosamund ignores her. Peace tries to make conversation, but Magda barely answers. The chicken salad is crunchy with pecans and sweet with cranberries, and Linda tries to remember if food ever tasted this good on West Tenth Street—maybe it did, but she never felt this safe, eating in a clean white room with a caretaking man who never snipes at her.

She thinks about the dented white Chevy pickup, about commandeering it for an errand. Ask always does the driving. "Peace, let me take you shopping," she says conversationally. "You're bursting. You need serious maternity stuff. And we can get things for Magda and Rosamund to sleep in tonight. Jeans, too."

"I'm right there, baby," says Peace. "I love Goodwill."

Magda slits her eyes, and Linda notices how closely Rosamund tracks her mother's expressions. "Do you wash everything first?"

Linda says, "Lord yes. Peace, get your purse." She watches Fern follow her mother out of the room like an imprinted duckling. Two days of that and Linda would be certifiable.

"Tampax," says Wanda brightly, "while you're at it."

Ask takes a swallow of milky coffee and says, "I'll drive them."

"You're sweet," says Linda, "but this is a *girls'* shopping trip." She beams at him like it's a settled thing.

He seems to get it. "Don't forget sneakers," he says. "For the dump. The ladies will need them."

"You expect us to visit a dump?" says Magda archly.

Ask folds his arms across his T-shirt, which this morning says *Don't Tread on Me*, and looks at her warmly. "It's a family business," he says. "We all go together."

Magda gets up, sets her plate in the sink, and walks to the kitchen window with Rosamund. She has the gait of a model with a book balanced on her head. Linda sends Peace to take a preemptive pee and waits out in the truck with Fern. Ask opens his wallet and holds out the Susan J. Fears Visa card, and Linda kisses him, quickly, on the mouth.

"You're happy," says Ask. "I like that."

"I like driving," Linda says lightly.

She goes up to their bedroom for her purse. It's a big, fake crocodile bag that she stole in Boulder one day from the Eden Emporium. Into it she stuffs in a bra and panties, a thicket of Rainey's letters, her hairbrush, a tiny vial of tea rose oil. She puts on two sweaters. From Ask's bureau drawer she boosts two hundred dollars, half the cash he's saved from his sporadic retail jobs. On a scrap of paper she writes the phone number of the farmhouse, though Peace probably knows it by heart. She adds the address for good measure. This scrap, too, goes into the purse.

Then she goes back downstairs. "Ta-da," she says in the kitchen. "What else can I pick up?"

THE TRUCK SMELLS like old sandwiches. Peace sits straight up in the middle, delighted to be out, green glass earrings shining against her coppery hair. "I'm so tired of wearing his shirts," she says, recuffing a fallen sleeve. "You think they'll have maternity?" Fern plays with her mother's fingers, counting to herself in a murmur.

Linda lets Peace chatter, sings with the radio as she drives.

Grace Bend's downtown is charming: rehabbed old townhouses turned into *shoppes*. When Linda enters the main street, Peace abruptly says, "Money," and closes her hands on her vinyl purse.

"Don't worry." Linda passes a strip mall and a King Soopers, then turns left into the Goodwill lot and parks. Fern has her hand on the door handle, and Linda says, "Hold on." She turns to Peace. "I have to get Wanda's Tampax first. I'll meet you inside." She opens her purse and pulls out the paper scrap. "You should always carry the farmhouse number. Here, stick this in your bag."

"You're joking, right?" says Peace. "I know it backwards." Fern clicks her tongue impatiently.

Linda jams the paper scrap in Peace's vinyl purse. "And take this." She pulls a bunch of Ask's twenties from her purse, enough to cover jeans and sneakers and even lunch and an expensive taxi back to the farmhouse, where Ask will provide food, shelter, and space enough for Peace, her baby, Magda's wariness, and that sense of privacy that Rosamund wears like a second skin, but yikes, no truck—which Ask can't afford to replace.

"Where did you get *that*?" Peace looks from the money to Linda as if she'd waved a wand or a revolver to produce it. "I thought ten dollars, maybe. It's just Goodwill."

Linda senses her mistake. "Oops," she says. "That's my savings from New York. Just take it. Give me back what you don't spend." So maybe she didn't think through about the truck. But how else was she going to get home?

When Peace hesitates, Linda shoves the bills, too, into the plastic purse. "Go," she says, ignoring Fern's window rolling up and down.

"How long will you be?"

"Ten minutes," says Linda. "Maybe twelve. Walgreens is around the corner. I'll find you in women's. Or shoes."

She watches Peace and Fern walk away from the truck. She watches sunlight explode on the glass door as they enter the Goodwill store. And then she reverses out of the parking spot, and turns.

She drives slowly on Main Street at first, as if she can't quite believe what she is doing. But then she hits the gas.

Ask was right—she had to leave home in order to go home.

But sitting on that torn front seat, gripping the hot steering wheel, Linda feels clammy with shame. She remembers this: In the first few weeks after she left her child, a tenuous bridge to West Tenth glimmered in her mind, so that Linda could still see herself taking a Trailways back home from Colorado. That notion made it easier, somehow, to commit to Bitter Creek.

She cruises past the little hair salon with its faded photos, the drug store with its Christian book stand and dusty English soaps.

What she didn't foresee was that every hour with Ask would make that faint, silvery bridge harder to conjure, till it simply blinked out of her brain. As it evaporated, so, too, did her right of return, her hope of reconciliation. And those few weeks hardened into twelve years.

Now the daughter who waits (she hopes) in New York is a grown woman. Does she still paint on the walls? It seems impossible. Did she ever become the master of her own gorgeous, radioactive self?

Can she forgive?

Linda is free to find out, that's for sure.

Peace and Fern must be freaking the fuck out. But they will abide. And there comes a time in a woman's life when she has to take care of herself. I-76 lies behind her. She can't make a

Uey without passing them again. So, yeah, she's aimed in the wrong direction, for now—but if she hangs a left at the old grain elevator and the first left after that, she ought to run smack into that gorgeous interstate, that most excellent runway to the rest of her life.

HOW TO STEAL A FAMILY

1984

Ever since he got locked out of the townhouse where he'd lived for twenty-four easy years, Gordy Vine has bunked with his mother uptown, in her single room in the Whitehaven SRO.

He doesn't contribute to the rent. She pays sixty bucks a week for a corner room with her own toilet and sink, so when Gordy wants to shower, he has to pad down the hall with a worn towel and his mother's shampoo. Easier to use her little sink and wash only the parts that touch—the pits and so on. His mother doesn't notice one way or the other. She likes having him here, someone to talk at. A woman who favors housecoats, solitaire, and *Dallas*, she likes her gin of an evening. She likes rouge. She likes Tony Bennett; she likes Ronald Reagan.

You need some sun, boy, she tells Gordy on bright days,

forgetting or ignoring the damage it can sear into pale skin like his.

But things are going to change, starting now, this very September evening.

Gordy Vine has been inching his way back into the West Tenth Street townhouse one shopping bag at a time. Inching, because it kills Rainey to let him back in. Tonight, a wet Saturday dusk, he's going to pry things wide open. Gordy has the golden ticket, and the ticket's name is Linda Royal.

Linda stayed away for more than a decade. Now she's home. Now she's *his*. Gordy remembers that fatal night last year, four in the morning after a gig, Howard jabbing uselessly with his key until the truth sank in. Rainey had changed the locks on her own dad.

And Howard's heart exploded. He was Lear dying of madness on the stoop, betrayed by a daughter. All Gordy could do, on the street, was grip his trumpet and flail at passing traffic for help.

Now, in the headlight-sparkled mist, Linda links arms with him and they walk toward the 125th Street elevated subway. He hadn't needed her help packing up at his mother's—only her safe passage back into the townhouse, or Rainey won't open the door. But ha ha! That's not a thing to be said aloud. They pass shops on Broadway selling tires and religious candles and striated cuts of meat. The paper bag of belongings grows moist in his arms.

Abruptly a swerve of headlights comes at Linda in the dusk,

or rather she walks into them, daydreaming, the silver sedan brushing her raincoat.

Linda jumps back and squeals. The car brakes so that a taxi nearly rams it from behind, and a voice shouts, "Fuck is she, suicidal?" Gordy pounds wetly on the trunk. His left rear molar has ached for a week, and it responds to this violence as if cracking open.

She stands so close Gordy can smell her tea rose oil, and beneath her transparent raincoat is that chunky light-blue sweater she knitted him on pearly clicking needles and keeps borrowing back. Under his own puffed-up jacket, he wears a plaid shirt Linda sewed for him it must be twenty years ago. She got those little buttonholes just right.

"Don't," Linda implores him, her face radiant.

"The fuck I won't." Gordy stalks around the car, waving his free arm as if casting seeds. "He almost killed you." Cars back up and honk. Yelling commences, the word *wife* flies out of Gordy's mouth, and on the curb Linda hugs herself excitedly in her shiny raincoat.

"You best apologize to *my wife*," Gordy says as the driver's window cracks open.

"Asswipe," says the driver, and his car screeches up the dark street.

"That was sexy. You stood up for me." Linda squeezes the arm holding the increasingly clammy bag.

He shakes his head. Linda is endearing as all get-out, but sometimes she does leave her brain in the bedroom. "Fighting isn't sexy, Linda. You haven't seen enough bar fights is all." Though maybe it *is* sexy, think of boxing, karate, all that flowing testosterone.

"Say my name again."

"Leen-da," he says, "you think your parents knew it means *pretty* in *Español*?"

"My very Jewish parents," says Linda dryly, "ya think?"

Gordy follows Linda up the staircase to the train, unzipping his jacket and holding the shopping bag close to his shirt, which is pretty clammy, too. The bag is starting to tear. Linda, fishing for tokens, comes up with one, which is one more than he has. Christ, musicians and their empty pockets. He gives her a nod, *go on*, and glances back at the token clerk. Linda pushes through one turnstile and he crouch-walks under another, forty-seven, he's still got the chops.

On the covered platform, Linda tosses back her hood and untucks her ostensible hair from the collar of her raincoat. Her wig makes Gordy, with his long lunar hair, feel especially tender. Linda's own hair vanished years ago. Her condition has a name, two names, they sound pretty, he can't remember. Steel rails shine in the rain and water streams from the platform roof, and it all looks so pregnant, like something about to change, down to the damp parcels in people's arms, umbrellas dangling from their hands like big sleeping bats.

Linda is bringing Gordy into the Royal family home by osmosis, over Rainey's dead body. Tonight is spaghetti, with a savory eggplant puree that Rainey invented where you roast a couple of those suckers with the skin off and churn them in the blender. Season, salt, and pour over rice. Linda is cooking it, though, because Rainey wouldn't cook for Gordy if he crawled up to her feet starving. Money's an issue. Rainey buys groceries from whatever she's got left. Linda talks about working as a dressmaker. Gordy brings home chump change from the clubs, when they need a horn player to fill in. Money always manifested, when Howard was alive.

What Gordy needs now is a key of his own, but he can't be pushy—Linda has to think of this herself. Rainey won't volunteer it and he won't lower himself to ask. He nervously watches Linda standing too close to the edge of the platform, bird-dogging down the tracks in the dusk as if she's never seen a train before.

"We should do this right." Gordy juggles the shopping bag and places his free hand at the curve of Linda's waist, ready to pull her back from danger.

"Do what right?" She looks so alive in that wet slicker, a woman aware of all her body parts simultaneously, tip of the tongue, soles of the feet. Here is yet one more thing he loves about Linda: her nerve. When she got back to New York in that truck she stole, she parked it by a hydrant so the city would tow it away for her. Free of charge. Brilliant.

"I mean us," he tells her earnestly. "Do *us* right."

She turns, green agate eyes lit from within, black lashes gripping the mascara in tiny clumps.

"Marry me," says Gordy, over the uptown train rumbling in across the tracks.

The rumble dies. He strokes her cheek and she gazes back at him, smiling. "I would love to marry you, Gordy Vine," Linda says. When no *but* is forthcoming, he realizes he isn't satisfied, not yet. What he wants from her is the spectacular.

"Gordy *Royal*." He's almost weeping as the train growls slowly off, and he grasps her arm. "I want your name. I don't have much family, Linda. And yours—it's everything to me. I lived in that house for a quarter century." He remembers Lala, the sweet grandmother whose house it was first, floating through the rooms with a Mona Lisa smile, as if unaware that sometimes young Rainey would knock at the bedroom door to find all three of them—Linda, Howard, and Gordy—tucked into the bed. Or not so tucked. "Your husband was my closest friend."

At the time, Howard and Linda slept on the second floor, down the hall from Lala. So Gordy got a room on the third floor, down the hall from Rainey, who was two.

"It's really Howard's name." Linda hesitates. "But Gordy Royal, if you can do that legally," and Gordy thinks: *I've done it, I've stolen a family.* He's loved them all for decades, every one. Howard, who loved his piano far more than he ever loved a human being. Linda, sweet and willing, who finally left while she still had something alive inside her. And Rainey, with her dark, bristly moods and that fucking obsession with museums. But his passion was never just for any one of them, male or female; it wasn't just for their beauty. It was for the Royals. He'd found the fountain of creativity in them, better even than the fountain of youth. And he wants to fuse with them the only way he knows, through the body, through his fault, through his fault, through his most grievous fault.

On the subway platform, Gordy embraces with one arm the pillar of light that is his beloved. Their train pulls in, the doors open, and the conductor barks out his static. Gordy has a good sense of timing. He gazes into her wondering eyes in the rocking subway car. "I have a confession," he calls into her ear. "You deserve a ring"—he presses her soft, damp knuckles—"and I can't afford one." Scrambling back to known territory, the empty pockets of musicians.

Linda visibly sighs and touches his face. "We'll reuse my wedding band," she shouts back. "And Rainey will give me Howard's old ring."

Gordy doubts it, but he squeezes her hand and smiles.

"I KNOW WHY you hate me," says Gordy softly, the next afternoon, addressing Rainey. His wet clothes still dry on hangers upstairs, Linda's gone for milk and groceries in the ceaseless rain, and now he presses at his jaw with irritation at the pain and slings himself into one of the parlor's bergères.

He used to sprawl like this back when he lived here. God, he's missed it. He taps out a cigarette and extends the pack to Rainey. Her feet up on the sofa, she practically spits at him. He shrugs and takes it back. If she's too good for Gordy's cigarettes, that's his gain.

"If you think I hate you," says Rainey, "stop bringing your stuff over." She slowly unbraids her dark hair, and he watches it fall about her oval face.

"You hold a long grudge," says Gordy admiringly, and strikes a match. He knows Rainey can't say no to her mother, that she's afraid if she kicks Gordy out, Linda will go with him. Outside the parlor's tall windows, the autumn rain beats down in undulating sheets, rattling a ginkgo. Gordy swirls smoke around his murderous tooth. Wet weather seems to make it worse. In all those years, Rainey never floated downstairs to listen to them play. I don't get jazz, she would say. What bullshit.

"Thirteen years old in the early seventies," he says now, talking around the smoke, "that was a full-fledged sexual partner." He exhales toward the Steinway gleaming like a scarred thoroughbred. "Thirteen-year-olds were screwing their brains out all over the country. I thought you were. You were all hormone and swivel and hips. Howard had you on the Pill at thirteen, if I remember right."

They might as well clean out the wound, since Linda is out. Talk it through. Make some peace. He never completely screwed her; what is the honest-to-God problem here?

"Fourteen. And you're in my living room." She combs her long hair with her fingers, sorts the tangles.

He worships this fervently creative tribe that makes its own rules, or did, when Howard lived, the leading one being that there are no rules besides *don't put anything on the piano*. Howard was a flame who burned up everyone in his orbit. He loved to yank Linda's fake hair off her head, and Gordy acutely misses him and his dry, wicked laugh. When Howard first installed Gordy down the hall from his little girl, it seemed to Gordy like he was opening a door of some kind.

God, those parents were a couple of innocents.

As Gordy watches through the windows, the day abruptly upshifts, liquid light pouring onto West Tenth Street like champagne down the side of a glass. He stretches his legs beneath the plaster angels on the ceiling. Gordy is here and not here, half his shit in bags in Linda's room and half in piles on the floor at his mother's. He has a virtuous collection of concert T-shirts, some signed by musicians and never washed. When Linda came home, Rainey instantly gave up the master bedroom, which she weirdly calls *Howardland*, and Gordy knows she never expected to find him in there, too, part of the Linda package.

He rolls the Kool between his pallid fingers with the bitten nails, quashing the filter. Rainey's hair fans out on the sofa; it looks furious enough to climb the walls.

"Jesus, Rainey, do you ever feel soft, or small, or—charitable?"

On his white carpenter's pants: a coffee stain. If he asks to use the basement washing machine when her mother is out, she might say no, and if there is one thing that makes Gordy cry, it's a public laundromat. Rain makes its *pit-pit* sound on the windows again, the weather changing like crazy, as if presenting both sides of an argument. Most of his attentions were little more than an uncle's, he thinks, watching the shaking tip of his burned-down cigarette. But he flushes, thinking, *funny uncle*, and brushes that cobweb from his mind.

"You're the one who should feel small." Rainey is sketching now. Above her is some old master painting, a biblical scene about feminine virtue that Gordy likes because one can almost see some nipple action.

Linda walks in the front door, laughing, carrying two net bags of wet groceries. She wears that see-through plastic raincoat with a hood; she never liked umbrellas. He remembers that about her.

"Hey, sweet pea," she says to Gordy. He rises to take the bags to the kitchen but Rainey beats him to it.

"Hi, Mommy." Rainey kisses her as if Linda had been out hunting down those groceries with a crossbow. What kind of grown person calls her mother *mommy*? It's as if she can't believe there's more affection where this came from, and more after that. Linda plays into it, too, nuzzling with her on the sofa, toying with her daughter's fingers. And Gordy—he has to wait for sloppy seconds. This is unfair, because until the lockout, Gordy fucking *lived* here.

"Hey, babe," he tells Linda, funneling extra warmth into his voice for Rainey's benefit. "Thanks for going out in the rain."

"It's beautiful out there." Linda beams at him through those emerald eyes. "It smells so *clean*. I'd forgotten the city could do that. Ozone, right?"

One thing Gordy knows for sure is that his early years in the townhouse were halcyon.

SUNDAY MORNING THEY have Linda's French toast, which Rainey sleeps through, and go back up to roll in the bed, which Rainey probably blocks out with that Pink Floyd record. Then they agree, more or less, to deliver the news.

"She's your *daughter*, not your mother," insists Gordy. "I'm only trying to be your one true husband. I'm only trying to live here as a family."

Linda nods and kisses him. "She hasn't exactly said no, you know."

"She's not exactly saying yes, either." Gordy thinks bitterly about the key he doesn't have. "Can you get us to yes, Linda? So I can feel welcome in my own home?" What he's thinking is, can she get them to yes without Rainey blurting out that ancient nonsense about some backrubs?

He stands behind his beloved as she knocks on her daughter's door. Everything feels like an omen this morning. The pain makes his fingers shimmer coppery around the edges. (Are there dentists in emergency rooms? Can he just *go*?)

Rainey's bedroom door has never clicked shut all the way. When she wedged it closed with a shim at fourteen—where the devil had she found a shim?—he was crushed. He wanted to beg for another chance. But she seemed dangerous after that, a snake lying across the only path he wished to take, and Gordy retreated, full of yearning and wasted love.

Now Linda calls, "Rain?" and nudges the door open. Gordy follows her in. Rainey sits up in bed, eyeing him warily. These parents, they let her paint all over the walls when she was a kid. A tree to the ceiling, with animals on the leaves. Pegasus, you can see every feather. Rainey leans back in her canopied bed, covers held high, hair thrashing the pillow. Gordy feels a melting pool below his solar plexus.

He watches Linda approach the bed and embrace Rainey, her own bewigged hair a mantle falling around them both.

"We have news." Linda wedges that fine bottom of hers onto the edge of the mattress.

And who is in charge of it, this news, who should speak? Gordy feels himself an instrument of pure love, yet here is Rainey bristling. He smiles at her tenderly.

"Raineleh," he says, "we came—"

But her look of hostility stops him. He lowers his high beams to meet Linda's gaze. *You try.*

Rainey says, "Mommy, I don't want his news."

Linda touches her cheek. "It's my news, too."

"Don't tell me you're getting married," Rainey demands. "Please say anything but that."

Gordy lets his feelings play on his face. Injury, resolving into sorrow, resolving into periodontal grief. He senses that Linda is watching his reaction, and that it wouldn't do to be caught observing her at this.

"Is it because of Daddy?" says Linda. After a silence, she goes on. "What if I *am* marrying Gordy, sweet pea? Wouldn't you be happy for me?"

Gordy wishes she could be more assertive. This thing has to come to a head. He watches Rainey chew her lower lip. At last she says, "No, I'd feel sorry for you. He's a creep."

"Ex*cuse* me?" Linda rises from the bed and looks down at her daughter. "That's so rude, Rainey. Gordy loves you. Can you explain yourself?"

No, no, that's the last thing Gordy wants. He tries to change songs. "Your mother," he says passionately, sitting on the bed by Rainey's knees, "would make me the happiest man in the world."

"There's things my mother doesn't know." He watches Rainey cock her head at Linda, who clenches her toes on the rug. "Things she's never asked."

"Like what?" Linda's almost shrill. "What have I never asked you?" Rainey starts to speak. "And why are you trying to ruin," Linda goes on, blessedly cutting Rainey off, "a beautiful and meaningful morning?"

Like she doesn't want the answer at all.

He feels a stirring against his hips as Rainey draws her knees up under the covers. "You've never asked me," she says, while Linda stands with her hands on her hips, "why I act like you brought a pervert into the house."

Then she pushes out hard with her feet and shoves him off the bed.

His spine scrapes the wooden bed frame and he hits the floor, landing on his bum. Pain ladders up from his tailbone; something tells him there's a rubber donut in his future. "Raineleh," he gasps. Linda kneels beside him, cooing and petting his back.

"What is the matter with you?" he hears Linda demand. "What have you got against him?"

Wrong direction. "Listen," he says urgently from the floor, one hand plastered to his back. "Who the hell else"—he rubs where it hurts and looks up fearfully at Rainey for due process—"thinks your mother is the ant's pants?"

Linda, still rubbing his lower back, gives a chirp of delight. But Rainey says darkly, "The *ance pance?*"

"The bee's knees." He struggles to get to his feet and rocks back down. "I sure could use some ice, little girl."

"It's in the freezer."

"You hurt him, Rainey, don't make him get his own ice." Linda sounds shocked. "And stop acting like queen of the house."

"I *am* queen of the house. He's your boyfriend, Mommy, you get his ice."

Linda sighs and rises from the floor and disappears into the hallway. Gordy listens to her tread on the stairs.

Finally he says, "There's no need to bring your mother into this, is there?"

The look Rainey gives him is both smug and serene. "There's every need," she says. They wait in simmering silence till Linda appears with a swollen plastic baggie, tied off.

"Not in my room," says Rainey, but Gordy pushes his face down on the shag rug, awaiting the unwelcome sensation of burning cold. As soon as he is prostrate, his throat feels prickly. Reactive. It feels like *cat*. He's always known Rainey wanted a cat. And she's always known he is deathly allergic. Did she foster one after she locked him out; is there one in the attic rooms even now? His breath quickens—probably, he tells himself, from imagined dander. His larynx swells and battens down the hatches.

"She does care about me," he tells Linda, the words muffled in the hostile rug. "She just doesn't know it yet."

"No," says Linda quietly, kneeling beside him. "She doesn't care about you at all."

Not good. He remembers Rainey as a child clutching a kitten from the street, being made by her mother to put it out in the snow, for his sake. He remembers her despair.

The baggie crinkles noisily around the ice. Linda says, "Lower your jeans."

"Not on my rug." Rainey sounds livid.

"He's wearing *boxers* for God's sake," says Linda, and Gordy lifts his hips and unbuckles. He's breathing carpet fibers and it isn't going well.

"He's defiling my rug," says Rainey, and Gordy feels the baggie settle on his tailbone. A frigid droplet traces its way down his butt and into the wrinkles of his shriveling scrotum. Is he any closer to getting a key? Surely Linda won't let him get expelled. But the daughter he loves is no closer to loving him.

Linda's hands stop petting his spine. "Why do you hate him?" he hears her say.

Struggling for breath, Gordy gasps, "She doesn't want a stepfather." But there is no deterring Rainey.

"Oh, Christ." Rainey's voice. "Seriously? He would bother me at night. What do you think, Mommy? In my room. Where were you? Why'd you put a grown man down the hall from a *girl*?"

Linda makes a high sound like something has struck or pierced her. "No," she says, and lifts her hands from Gordy's back. She must be touching Rainey now. "You never *said* anything."

"I was like eleven," says Rainey. "And twelve and thirteen. What was I supposed to tell you?"

Nothing he can say in his own defense will sound truthful, not now. He waits it out, hears Linda's long sigh.

Then she says quietly, "How far did it go?"

"Fucking far enough."

Everything he's struggled for is lost. The regal, crumbling townhouse. The blue bedroom with its windows full of leaves. The free-spirited woman he adores, widow of the man whose shadow he was happy to stand in. Linda will never forgive him now. He'll be back at his mother's with his signed T-shirts and his trumpet and his shopping bags; he'll be alone, bereft of the Royals. He eyes the fuzzy pink carpet fibers and waits for the end, his tooth throbbing.

Linda makes a little mew of distress. It's over now.

"Sweet pea," she says, and Gordy hears the plea in her voice as she is about to beg Rainey's forgiveness.

Instead she says, "That was all a long time ago, wasn't it?"

A sharp intake of breath from Rainey.

"Things were so different in the seventies," says Linda. "We didn't have *rules* about these things. He didn't mean to hurt you. If there's one thing I know about Gordy it's that he loves you."

A long silence from Rainey. He's glad he can't see her eyes; they must be smoldering.

"Maybe he lost control a little," says Linda, pleading. "But he's changed. He's a good man. I know he is or I wouldn't be marrying him."

Again Rainey does not respond. Three times now Linda has denied her, as Peter denied Jesus; what more is there to be said? Beneath his prostrate body, Gordy feels the room tilt. He sees a golden key in his future. His luck is unbelievable. If there is a cat here, he will get rid of it.

"Please, Rainey," says Linda. "Don't be like that."

"Too late," he hears Rainey say. "I am like that."

TATTOO

1985

Rainey's husband, Hugh, goes to the dinner party straight from work with Becca van der Vliet, his partner from their architecture firm. A woman Rainey struggles to like. And to trust.

And to steal from.

She takes the bus alone through the December drizzle to the Upper East Side, and finds herself staring at Becca's parents' doorbell late, swirling her damp cape close around her. Becca answers, her teeth shooting off sparks.

Late twenties, like Rainey. Those teeth are expensive Yuppie teeth. And those high pink cheeks! All she needs is a beret.

"Last and best," says Becca warmly.

"Back at you," says Rainey, because Becca calls every night at least once, interrupting dinner and bedtime. She glances past the foyer into the living room and sees two older people talking with Hugh. He looks at her eagerly and rises from a long white sofa.

Down at her feet is a jumble of shoes—so it's one of those households. Tough titties. Rainey looks great in heels. She hands Becca her cape and strides past the shoes, poses under the arched entry to the living room, and beams at the others in their stocking feet. Becca's parents, whom she hasn't seen since her courthouse wedding, are talking with Hugh. He looks at her eagerly and rises from the long white airplane wing of a sofa.

Madonna plays on an unseen stereo, infectious.

"Hello, sweet pea," Rainey says to Hugh. He is the man she cheated with when she was engaged to Flynn, the oncologist. One of the men. One of the men she cheated with. But that was then.

He comes over, kisses her on the mouth, and leads her into the little group. Hugh Doyle is the Rainey Royal antidote. His flame never goes above a simmer. His dark red hair is endearingly choppy because he sticks his hands in it when he thinks, and he wears the asymmetrically cabled blue sweater she knitted him, though pattern is not his first love. Rainey thinks he floats above details of everyday living because his everyday living is so cerebral. He is everything her late father was not—kind where Howard was sardonic, gentle where Howard was cruel—which is probably why she married him, seven months ago.

Face it, married him and Becca.

"Did you get a lot of work done today?" Hugh knows she is struggling with a deadline for a show, making a series of tapestries based on rose windows, each studded with tiny objects. He does not know the objects are all stolen; that's the whole point.

Becca waves an arm around the living room. "We just got all my mother's paintings hung." Rainey looks around. Hugh and Becca just finished renovating the place. The paintings are taller than she is. They look like bleached geodes. Dierdre has her own frosty elegance, white jeans dabbed with gauzy hues of paint, silver hair swept up in a disciplined knot.

Hendrik rises stork-like from the Scandinavian sofa and embraces her. No wedding band on his long, sculptural hands. Hugh is always taking his off, leaving it on the sink, on the nightstand. It makes her nuts. "Hey, Chef," says Becca, and Rainey turns to see a young man emerge from the kitchen. His apron reads *I am the secret ingredient*. Blond, with spiky eyebrows and a tufty little triangular beard, Will makes Rainey think of the Narnia faun, but barefoot instead of hooved, with blessedly presentable toenails.

"I think they seated us together," he tells Rainey in a low aside. "We're both artists." So Becca gets to sit with Hugh? Are they fucking kidding? Becca sits with Hugh all fucking day long.

"We just installed Will's new sculpture," says Becca, and Rainey takes in an argumentative chunk of nails, wire, and charred wood by the window that seems to comment on the sorrow of empty lots.

"That one's about man's inhumanity to man," says Will cheerfully. Rainey thinks the sculpture looks more like Will's inhumanity to Becca's parents, who surely can't love the thing.

She knows this from Hugh about their marriage—Becca permitted only one of Will's wiry entanglements in the Sutton Place co-op they share.

"Dinner awaits," says Will, loosening the apron. Rainey is late—she's always late; dinner has probably been waiting a while. Dierdre follows him into the kitchen and Rainey follows the others toward the dining room, where the table, a white slab shaped like an airplane wing, seems to hover without support.

And Rainey knows this about Becca: She gets her best ideas in the dark. She calls their apartment late at night to talk with Hugh supposedly about things like corbels. Or countertops. Or I beams. His voice always drops to a monosyllabic murmur, as if these things are somehow private. You work with her all day, isn't that enough? Rainey once snapped, but apparently it is not enough, because Hugh and Becca also have dinner every Thursday, which runs late, into after-after-dinner drinks. Becca is Hugh's other wife.

But forget all that, because tonight Rainey is going to seduce her own husband, make it clear whom he belongs to. Tonight she is ready for the competition. She looks fantastic, swaybacked in heels, and over her tight black dress she wears the Jacket of Theft, a black denim jacket she's quilted with alternating black velveteen diamonds. Between the diamonds she's sewn small, meaningful, glinting things. A wedding band. Many earrings. A Traveler's pen. A silver dollar, drilled at the lumberyard. A baby bracelet. Chandelier crystals, unhooked from various chandeliers.

Everything stolen, which is her little secret.

She can't help it if things stick to her, or maybe she sticks to them, because it's all part of her art, both the act of purloining and the finished object. If stealing the stuff feels triumphant, wearing it out in public makes her feel like a billboard for her own stealth and fantasticness. Becca's short black dress has a faint sheen and a snug fit. Did she wear it to work? Around Hugh, for Chrissake? "Rainey, I *must* examine that jacket," she says, fingering it. "If you take it off, I can put it in the bedroom."

"It's surgically attached," murmurs Rainey. She likes the attention the jacket brings, and she likes the secret pocket in the finch-green satin lining, which she sewed herself to hide the things she steals.

But she hands over her purse, and Becca disappears with it down a hallway.

Hendrik moves toward her. His slicked-back hair makes him look like a man leaning into the wind. "You must help us resolve an old design debate," he says.

"Ancient," says Will, as Becca returns without the purse. "I always lose."

"Take it to the table," commands Becca. She links her arm through Hugh's. We're just business partners, Hugh would say. We're just best friends. He doesn't encourage her, but neither does he disengage his arm. It's mere passivity, but isn't passivity a choice? Perhaps Rainey mistook it for that gentleness of his when she married him. She drifts along behind them, squinting at Becca's fleshy but firm triceps. She's a big girl; she isn't Hugh's type, so what is the problem, besides a pinprick in Rainey's head?

Hugh, who is built like a lamppost, likes women with gorgeous bosoms who look ten pounds underweight for the camera everywhere else. In other words, he likes Rainey. She should feel fine.

She *does* feel fine.

In the dining room, Hendrik draws the white silk curtains closed and takes his seat. Rainey steps close to Becca; her fingertips can almost feel the silvery beads along Becca's neckline. "I made it," Rainey confides, touching her jacket. Becca gives a trill of pleasure and reaches out, fingering the stolen bits, a baby-name bracelet that spells out LULU and a braided cross of Mexican silver. Her fingernails are long and red, not bitten like Rainey's.

"People give me these things." Rainey loves telling lies. She loves the way stealing and lying and sneaking around make her feel even more filled up with herself. That's why she consolidates it into her art, makes it part of the performance.

Will carries in the salad. Dierdre gingerly sets down a platter bearing slices of poultry. Rainey wants to peel off the glistening caramel duck skin and eat it, salty and crisp. She pulls out the chair beside Hugh's, but Will, laughing, steers her to the opposite side of the table, so she gets to watch Becca slide in next to Hugh.

"Where were we." Will turns to Rainey. "Before you got here, I was saying that I love Becca's work, it's ascetic and clean, but I also believe a house should be about the human heart." He looks at her hopefully.

Did Hugh always let women take possession like this? Does he make his truest and most secret decisions like this, by letting the other person act for him? Becca has her hand on his arm, her décolletage in full flower as she leans in. Rainey decides to bomb them apart. "Hey," she says, "I never get to sit with my husband at parties." She pushes her chair back. "How about switching seats, Becks?"

"It's Becca," says Becca, not moving. "And Hugh and I have news." Her fingers tighten on his arm. "Stay tuned!"

Rainey knows one thing from growing up with her father—the person with no conscience has all the power in the house. What would it feel like to have one? She smiles sweetly at Hugh as she brushes Will's thigh under the table with her fingertips. A revenge caress. His spine straightens and he flashes her an anxious look. Becca, unseeing, rests her chin on a dimpled fist, spilling hair and laughter and a flash of green from an emerald ring. Her laugh sounds like braying; it's the laugh of a woman announcing that she's having more fun than anyone in the room.

"Child of mine?" says Hendrik, and fills Becca's wine glass, then Rainey's.

"And what about color from artwork and books?" says Will. His voice has taken on a slightly desperate tinge, with Rainey's hand resting on his upper thigh. "I'm not so sure that should be banished." She watches his Adam's apple bob as he swallows. "You can end up with a museum," he says.

Casually, he drops his hand under the table, touching her own—but then he only disconnects her fingers from his leg.

Rainey is both amazed and disappointed at his willpower. She thinks he has a point about the museum, though. She glances back into the living room, where all the books in the shelves have been covered in white paper, the titles hand-lettered in black ink.

"As an artist, Rainey, do you agree?" says Hendrik. "Is that what Hugh and Becca designed for us here, a museum?"

Hugh laughs. "Rainey's too smart to get drawn into that." He gives her a lit smile. "Tell them about your last show, Rain."

But Dierdre interrupts, clinking her glass with a knife whose handle is almost too thin to grip. Everyone falls silent but Becca, who murmurs another moment, then expels her metallic laugh.

"Beloveds, this is a turducken." Deirdre, presiding. "It flew up from New Orleans. It's a chicken inside a duck inside a turkey, or it was till we took it apart, and it's stuffed with crawfish and jambalaya and corn bread dressing."

Like a matryoshka doll, but with poultry, thinks Rainey, a little queasy. *There was an old lady who swallowed a fly*—Rainey remembers her mother, more than two decades ago, chanting for her daughter at bedtime. *She swallowed a spider to catch the fly.* Then *How absurd to swallow a bird! She swallowed the bird to catch the spider . . .* a human turducken, hiding in plain sight.

"Good God, is that fragrant," says Hugh. "What's the wine—let me guess—a Riesling inside a pinot gris inside a sauvignon blanc."

"A ries-pin-blanc." Becca sounds it out. Those pink, fleshy cheeks! They are asking to be slapped. "And what's dessert? I'll show my tattoo to whoever comes up with the best dessert."

Of course she will.

"A pudding inside a cake—" says Will.

· TATTOO ·

Deirdre wrinkles her nose and says, "Becca darling, when did you get a *tattoo*?"

The mystery of the evening. Hendrik starts serving. Dierdre goes back to the kitchen and returns with a plate of green beans and slivered almonds. Rainey sips and watches. Her plate leaves her hand and comes back aromatic with bird.

"What's it of, this tattoo you're sporting?" says Hendrik, looking amused. "An architectural wonder of the world?"

"Yeah, you don't seem the butterfly type," Rainey says dryly. Hugh has a tattoo, inked in sans serif, not a flourish about it. The typography suits him.

Will turns to her and says, "No butterflies for my wife. And you're not furthering the debate, Rainey." She notices a hole in his white sweater that could have been poked with wire in his studio. "As an artist, what should home be like?"

She looks around the dining room. White walls, white table, white leather chairs. A white Murano chandelier with voluptuous glass droplets, and more cool abstract paintings by Dierdre. She thinks about the first and only time Hugh visited the townhouse, how his neck and arms broke out in streaky hives—it wasn't dust, she understood, but fuss, the red curtains, the antique furniture, the grand piano, the Oriental carpets, the ornate moldings, the *stuff*. Later, when they got serious, he refused to move in. Now they live in Hugh's apartment, which looks relentlessly like this one: white. The exception is the top of Rainey's bureau, an altar of candles, incense, old photographs of her mother, earrings arranged in a kind of mosaic. Around it hang watercolors she's done of rooms she's loved. Her closet is painted pink inside: a shell.

"As an artist, I'm partial to color," she says carefully. "Pink, violet, even black . . ."

"You sure married the wrong guy," says Will, but he blunders into it, and the laughter sounds uncomfortable. Did she marry the wrong guy? She's known him barely two years. It is true that she wishes they could live in the townhouse she grew up in and which her best friend, Tina, now rattles around in alone. Rainey takes the subway to Union Square every day, when Tina is delivering babies at St. Vincent's, and works on her tapestries in the dining room on West Tenth. She leaves all her fabric pieces out overnight, which she could hardly do at Hugh's. Tina doesn't break out in hives over it. Hugh might.

Something deliciously soft slides along her left ankle: the Van der Vliets' cat, Missy.

"This turducken is fabulous," says Hendrik. "They ought to breed it."

Becca taps her glass with a spoon. "We have an announcement," she says.

Hugh looks straight at Rainey, and she holds his gaze. She prays it is something fantastic, an architecture prize, a job with big prospects.

"We have a new client with a SoHo loft," says Becca, and when her parents start clapping she raises a hand to stop them. "That's not the real news," Becca crows. "She's sending us to France next week. She wants us to bring back these perfect little white river stones from a town in the south where she grew up. She wants them embedded in the shower floors. Not bad, huh?"

Hendrik and Dierdre start crooning. They're full of questions. Rainey leans across the table and says quietly to Hugh, "You're going to France." She means you're going to France *together*. Hugh nods. No wonder he didn't tell her himself. When did he think she was going to find out—when he was packing?

"I'm going with you," she says.

"There's no room, sweetheart," he says. "It's just a cottage. I'm sleeping on the client's pullout sofa."

She bites the inside of her cheek and wonders if he really will be sleeping on the sofa, if Becca won't come down in her little nightie and beckon him upstairs, if it's actually a château.

"So tell us about that show you had, Rainey," says Becca, prompting. "Hugh says you were inspired by your aunt."

Let it go, Rainey tells herself. He talks about you to his partner—isn't that proof of fidelity, of a sort?

"My amazing Aunt Laurette," she says, looking around the table, "collects just about everything. I used bits of her jewelry, and tiny objects, and snippets of letters and photographs to create a series of small tapestries." She holds her hands apart to show the size. "They're portraits, really, in her honor."

Some kind of haunting violin issues from the stereo. Rainey hadn't realized till now that Becca's parents had silenced Madonna.

"What a concept," says Hendrik. "It sounds quite beautiful. Why did you choose your aunt? Not your mother, or Hugh?"

Rainey starts to speak, but Becca lifts her glass and breaks in.

"I can answer that," she says. "Her aunt is one of those clutterers. She has all that *material*."

Hendrik looks puzzled. Rainey twirls Becca's image in her wineglass till it drowns. "My aunt is a collector," she corrects. "She sees the poetry in objects."

"A lot of objects," suggests Hugh gently. He went to Aunt Laurette's once with Rainey and fled.

It is true that Aunt Laurette might technically live in a hoard, which Rainey likes to pick through and extract from when her aunt isn't watching. Laurette mostly barricades herself inside, and Rainey started going there for maternal affection after her mother split. Sometimes Laurette will stroke Rainey's hair or braid it and talk about her girlhood with Linda, how they grew up in a strict Orthodox family that had rules up the wazoo. But Laurette caught her once trying to smuggle out old, grainy Polaroids of Linda. She cried out and had to lie down for an hour, impervious to Rainey's promises. No way will Rainey discuss this at a dinner party.

"Hugh made it sound *fascinating*," says Becca, tossing her hair. She looks around the table as if for agreement. "He said your aunt is a clutterbug, and that your artwork is all about visually recreating and organizing that experience."

"I don't love that word," says Rainey carefully. Maybe it's the *bug*, the association with roaches. Maybe it's the *clutter*, the utter loss of control. She'll have to talk with Hugh about this; it feels disloyal for him to say it.

"Your aunt is a *what*?" says Hendrik, his arms outspread at the head of the table, and Rainey wonders if there is a word for it in Dutch.

"Becca is talking about hoarders," she says, and Hugh nods at her encouragingly. "People who fill their houses with newspapers or cats. Which my aunt does not." A real clutterbug, she thinks, would have towers of food-encrusted dishes, which Laurette does not allow, would have piles of newspaper and luggage and junk that have collapsed to the floor in heaps, whereas Laurette keeps her newspaper piles straight and her pathways clear. She keeps her personal things in piles of boxes, which to Rainey are full of stories and secrets.

"I know about this," says Hendrik. "We had a famous case in Utrecht. Three firemen died because of them. Unbelievable."

Hugh grimaces, toggling his fork back and forth. "Hendrik," he says.

"People, my aunt is a collector," says Rainey.

All five of them look at her, waiting. She's prepared to defend Aunt Laurette into dessert and beyond.

"I'm sorry," says Becca sweetly. "I didn't mean to open a can of—clutter."

Will stops eating, attentive. "Is she an artist?" he says. "I've heard you can barely walk through some of Andy Warhol's rooms."

"Seriously!" Rainey's excited by this. "How did you guess? She used to paint gorgeous portraits." She doesn't say there's no longer space to set up an easel and step back from it, no room to lean the canvases to dry. Now Laurette is like an outsider artist who simply collects material—cartons of clothes and earrings and dolls and books—then forgets to make any sculpture. But the material excites Rainey, who loves to work with it.

"She *was* an artist, a gifted one," she says. "Now she just collects."

"Collects what?" Dierdre tilts her head, the silver hair falling straight.

"Lady's head vases?" Rainey suggests.

Hendrik and Dierdre look at her blankly from the ends of the table.

"Vintage paperbacks, for the covers," says Rainey. Dierdre's face brightens as she nods. "Bottle caps, some of them decades old," and she thinks, *Stop now*. "Chopsticks. Souvenir pens. Beads of all kinds," she says, unable to stop herself. "Heads from tiny baby dolls. Hands, too."

"There's a little doll's arm on your jacket," says Hendrik.

"What about the rest of the doll?" says Will, smiling. "Does it get a proper burial?"

"It's such a tribute," says Becca, "that you're doing tapestries with her . . . stuff. She must have been proud of your show."

Rainey smiles. She never brought Laurette to the show; her aunt would have felt exposed, humiliated, enraged by the theft of her belongings.

"How do you get things out of her apartment?" says Will. "Hoarders are notorious for holding on to their stuff."

"She's not a hoarder." Rainey feels the wine now; she's floating a bit, and she wouldn't mind floating further from the conversation.

"But it's brilliant, Rain," says Becca. "You have to tell it." She folds her hands behind her neck, looks around the table with bright blue eyes, and says dramatically, "Hugh says Rainey is decluttering her aunt's apartment—by *stealth*."

"Becca," says Rainey sharply, "let's stop there."

But it's too late. Dierdre says, "You take things without her knowing?"

"These aren't exactly *things*." Rainey inhales. She wants this line of questioning to end now. She feels goaded; she has exposed her aunt to surgery by strangers. "These are *bottle caps*," she says. "Broken watches. Stuff she's forgotten about for years. It's not stealing. It's . . . helping her clean up."

"But it's not exactly trash, is it," says Deirdre delicately. "These are things she cares about, yes?"

Rainey downs the last of her glass and reaches for the bottle. "I think I care about these things more than my aunt does," she says coolly. "And I create art with them. Even beauty." But there is another truth, namely that she's stealing from a person she loves. This should bother her, shouldn't it? She loves Aunt Laurette like a daughter would, and the stealing has nothing to do with the love, or perhaps it has everything to do with it.

After a moment's silence, Will says, with a note of despairing cheer, "Change of subject? Give Rainey a break?" No one objects. "I think we were talking of tattoos." He gives Becca a significant look. "Yours, darling, to be precise. I don't know about the *show* part, but you can at least *tell*."

"Sure, let's have some skin art." Becca looks delighted. She turns sideways in her chair, presenting her back to Hugh. "Would you?" she asks him, and lifts her dark, heavy hair off her shoulders.

"Becca, at the table?" says Dierdre sharply.

The intimacy, the unzipping, flies by so fast that Rainey almost misses the shock on Will's face. She doesn't miss Becca's black satin bra strap. Becca stands, turns from the table, flips her hair to the front, and pulls the flaps of her dress apart, revealing her shoulder blades.

Her skin is seemingly without imperfection, and the lettering is black sans serif. It arches between Becca's shoulder blades and reads:

SKY SPACE TREES

Rainey closes her eyes. When she opens them, the tattoo still reads the same.

"I don't understand," says Dierdre.

Hugh watches Rainey drink. She sees him watch. She still is not drunk.

Becca sits again, the dress sliding off her shoulders.

"Zip up now," says Hendrik, with a sharp note. Rainey knows from her husband that these people go to church; maybe they're puritans at home.

Becca shoots Rainey a surmising look. Then she smiles at her. "I bet you know."

"It's Le Corbusier." Rainey looks around the table and catches an expression of pain on Hugh's face. "Le Corbusier said these three things were all he needed to bring joy to human beings. Sky, space, and trees."

"Becca, *zip*," says Dierdre.

Will turns to Rainey, puzzled. "How do you know what Le Corbusier said?"

"I read a lot," she says dryly.

She remembers the first time she and Hugh made love. He peeled off her T-shirt, and after some fooling around she peeled off his. Then he stooped to pull his sneakers off and she saw the lettering, the three words, across his back.

What is that, the three things that make you happy? she asked, and he said, Close, and explained the quotation.

They must have gotten matching tattoos back when they opened the firm, before Hugh and Rainey met.

Now she thinks: It would have been better if they'd just gone to bed.

"News flash." Will gives her a friendly nudge. "Rainey's getting one on her back, too."

She almost smacks him. Instead, she pushes her chair back and stands.

"Excuse me," she says. She walks down the hall a little unsteadily and passes the powder room. Then she turns left into Hendrik and Dierdre's bedroom, as if headed for the master bath.

When she closes the bedroom door, the noise of the dinner party turns to cotton. Her things and Becca's lie on the white leather bed, and a bowl of parchment-colored roses rests on the pale wood bureau. Reading lights affixed to the walls, a clock on a nightstand. Nothing else. Where is their *stuff*? She opens a bureau drawer. In the back is a silk Pucci scarf of a good weight.

She slips it into her secret green pocket, keeps rummaging, and finds at the bottom of the drawer a piece of blue sea glass. It's a nearly perfect triangle. Scalene, she remembers, not isosceles. If she wraps fine wire around it, it will be easy to attach.

She drops it into the secret pocket on top of the scarf, and has just closed the drawer when she hears the doorknob. She turns; did Hendrik see? He looks as startled as she feels. Immediately she begins checking her hair in the mirror over the bureau.

"Hunting?" says Hendrik soberly. "Or fishing?"

Rainey flushes with heat. "Neither," she says. "Lipsticking and peeing. I was hoping to find a comb."

"It's best not to share combs, don't you think?" He studies her and finally smiles. "Come on back. We promise not to talk about your aunt. If you're using this bathroom . . . ?"

"Yes, please," she says.

"I'll use the powder room." Hendrik ambles off, leaving the bedroom door half open. Rainey uses the bathroom, flushes the toilet, runs the water noisily. When she comes out, she puts a knee on the bed and unzips Becca's black Prada purse.

She has to move fast.

Becca has the matching Prada wallet; of course she does. Rainey rummages quickly past a batch of mail, a boar's bristle hairbrush, a Cross pen, a Chanel lipstick that she knows from Becca's mouth to be wine red, a massive set of keys on a Mercedes key ring. She hadn't known Becca owned a car. Of course she does. And of course it's a Mercedes. Where is all the junk of life, the chewing gum, the battered little notebook, the aspirin, the chewed-on pencil and collection of BIC pens? Where is the ink stain on the rich blue lining?

Rainey takes the keys from the bag. They're heavy, and before she can drop them into her own purse she sees that Becca's Harvard ring is part of the jangle on the key fob. The ring is gold all over, no stone, and engraved on its face is a single word. Rainey takes a closer look. VERITAS, it says. Truth! This thing would be a joy to steal.

Then she spots a zippered pocket she'd missed in the Wedgwood blue lining, and opens it. Something stiff lies inside. She pulls it out.

Becca's passport.

This is pure, gorgeous sabotage—without the passport, Becca can't go to France, not for the months it will take to get a new one. So either Hugh goes alone, or the client finds her dumb stones someplace else.

Rainey locates her own bag on the bed among the coats and opens the flap to slide the passport inside.

But then an image floats to her of Hugh in France. He isn't making love to Becca, not at all. In her mind's eye, her husband pulls up a white matelassé coverlet on a narrow foldout cot. He is bone-tired from gathering small white stones with Becca all day, stones that now collect in a handwoven basket by the hearth. His back aches from bending, and tomorrow it will ache worse. This half-asleep Hugh nurses a dreamy image of his own: how he misses bedding down with his wife at home—he's the outside spoon, his right arm flung around Rainey, his right hand a goblet for her breast.

"Oh, baby," murmurs Rainey. She flips through the heavily stamped passport. Italy flies by, Morocco, Brazil—okay, so the witch gets around, but Rainey has her own life to live, right? Not without regret, she slides the little booklet back into the pocket of Becca's Prada bag and zips it shut.

Because the only thing she wants from Becca already belongs to her.

Oh, what a load of crap.

Rainey looks down at the new bleached floorboards. Sky, space, trees. Why hadn't he told her? Because it was private, because he knew it was too much?

Quickly, she takes the passport out again, slides it this time into her own purse.

By the time he has to ask, it will be too late for them all.

HEART JAMMED OPEN

1987

Rainey brings the sandwiches to Aunt Laurette's apartment because Laurette's fridge is impassable, all those boxes and bags of oddities and piles of newsprint in the way. That fridge must now be lush with mold, a rainforest cultivating lumpy orchids. If Rainey could even reach it to crack it open, she'd hear parrots shrilling deep in the vegetation.

Pulling off her snowy boots in the foyer, she hears her mother trashing her aunt's belongings. Rustling, swishing—that's Linda in the living room, deep in the newspaper stacks.

Aunt Laurette is away, in San Francisco, and Rainey and Linda take the subway uptown from West Tenth every day to feed her cats. Also, they are cleaning house. Without permission. Laurette would freak if she knew. It agonizes her to see a thing thrown out:

One day you'd want the paper from some special date and would be anguished to find it gone. Everything is potentially precious.

"Fill this, would you, sweet pea?" Linda shakes out a Hefty bag so it balloons, creating an ecstatic twirling mushroom of dust motes. Chaos inside, chaos outside. All over Manhattan, Yuppie money deluges the avenues while crack poisons whole swaths of side streets, strewing bodies in stairwells and crunchy vials underfoot. The Royals, both uptown and downtown, live in the in-between, at good addresses in pockets of brokenness. They eat things past their expiration dates. No one in this family, thinks Rainey, buys anything new. Her thrift shop boots are too thin for this cold.

She winds her way into the living room, which is still a wreck. Deep stacks of newsprint are depleted after days of work, but heaps of knotted Hefty bags have yet to be dragged to the basement. Ardelio, the super, is going to kill them. Clearly he's been snitching to the landlord. And what will they find at the bottom of it all—a mummified lover, a fortune in silver dollars? Or, if Rainey is lucky, a brittle diary in which Laurette unspools the mystery of her days.

"The landlord called again." Linda waves open another bag, attacking a newspaper stack that rises to her waist and sniffing wetly as a veil of dust levitates. Her wig gets hot, so she's taken it off and wrapped her bare head in a green chiffon scarf. "He's starting eviction proceedings."

If Aunt Laurette gets evicted, she might try to move in to the townhouse with Rainey—God forbid. She'd start collecting again. The weight of her *stuff* would bring the floors down. She'd bury them alive.

"Landlords can't just *do* that." Rainey picks up the black cat, Ticket, that's twining around her ankles. She's stalling; she hates the dust. "Seriously, doesn't he have to go to court?" Beyond the gray, sleeted windows lies the blade of the Hudson River, rippled with unforgiving light and patrolled by a lone helicopter.

"He seemed open to suggestions," her mother says cheerily. "I'm not worried."

"You should be." Rainey sets the vibrating Ticket on the coffee table, where he topples a tower of unopened mail and springs away. She crams newsprint into her Hefty bag, looks at her dusty hand in dismay. Above her, oil portraits painted long ago by Laurette gaze distractedly from the walls. In one, a thin teenage boy with straw-colored hair peers out with a blue, catlike wariness. He is Laurette's son, Elihu, who fled the hoard for Yale at seventeen and never came back.

Now Elihu, at twenty-nine, a year younger than Rainey, is dying out in the Castro, and Laurette has managed to get her claustrophobic self on a 747 to fetch him home. Rainey knows something Elihu doesn't, namely who his daddy was—a stranger who dragged Laurette into an alley at knifepoint. This is the kind of oversharing Rainey's mother sometimes does. "Mommy, you seem to have the living room under control," Rainey says. "Why don't I blast through the bedroom?" What she really wants is to burrow in private through the cartons heaped with her aunt's wonders and portents: the keys and doll arms and watch faces and mismatched earrings that Rainey has pilfered for years and stitched into her tapestries. Laurette amasses it, Rainey steals it, now Linda transforms it to garbage. They are three goddesses spinning trash into treasure into trash again, all working behind one another's backs.

"How about not," says Linda, just as the phone rings. She wipes her forehead with the back of her hand, leaving a gray mark below the bright green scarf. "Man oh man, Death himself couldn't reach Laurette with a pitchfork through all this shit."

"You mean a scythe." Rainey digs the phone out from under the spilled mail. It's her aunt, calling from Elihu's.

"They're still canceling flights," Laurette says on the phone. Her voice is melodic, exactly like Linda's, with the same distant undernotes of rustling paper or crunching glass. "It's all the ice," she explains, and it hardly matters, Rainey knows, whether Elihu gets back for Christmas. "Are you ladies cleaning the cat box?" Laurette can barely reach her own bathroom but she's pristine about the kitty litter.

"We hand-wash every grain of sand. How's Elihu?" Rainey rarely saw her cousin growing up because her aunt disapproved of the drugs, sex, and live music all night. She remembers when El was a slip of a thing, visiting the townhouse with his mother, and she and Tina Dial, who were twelve, made him up like a doll at Rainey's dressing table. Then Laurette burst in and had to be consoled in the hall. Now Laurette could care less who he fucks—she just wants her son in her life. Instead, she has an ailing replica who looks like the withering Christ, with sores instead of thorn holes.

"He's lost forty pounds. And about ten friends," says Laurette. "Maybe Thursday we'll fly in if the weather breaks."

"Put him on." Rainey's prepared a bedroom for Elihu in the townhouse. *Don't make me die in that squirrel nest* was how he put it on the phone, after Laurette first decided that her son should end his days at home. God knows beautiful young men are dying in New York, too. People are starting to talk about T cell counts with the fervor once saved for the scarcity of rent-controlled apartments.

There's fumbling on the line, then El's voice, dredged up as if from a deep, dried-out well with stones and leaves at the bottom. "Hey," he says slowly, making a meal out of it.

"Hey you," says Rainey. "How you feeling, babe?"

Elihu seems to consider this. "I hurt," he says finally, "and everything is very detailed and close-up." Of course he's super visual, he's a film editor or something for Francis Ford Coppola. Or was. "Assuming I can get on that plane," he says, his breath ragged, wind rushing under a door, "you know I'm bringing a cat, right?"

Oh really.

This is divine vengeance. Gordy Vine, who has married her mother and sleeps with her in the blue bedroom now, is allergic. He's beyond allergic—he practically goes into anaphylactic fucking shock. It would be a joy to suffocate him.

"You do whatever your heart desires," Rainey says. Let Gordy Vine wheeze himself to death.

* * *

ON WEST TENTH Street that night, she finishes her hand stitching at the scarred dining table. At her feet, an electric heater whirrs. A Bloomie's bag of Laurette's baubles stands by her knee. She's finally at the end of this piece—affixing the last few snippets of fabric to a circle on her fifth rose window tapestry.

Not that people really see the circles. They're drawn to the petals, the dazzling spokes of the complicated rose design.

A few flakes of ceiling plaster fall onto her work. She blows them away. What's a little plaster snow? The townhouse is slowly falling to pieces, and since her father blew through most of the trust before he died, there's no cash to fix things up.

To make her pattern, Rainey spent hours in Saint John the Divine on 110th and Amsterdam, twisted around in the pew, staring at the window, sketching, until positive became negative. She pasted postcards into her sketchbook. She found a book on rose windows in the NYPL and copied out drawings—she almost stole the damn thing but it didn't fit into her pack.

She can't get enough of it.

In the end she laid out nineteen circles total for this tapestry. One lies outside the rose itself—how cool is that? Then came the stars, the squares, the sixteen rays. This all had far more to do with geometry than roses, and filled her with awe.

Even with Linda's old yellow Singer, it's punishing work to make one tapestry. But as it comes together, slowly, each rose window is a mandala, a womb, a closed system—a snowflake, world within a world. Some are called *Catherine wheels*, patterned for the one on which Saint Catherine herself was to be broken, bone by bone—though that wheel shattered when she touched it, so they had to lop off her head.

And ultimately all the windows she copies are roses, and Rainey can't help thinking that her mother wears tea rose oil.

She stirs up a box of fabric scraps—some cut from Linda's old clothes and some from blouses nicked from Laurette—till she finds the final piece. It's the one she's saved for last. From her childhood, a snippet from the first real project she and Linda sewed together, back when Rainey was maybe ten and learning about bobbins and the presser foot. She threads her needle, trims the scrap, folds the edges under, then works it into her tapestry like code.

The half-hidden inch of wool is as green as the first spring caterpillar.

It's a gift to her mother, if only her mother would *see* it. Yet it's impossible that Linda would remember it now.

Schirmer Shapiro, the SoHo gallery, is waiting for delivery of the ten tapestries she has promised. If she can produce those, they'll give her a show. If she can produce them before they forget she exists.

Every piece is named *LINDA*, for they are all about the search.

THE NEXT DAY Rainey is back on 106th, helping her mother tornado through more of Laurette's belongings, when the landlord calls again.

This time Linda pretends to be Laurette on the phone. She's clearly enjoying herself.

"Wait one minute, sir. Just hold your horses." Linda has raided Laurette's closet for her vintage thrift store finds—today she's borrowed a green dress dotted with rotary dial telephones. She's trying to pace but the curly cord restrains her. "You can't evict me if I paid two months in advance." Pause. "Whaddaya mean it doesn't matter? You've already *filed*?"

Rainey sits on the sofa stroking the other cat, Quibble, and sipping a Coke. She's trying to make sense of a piece of mail that the landlord, on yesterday's call, told her mother to dig out. At the top of the paper it says NOTICE TO CURE in bold, and below that, essentially, that Laurette Barbanel has violated her lease by creating a nuisance and she has ten days to blah blah blah. If she fails to clean up, she will be served with a thirty-day Notice to Terminate.

"You know what? You're absolutely right," Linda-as-Laurette says into the phone. "I'm sick of living like this. I'm getting rid of all my shit." Pause. "Yeah, dead serious. I've already started. Come by in a week and see for yourself."

What if everyone got a Notice to Cure, like in some Kafka story? You'd be forced to puzzle out what it meant. You'd excavate your most existential and personal problems and try to fix them before that Notice to Terminate landed in your life. It would all be very mysterious and deep. Like for Rainey, she'd have to stop hating Gordy. She'd have to stop feeling as desolate as an orphan, especially when her mother was standing *right there*.

"I promise," Linda-as-Laurette says, and hangs up. "We're old buds now, me and that landlord," she tells Rainey happily. Though the atmosphere outside the living room windows has dulled to an ash gray, her green eyes are full of light. "And don't I sound just like her?"

Rainey laughs. "When you were gone, I sat through a million tuna fish sandwiches at Tom's with Laurette just to hear her talk."

She looks again at the Notice to Cure. All that tight lettering jammed up against itself. "You do realize the ten days is expired?" she says. "It's too late to throw shit out, Mommy. That's why he started eviction proceedings. Where's the Notice to Terminate?"

Linda gestures vaguely at the coffee table, or maybe she means the floor by the fireplace, where months or years of mail have accreted into a small mountain. "Legal mumbo jumbo doesn't worry me. I love it when you call me *mommy*," she adds.

"Seriously, stop cleaning," says Rainey. "She has less than a month to move *out*. We should be looking for a new apartment." Not the townhouse. Anywhere but there.

Linda stops trashing newspapers. "Why? The landlord told me to go ahead and get rid of things."

Rainey grips her Coke so tightly she dents the can. "He wants you to clean up so he won't have to hire a crew."

Her mother looks at her indulgently. "Ye of little faith," she says, smiling. "Did you know that when you leave or enter a place that shelters you, you're supposed to express your thanks?" She presses her palms together as if in prayer. This seems a lousy solution to eviction, but Linda has the weirdest ways of solving problems. "I connect my feet with the ground," she says reverently. "And I express gratitude."

Linda bows.

"Mommy," says Rainey, "focus. *Landlord.*" Why can't she pin her parent down to address the situation—or, really, anything Rainey cares about? Linda is a butterfly; no sooner does she alight on one thing than she's thinking about her next perch.

Her mother speaks over clasped hands. "I already talked to Legal Aid, sweet pea. Laurette's not here to go to housing court. So I offered to clean house. Somebody has to."

"Without telling her," says Rainey pointedly.

Her mother smiles in brilliant acknowledgment of this fact. Rainey eases Quibble off her lap and starts filling a bag with mail. "Look, if you are throwing things out," she says, "I get to see everything first."

"Go for it." Linda reaches for another stack of ancient, yellowed newsprint.

She hesitates. Linda hasn't seen the rose window tapestries that practically glitter with items of Laurette's, bits and fragments and ephemera that Rainey has been sneaking out of the hoard for more than a decade. "You know," she tells her mother, "I use her things in my artwork."

"Oh?" Linda turns, holding a handful of upside-down *New York Times* headlines. The words *heart* and *transplant* flash through Rainey's vision—is that paper two years old or what? Maybe the patient's new heart came from someone who was loved. Maybe when the anesthesia lifted, the patient consulted his new pulse, stopped cheating on his wife, and tried to be a worthy husband. Huh. "Does Laurette mind?" her mother asks, and Rainey opens her mouth, trying to say about five things at once about the stealing. Nothing comes out. "Does she *know*?"

Laurette has built a fortress out of trash and secreted herself inside it. But trash turns out to be dangerously permeable. Landlords can clear it with Notices to Cure, death can pierce it with a spiky virus, and a sister and niece can dismantle it all in ten days. Two weeks, realistically. Or you can turn it upside down and shake it till the shiny bits fall out, and make a tapestry called *LINDA*. Everything is mutable. Everything is part of a cycle.

Defensive, Rainey says, "You're junking it, right? Isn't it better to turn some of it into art?" Fiercely she jams another handful of mail deep into her Hefty bag. She still can't see the surface of the coffee table.

Her mother seems to consider this. After a moment, she says, "Point taken. Knock yourself out. Tell me if you find our mother's wedding silver—we'll save that for Laurette."

Rainey can't wait to search the hoard. Her mother has just opened an entire department store for her alone, all the merchandise free: photographs, jewelry, dolls, bottle caps, keys, old letters, polished stones—all the pretty detritus of which Laurette has made this crazy armor they are now dismantling.

"I want you to do something for me," she tells her mother. "You can take a little break, right?"

• • •

FIRST THEY GO home to pick up the finished tapestry. Rainey's rolled it up in plastic sheeting against the snow, so all Linda sees is the shiny tube, thick as a man's arm and about as long. Rainey tucks it inside her coat. Then they take the R to Prince Street and walk.

The sky over SoHo looks like dirty water. On the corner by the Schirmer Shapiro gallery, a woman stamping her boots sells Christmas trees trussed with twine, and next door, a man with a battered coffee cup huddles in a sleeping bag beneath a shoe store awning. His gnarled gaze meets Rainey's. She falters, then pulls a thrift store scarf from the neck of her peacoat and thrusts it at him.

Inside, the weather immediately shifts. The space is clean and brilliantly lit. A glass chandelier by Dale Chihuly dangles orange tentacles over the front desk.

Rainey slots their umbrella into the bin, and Linda, unzipping her down jacket, walks straight to a mazelike picture, maybe a crazy notebook doodle by some high schooler with Magic Markers who didn't know when to stop. "Oh my," says Linda. "Someone was speeding."

The man at the front desk laughs. He has lit, inky eyes and feathers braided into his black hair.

"Hey, Michael," says Rainey. "I brought you a present." She holds out the tapestry in its roll of damp plastic.

He comes around from behind the desk and takes it, squeezing her hand. "This is an occasion."

"My mother is the occasion." Rainey savors the hand. "Mommy, Michael runs the gallery."

Her mother turns from the framed doodle, drops an arm around Rainey's shoulders as if they were sisters, and beams at Michael. "I'm Linda. Very dusty, excuse me. I was clearing out a hovel. Not mine," she adds. How amazing to have this radiant new sister-mother beside her, not looking remotely dusty.

"I see you like the Tara Galanis." Michael's voice is silky, the gallery so silent it almost hums. "She's one of our best artists. And present company, of course." He turns to Rainey. "So, show me."

She hopes her mother won't be disappointed to find her tapestries only in flat files in the back room. No fancy Chihuly chandelier here, just a halogen ceiling light. Along the walls are tall wooden racks holding upright canvases, and stacks of metal drawers.

Michael unfurls the plastic and lays the fifth rose window tapestry flat on a table. Rainey unpins a handwritten index card from the back and sets it on the laminate. *LINDA 5*, the card reads, and beneath that, *Cloth, metal, plastic, glass, paper, jade, pearls*. Rainey catches her breath. If her mother spots the title, she might grasp what it meant to disappear on a thirteen-year-old daughter.

It's almost embarrassing. Maybe it's better if Linda doesn't see.

Her mother bends to the tapestry, inspecting.

"Holy hell," says Michael. "You've outdone yourself, girl."

LINDA 5 is almost three feet high and three feet across, a many-pieced, brilliantly colored, sixteen-petaled rose with round medallions, spokes, pointed arches, elongated teardrop and petal shapes. Stitched to it are miniature objects, all of them stolen, many purloined from Laurette's: pearls, keys, earrings, tiny ceramic antique doll hands, the tiniest souvenir teaspoon, shards of teacups and lady's head vases that Rainey gingerly cracked apart, faces cut from old Polaroids and black-and-whites, snippets of letters bearing single words—*field*, *miss*, *yurt*—that Linda wrote home to Laurette from Colorado.

"Fascinating." Linda, whispering, touches the appliqué. "It's like a stained glass window, isn't it? And these are Laurette's? You were always good at art, but this is astonishing."

Rainey strokes her mother's wrist. *Look at the placard.* She could stand here all day, watching Linda soak it up.

Michael opens a metal drawer and extracts *LINDA 1*, cradling it.

"So original." Her mother straightens. "Remember that acid-green pantsuit we made Laurette?" She laughs. "That was egregious. But she wore it, by God. Your father said she looked like a parrot."

Rainey takes her mother's hand; it's warm and fleshy, the veins standing out like a blue map of the roads she traveled when she ran away from home. She places Linda's forefinger on the tiny remnant of finch-green material. There, right there, next to a snip of azure.

"I was ten," she says softly.

Linda falls silent, seemingly mesmerized, stroking the fabric as if it were fur.

• • •

HUGH, HER EX, invited them to the party.

Rainey and Hugh get to be actual friends now, since she no longer has to live in his white apartment or sleep in his white bed or deal with his other wife, Becca, from work. Sometimes they even fuck.

Linda is her plus-one. All the women will wear black, Rainey warned her, but here is her mother in yet another vintage Laurette, this one a full-skirted turquoise dress patterned with little steam irons. The Upper East Side condo is packed with murmuring collectors, which Hugh thought Rainey might take advantage of somehow, chat them up, whip photos out of her bag. Linda's on her second White Russian. Rainey's nursing a Black Russian, watching her mother frown at the living room's bare surfaces. Where do these humans keep their stuff? Linda asks—keys and photos and shit? Under the freaking *bed*?

Hugh and Becca van der Vliet, his architecture partner, did the reno for her parents. The condo is creamy, spartan, rooms like interlocking white cubes, like some future exhibit in the Cooper Hewitt of how rich people lived in the '80s. If only they had messy secret rooms, concealed behind hidden panels.

She tugs Linda away from a laughing knot of people with drinks.

"Guess where Hugh wants to go when he dies." She leads her mother far down a hallway to the former maid's room, now a study belonging to Becca's father, Hendrik. Hand poised on the door, she says, "Ready? Check out the vanishing point."

Linda gasps when she sees it. "It's got *three walls*," she says, laughing, and in fact the room is a perfect isosceles triangle. Notched into the far end is a three-sided black desk, the point of an exclamation mark. "This is Hugh's idea of heaven?"

"The townhouse gave him hives," Rainey says.

They drift back to the crowded living room. Hugh and Becca are talking with her parents and a few other people by tall windows dressed in white silk. They took the whole condo down to the studs for her folks, and Rainey has to give them credit. It's pretty meditative. An oasis. Bleached floorboards race on the diagonal; doorways nearly scrape the ceiling. In the living room, books are all covered in white paper, a phalanx of teeth, retitled in neat black ink—apparently that is what interns are for. Huge pearlescent canvases painted by Becca's mother, Dierdre, glow beneath eyeball spots.

Rainey nudges her mother, meaning *Get a load of the tree.* Tucked in a corner, it's sprayed white, baubled with white, gifts below it wrapped in white—except for the trespassers, a bunch in bright paper that guests must have brought.

Aunt Laurette would dry up here, an unwatered plant. So would Rainey, honestly. Don't these people get mail, and what do they *do* with it? What about pens, eyeglasses, cloying ceramic owls that arrive as dumb gifts? Their white laminate coffee table is barren, flanked by butterfly chairs in buttery ecru leather. Becca's husband, Will, has poured himself into one, and gazes at his wife over a glass of bronze liquid.

Rainey and Linda ease into the little group next to Hugh. Someone's critiquing a scribbly Cy Twombly over the fireplace, but now the women turn, magnetized by Linda, who twirls in her steam iron dress. Rainey herself wears a coal-black sateen sheath she sewed herself, with black tights and boots, her mink-colored hair worn long and loose. But it's her mother who's the cool girl, everyone admiring the little irons, which are also kind of isosceles.

And suddenly—Rainey should have seen this coming—Linda is telling inappropriate stories about the Colorado farmhouse, clearly digging the attention.

"We did have an unorthodox idea of work." Linda smiles mysteriously, and Hugh, who's fond of Linda, winks at Rainey. He seems to know where this is headed.

"*Jesucristo*," says Rainey theatrically. She knows where this is headed, too. She's perversely proud of Linda's criminal past, but she'd also hoped to pull out those photos of her newest tapestries, show them to Hendrik and Dierdre, who might talk them up among their guests—and that particular moment seems to be sailing out the double-paned window and over the snowy park.

"*Tell* me this is someone else's mother, please," she says. But Linda doesn't get the hint.

"So how did you all live?" Dierdre is obviously not going to let this drop. She wears an unchallenging mauve lipstick, and Rainey wants to hand her a bold red that will stand up to her silvery hair.

Becca gulps her red wine and licks her lips. She is the human equivalent of a Georgia peach. It once made Rainey crazy that Hugh worked till late with her and traveled with someone so—no other word for it—luscious, a woman who called at all hours of the night. Well, practically. "I love unorthodox," says Becca, beaming. "Tell us everything." Hugh smiles, too. No wonder their dinners used to go on for hours.

Once Linda opens her mouth, there is no going back. "We stole credit cards," she says brightly.

Deirdre links her arm through Hendrik's, her mouth flicking into a slight grimace.

Linda laughs and tips hair out of her face. It swoops back in. The hair looks like she just woke up, and she is wearing last night's smudged eyeliner, too. She could not look any sexier. "Any more White Russians where this came from?" She waves her glass, and Hugh takes it to the bar. His azure sweater is a rupture of blue in this milky room.

"Bless you and thank you," says Linda, taking her glass back. "Actually, what we stole were *applications* for credit cards. We changed the addresses, and when the cards arrived we bought clothes and gas." She smiles at each of them. "And a TV for the bedroom. I'm not a saint."

Rainey slings an arm around her mother. "You sure aren't. You stole the pickup you got home in, too." She just dares Dierdre to make something of it.

Becca laughs, an abrasive, happy sound. Hendrik looks at Linda as if she were a puzzle missing a final piece. Hugh stretches to the sideboard and picks up a mound of hard cheese and a dried apricot. "What happened to the truck?" he says, as Linda plucks the apricot from his fingers and nibbles on it.

"Ha!" says Rainey. "Parked it at a hydrant. Made it vanish. Poof."

"I want a fake credit card," announces Becca. "I want to take it to Bendel's."

"I'm not bailing you out," Hendrik says affably.

"I'll bail her out," says Hugh, and Rainey sees Hugh and Becca two years from now, drinking Illycaffè on crisp white Italian sheets and parceling out the Sunday *New York Times*.

"If you want one, Becca, go get one," says Linda, while Dierdre's face turns as rigid as a clamp—*no daughter of mine*. "People do throw out applications. We found ours in the county dump."

"And you never got caught?" Becca swirls her wine, a wash of red.

But Rainey thinks this has gone far enough. "Can I ask a question?" She turns to Dierdre and Hendrik. "Where do you keep all your personal shit?" With satisfaction she sees Dierdre wince. But no—there goes her chance to whip out the photos. "Like family photographs," she says, bulldozing ahead, "or throw pillows, or if your nephew makes you a ceramic frog?" What if a cousin were having his whole life stolen and needed a place to die—could such a love be installed in such a place as this?

Hendrik smiles at her. "Oh, we have our things, but they're tucked away. It's better for the art. We like to keep the sight lines clear," he says, as if that were the real question.

"But what about *wabi-sabi*?" The woman with chunky amber beads has been pressing her palms together, waiting to interrupt. "The Japanese ideal that beauty contains imperfection—don't you need that?"

Rainey looks at Hugh, adorable, with that easy stance, hands shoved in his front pockets. "Yeah," she says, "if you take out imperfection, what've you got, death?"

Dierdre inhales sharply.

"But it isn't perfect," says Hugh thoughtfully. "The humans in the house are flawed, and so is the art. Art might be sublime, but it's never perfect."

"And the reward," says Dierdre coolly, "is an uncluttered mind. We like to think we practice serenity here."

Rainey barks out a laugh. How serene can a person be in a vanishing point? But maybe she's missing something—maybe Hendrik gazes into that vertical seam where two walls meet in eternity and finds his center and his sanity every morning anew. She only feels sane like that when she's working. And not always then.

"About those credit cards," says Dierdre. "It's also mail fraud, isn't it?"

Has Linda ever considered this? But her mother shrugs and smiles. She's sloughed off Colorado like an old scab.

"I wouldn't make much of that," Hugh tells Dierdre mildly. "There's a statute of limitations."

Of course, a statute. After which Linda will enter a state of grace, and start fresh—what a concept. Rainey drains her Black Russian. Maybe there's a statute of limitations on hoards, and loss, and Laurette will recover from her shock at the soon-to-be-empty apartment—an apartment she hasn't yet seen—to find it refilled overnight, dust and all. Hey, maybe there's even a statute on marriage, and Rainey will awaken one day with windows for eyes and the cry of a new heart.

IT'S NEARLY MIDNIGHT, time zones and checked baggage being what they are, when Elihu and Laurette ring the bell.

"Elihu," Rainey breathes, opening the front door to a wash of cold air. Fat white flakes drift down around her cousin and her aunt like fairy pearls but evanesce when they land on the salted steps.

Elihu is a wraith, a mere transmission of himself from a distant planet. Raccoon fur on his hood wreathes his face, and his blue eyes look out at her from deep in his skull. His parka hangs loose as if on a child. On the stoop at their feet are duffel bags, a blue suitcase, and a cat carrier, and behind them Rainey sees humps of dirty snow at the curb, baring their ugliness under the yellowy sodium streetlamp.

Laurette lets Elihu walk in ahead of her, which shows the sad new order of things. "New York two, San Francisco zero," says Linda in the foyer, and hugs Laurette hard and Elihu as if he might break. Gordy starts to speak and sneezes instead, then can't stop sneezing.

Elihu lets Rainey kiss him on his mottled cheek. "Can you make it up two flights?" she says. "I'll bring you up some food if you like." She wishes suddenly that she'd hung a wreath, bought a gift, done something to mark the season.

"Maybe some juice for his meds," says Laurette.

"I told you, Ma," says Elihu, but he doesn't finish.

"I'm having trouble breathing," Gordy says to no one in particular, and now he is wheezing on the inhale, a kind of suffocated whistle.

"I remember you." Elihu looks suddenly awake, as if he might bloom again. "You showed me how to blow the trumpet." Gordy bows slightly and wheezes again. "Howard said, 'Remember the man's name, son.' You're Gordy Vine." He deflates. "Yeah, bed would be fantastic, Rainey. Thanks."

A doleful song issues from the cat carrier. Rainey heaves it up and starts up the stairs, her cousin sluggish and breathing hard behind her. Below she hears Gordy going, "Oh, no. Oh, wait just a minute here," her mother fussing about an inhaler. Dragging sounds—that would be Laurette with the rest of the bags. Rainey can't wait to meet this cat. Elihu's going to love his room, with the green William Morris wallpaper facing front into a plane tree, or at least into its dead, wet branches. When she was young, this was Gordy's room. But now Gordy is her mother's problem in the blue room downstairs, and the green room is a place of beauty where her cousin can shift through whatever dark changes loom for him.

Elihu belly flops onto the middle of the bed, between the four posts rising as inerrant as oaks. His parka gives out a *whoosh*. Laurette drops her suitcase, sits at the foot of the bed, and rests a still-gloved hand on his back. Rainey sets the cat carrier down. The tag on the handle says *Byron*.

"You need your meds, hon," Laurette says. Though she seems too exhausted to move. "I'll dig them out."

"Ma," says Elihu sharply, but his face is buried in the bedspread.

It can't be easy, being Laurette. That carapace of an apartment, her son resistant, apostate. Rainey smiles at her. She'll deal with the cat when she gets these people settled. "Why don't I fetch the juice?" she says, but when she comes back up with the OJ and a bowl of water plus an extra saucer for Byron, she finds her aunt now lying beside Elihu, still in her buttoned cloth coat and gloves, eyes closed. Are they dreaming? The room is now hushed except for the radiator, which gives out its steady hiss and, beneath that, a distant knocking sound in its pipes, which might be transmitted from the laundry room, or from the bottom of the Hudson River, or from St. Vincent's Hospital a block away where men like Elihu lie on coarse white sheets with IVs in their arms and hollows in their cheeks.

Rainey quietly closes the bedroom door, sets the juice on the nightstand, then turns her attention to unzipping the cat.

The tabby crouches, hisses, and skulks out of the carrier and under the bed. She nudges the water bowl after it, then finds Purina cans stashed in Laurette's suitcase, and a can opener—of course the crazy cat lady would travel with a can opener. She lifts the bedspread and offers dinner, but Byron just looks at her with shocked emerald eyes.

Rainey locates Elihu's pills in his rolled-up jeans. She sounds the name out in a whisper. *Zidovudine* might be the title of a particularly virulent piece of jazz her father would have written, or a tapestry for Elihu. She ekes out a blue-and-white capsule and places it by the juice.

"It gives me diarrhea." Elihu's voice is gravelly and slow. Somehow he sees what she is doing through closed eyelids, a gift of vision that must arrive at the end of days. "And I'm resistant."

"Oh, babe, you don't know," murmurs Laurette, and Rainey watches her hand grope for Elihu's, the fingers traveling after his. "How can you really know such a thing?" Till he dies, Laurette will sleep down the hall in Rainey's room, living out of her suitcase, and Rainey will be vigilant. She will sneak in every night and throw out the newspaper or whatever damn thing Laurette brings in to insulate herself.

Elihu rubs his mother's thumb with his own; Rainey hears him murmur, "Squirrel." His damp hiking boots hang off the edge of the bed, and she unties the laces and tugs them off, revealing red wool socks. His feet are long and narrow—dancer's feet, film editor's feet. Her aunt and cousin show no signs of getting up. From downstairs, Joni Mitchell's soprano rises as high as a lark's; she sings of love and taxicabs, which never go together well. But if there is anything else to be done here, Rainey can't think of it.

She switches off the overhead light, leaving a pool of luster around the nightstand lamp. Then she climbs onto the bed and lies on Elihu's other side, trying not to jostle. Though she barely knows him, he's her cousin. She reaches for his free hand. Reflexively or not, his fingers curl toward hers. Capillaries almost touching, blood whispering to blood.

For a while the three lie in silence while the radiator brings them one-way messages from the next world.

After a few minutes, Elihu says, "Ma?" His voice so low it's as if he hadn't spoken.

"Mmm?" says Laurette, and then, "What is it, hon?"

Rainey wonders if he will ask about his father before he steps off the thin edge of the planet. She wonders if Laurette will read that particular Notice to Cure.

"I'm sorry," says Elihu.

"I know," says Laurette. "I'm sorry, too."

When Rainey wakes, still in her clothes, the sky is a washed-out black that's almost gray, and the cat is asleep on the base of Elihu's spine. Rainey can't help herself—she rises up and touches Elihu's back through his parka to see if he's still alive, because if she's honest with herself, it would be so perfect if he'd died when there was nothing left to say. But her fingers keep rising and falling, and she leaves them there a long time, feeling the ebb and flow of his life, of her life, of her life with her mother back in it, of life that will mercilessly roll on with one less willowy, ironic, cat-loving film editor, and she finds herself looking down from the ceiling onto the floating bed with the three survivors, one who will blink out any day, one who will cry for him with her heart jammed open like a mouth, and one who accepts the great gift from the dying to the living, which is to feel joystruck at being alive.

ACKNOWLEDGMENTS

My gratitude to Joy Harris and to Jim Krusoe, always.

These stories were honed by perceptive and generous readers: Dean Baquet, Natalie Baszile, Samantha Dunn, Janet Fitch, David Frances, Tara Ison, Julianne Ortale, Heather Sellers, Thomas Tetreault and Rita Williams.

For their expertise, I am grateful to Steve Schneck, who vetted the trumpeting scene in "Embouchure"; to Heather Hartley, who vetted my French; and to Michael Bernstein, who explained how Rainey's trust might operate. Any errors are entirely mine.

I also want to acknowledge the artists and works of art that went into the making of Rainey's world. The story "Mr. Apology" was inspired by the Apology Project, a conceptual art piece by the late artist Allan Bridge. Running his Apology Line, he became a kind of confessor—what the writer Lydia Nibley called a "secular priest." The flyers I describe were his. The project inspired a museum exhibit, essays, a novel, a film, even a podcast (*The Apology Line*) hosted by Bridge's second wife, the artist Marissa Bridge.

The little study with the vanishing point in "Heart Jammed Open" was designed by architect and critic Joseph Giovannini, and mesmerized me years after I saw it—a triangular room? You could do that? I came up with Rainey's tapestries after witnessing set designer Stephanie Kerley Schwartz salvage a teeny scrap of metal from the street for her own beautifully detailed paper quilts. The poem in "Bernard Landry, Save Me" is by my late father, Bern Landis.

Also, if anyone appears to be quoting (or nearly so) the King James Bible, or Shakespeare, especially in "String Tension," they probably are.

My thanks to Lisa Lenz and Cheryl Arutt. And to Liza Mackeen-Shapiro, and as ever, to Adam Reed.

I am grateful to Soho Press and Bronwen Hruska for reissuing the previous two works in the Rainey Royal Cycle—*Normal People Don't Live Like This* and *Rainey Royal*—as deluxe editions alongside this book. Deepest thanks to my surgically brilliant editor, Mark Doten, and to Janine Agro, Rachel Kowal, Paul Oliver, Hanna Richards, Liza Voznessenskaia, Alex Willcox, Alexa Wejko, and Vivian Lopez Rowe. And to Judith Freeman for the introduction.